KT-524-891

To my parents, Anne and Peter, and my husband, Dara

A Good Father

A Good Father

CATHERINE TALBOT

PENGUIN
IRELAND

PENGUIN IRELAND

UK | USA | Canada | Ireland | Australia
India | New Zealand | South Africa

Penguin Ireland is part of the Penguin Random House group of companies
whose addresses can be found at global.penguinrandomhouse.com.

First published 2020
001

Copyright © Catherine Talbot, 2020

The moral right of the author has been asserted

Set in 13.5/16 pt Garamond MT Std
Typeset by Jouve (UK), Milton Keynes
Printed and bound in Great Britain by Clays Ltd, Elcograf S.p.A.

A CIP catalogue record for this book is available from the British Library

ISBN: 978–1–844–88484–1

www.greenpenguin.co.uk

MIX
Paper from
responsible sources
FSC
www.fsc.org   FSC® C018179

Penguin Random House is committed to a
sustainable future for our business, our readers
and our planet. This book is made from Forest
Stewardship Council® certified paper.

It is possible to have an overwhelming love.

1. Can Anybody Hear Me?

December 2016

By the end of next summer, before the kids go back to school, I will kill my family.

After I kill them, I will cry bitterly and make some freshly squeezed orange juice using the electric fruit juicer that I bought in Lidl with my daughter, Maeve. It cost €13.99. We made juice as a family every morning for two weeks, but after the initial healthy buzz, we kept forgetting to buy oranges. After I make the juice, I will put on my Lycra training gear and run up and down the Cat's Ladder (my favourite set of steps) for a while. I often meet other like-minded people there, covered in Lycra. When I finish on the steps, I'll make my way up to the Obelisk at the top of Killiney Hill.

Once there, I'll see Dalkey Island set majestically, frozen to my left, and the long sweep of Killiney beach on my right. I'll squint and make out the shaft of light that marks the beginning of the tunnel through Bray Head to Greystones. I'll allow myself a moment to consider the similarity between the beaches in Killiney and Greystones. And wonder, as I always do, why I have never set foot on Dalkey Island, despite its proximity. I'll start on my set of stretches taught to me by my friend Maurice, who helps me out with the under-elevens football team that I coach, mainly because my twin sons, Mikey and Joey, are on the team. These stretches encourage my muscles to retract to the place where they are more comfortable. I'll be aware of my breathing, and if it's sunny, I'll be able to feel a warmth on my back while pondering why I couldn't get rid of myself. This will provide me with the complete understanding that I am a coward. In the rural parts of this country, men who perform such acts on their families generally finish themselves off. But the truth is that they often have far better access to more suitable tools – a shotgun for starters. I might well consider how many times I have studied Jenny's woodcutting implements and wondered if they would be suitable for inflicting sufficient self-damage. But I know that long ago, I came to the conclusion I wouldn't be able to go through with it.

I am not insane. I am afraid. I don't want to live and have to keep worrying about all the shit about children being bullied online and I'm holding off on getting mine mobile phones. I fear that Mikey and Joey may not make good men, and I worry that Maeve will fall for a weak man. I could leave them, I could move to another part of the country, I've always had a yen to set up in Connemara, but they would still be here, in this house.

I am an educated man. I do not take drugs, prescribed or otherwise, nothing to combat loneliness or a general reluctance for life itself. It's just that I am living in fear. The fear is like a crazy person running after you as you sleep. Tearing away, you are in grave danger of being attacked, and you try to run from him but your legs won't work. And in the dream you cannot fathom why your legs have become paralysed. They worked before, why not now, when you so desperately need them to? And when you toss and turn and try to breathe new life into your immobile legs, you wriggle in your bed, and as a child, you eventually fall out, but as an adult you simply wake up. And you start another day and the semblance of terror that you felt in the dream isn't tangible any more but it leaves a bad taste in your mouth.

I look around my house and I see a place of comfort, not excessive abundance, but a pleasant place to be. There are books lining the walls. Our children sometimes colour and read in their spare time and play rounders on the green. Jenny is in her forties now. She is a little too thin but very attractive. I love the way her hair falls about her face as she works on her carving and her sketches. To me, she is still beautiful. She will not have much sex with me though, and that doesn't cause me any great degree of anger per se, but sometimes I become tired of pleading with her to feel me. When she agrees to my request, it isn't very pleasurable because her hands are not as smooth as I would like. They are calloused right at the bases of her fingers, just where they ought to be soft.

Jenny is an artist of wood but she sketches too. I adore her sketches, pencil scratchings, etchings almost, of things that she finds when she beachcombs: Budweiser cans and Pražský cans and Fanta orange, stones and feathers and bladder wrack. I never forget that the Latin name for bladder wrack is *Fucus vesiculosus*. I often compliment her on her work. She brushes my praise away as though it doesn't mean a thing.

I brush my teeth assiduously every morning and every night. Jenny is more lax and, as a result, the kids are also negligent. Jenny's teeth are often stained from coffee.

Play with me, Daddy, tickle me.

My eleven-year-old daughter, Maeve, tickles me and runs away from me shrieking, urging me to chase her. I take after her, giant steps at a time. This is our snatch and grab and tickle game.

Jenny can never let anything go. There was the time Maeve was almost knocked down by a car driven by another child's mother. This mother in question is always talking about how desperate the weather is. My kids call her 'desperate weather'.

It has a kind of depressing comedy. Inches away from an impact with Maeve, she tried to blame the ice and the desperate weather. I hadn't dwelt on it, but I was really angry at the time. Jenny ranted to high heaven about the school, and the parents, and how they didn't give a flying fuck about other people's children. I endured as much of it as I was capable of, and then I stopped listening.

Sometimes things become too much for me, and I break out of the circle temporarily, and when this happens I could be justified for taking the opportunity to hurt her pretty face, although this is never my actual intention.

When I hit her, which isn't often, I am careful not to go too deep around her cheekbones because her cheekbones are a great feature of hers. Delicacy abounds.

I often watch her in the kitchen as she plays cards or Scrabble with Maeve. Her hands rest on her cheekbones, slightly curled. Such long fingers. They talk while they play.

2. The Under-elevens

January 2017

I like to lead out the football team on a Sunday morning in the coldness of the winter months.

This particular Sunday, we are well braced, ready for the onslaught of a team from a place that no one has heard of. Lots of shouting and screaming and my team of psyched-up kids in a heap of frustration and bruises. I keep their spirits up by dishing out mini Mars Bars at half-time.

There is only so much chocolate can do.

Mikey and Joey try to score an extra Mars Bar each because I'm their dad. I stop them in their tracks.

I don't mind the banter with Maurice, it is well-intentioned. That ad, he says to me, with your man sending a text when he's on the road and the old crash bang wallop routine and it wouldn't kill you to put it away – it hits home, don't you think, Des? Its impact has to be rewarded. Not many ads these days do that to you.

I have a dream, Maurice.

What's that, Des?

A dream of the day that we'll beat this shower of fuckers and they'll go back to where they belong, with nothing only the memory of how our boys have thrashed them.

Maurice nods. I reach into my large kit bag. Lads, here's your bars. I'll be back in a jiffy. Hold the fort, Maurice.

*

In the clubhouse I stick my fingers down my throat and with a heave comes the bile. I flush the toilet. I feel a sense of regret. The first time I allowed myself to vomit up my lunch, I got away with it, despite the cuff ends of my hoodie being streaked with flecks of smoked fish from the chowder I'd downed in Vaughan's. Jenny knew no different. On holiday, free from the confines of the office, locked into the wilderness of Connemara and its restful arms, I felt a sway like no other sway before. My body had over-indulged and the purging was strange, and yet I was somehow indifferent to it. I risked it twice or maybe three times during our week's stay. I dry my hands on the crusty towel scrunched in a ball on the sink. Its hardened edges chafe my skin.

Back out on the pitch of woe, the pull of the West is still in me.

Here, lads, have you finished your bars? You lot are as lucky as hell, do you know that? In my day we got oranges cut into quarters and we had to suck on them so hard that the bits of flesh would get rammed in between our teeth. Don't get me started on energy drinks.

The kids wait.

They didn't exist, energy drinks.

The lads snort and there is a kind of a release in the air.

Good now, lads, I say. Things are coming on very nicely indeed.

They're hammering us, Dad, Mikey says.

A hammering is not what we'll call it, got that. I say, there's no such thing as a hammering. It's a day out, a morning away from television. Consider this: you're lucky to be out here in the air. Now brace yourselves, lads, for the onslaught. We'll get a few back.

It's four nil, says Joey.

It'll be five nil in about two seconds, says Mikey.

It's a fucking disaster, says Dano, the fat kid.

Any more of that language, Dano, and you're off, do you hear me?

I tell Joey to blow his nose because he's always got snot oozing from it and it drives me mad.

The football is fierce and it is windy and the air is brisk with it. None of the boys shiver though, they are red in the face. The determination not to let myself and Maurice down. We scream our instructions at them from the sidelines and our voices begin to falter, and soon I feel that they are nothing more than rasps in the wind.

Fuck this wind, Maurice, I say.

It's going to flatten them, it's against them. Fuck, Des, that's another one in.

I shout for the goalkeeper to be changed. I wave my arms. The boys do their best. They lean in hard and for under-elevens they show a tenaciousness. They play entrenched in the mud. Mud leaves the pitch and lands on legs, arms and shorts. The opposition up their attack, their coach curses blue murder and he paces the ground as though he is dealing with the national squad.

The full-time whistle comes, and everyone tries their best to act like it doesn't matter.

Look, lads, seven one. That's not a bad place to be, not a bad score, hang in there, lads, you showed true spirit. Right then, that's it, let's wrap this up.

On the way home in the car, Mikey and Joey joke about in the back seat, doing bottle flips. I tell them to stop doing bottle flips in the car because it's distracting me. Joey says he's hungry and Mikey talks about rashers and sausages. I hope Jenny is preparing our breakfast. I look at my sons through the rear view mirror and stroke my beard. There's a

7

bit of spittle at its end on account of all my shouting. I rub it out and the radio is on in the background.

What is this shite? Don't worry about being broken into. Everyone has that fear, let them be, I say to myself.

Dad, you're talking to the radio, says Mikey.

No, son, the radio is talking to me and it's talking a whole load of shite, like I said.

I am a damn good father and a damn good husband, and a damn good cook.

I pull up at the house and kill the engine, but I leave the key in the ignition so I can still hear the radio. I tell Mikey and Joey that I have a bit of work to do this afternoon for the office, and that they had better be quiet and just play about without annoying me. I suggest that Mikey makes a start on the new *Diary of a Wimpy Kid* and that Joey might consider reading anything other than football magazines. I tell them that we lost the game because we were sloppy but to tell their mother that it was a draw. She doesn't like tales of failure that much. I don't know why, exactly, but I go along with it. It's easier that way.

I have difficulty opening the front door with my key. The loss of dexterity in my fingertips from standing about is a killer. I call out, telling Jenny that we're home, but she doesn't respond. I tell Mikey and Joey to leave their muddy boots on the front step, because I am sick of mud being walked all over the house. The boys pull at their boots and leave them in an untidy pile outside and we go into the kitchen. Who is in the kitchen drinking coffee like a lord? None other than Jerome Fagan.

How are you, Jerome? I say.

I don't give a fuck how he is, but I want to know what he's doing here in my kitchen and how long he's been in my kitchen while I freeze my balls off and lose my voice at the football. I remove my winter coat and leave it hanging on the kitchen door. I know this annoys Jenny. That's why I do it.

Jerome Fagan is Jenny's ex and he's a persistent cunt. He has an air of self-confidence that goes brilliantly with his white-starched shirt. Jenny maintains that I should be kinder to him because his wife is dead, and he's rearing a boy on his own. I find it hard to believe that a man who has the audacity to sit comfortably at my kitchen table while flicking his fair hair back from his tanned face and charming my wife is in any kind of serious mourning.

I'm making eggs, I say to Jenny, assuming that Jerome will take the hint and be on his way, but Jenny only goes and offers him more coffee. I am sick. I tell them that it was Baltic at the pitch, and that I don't know what they were thinking of picking Maxwell's Park as a suitable venue for a club. I describe how I cannot possibly think of a worse place and then I go on a bit about the wind and how it cuts you in two. I mention how hard it was for my fingers to work. I crack half a dozen eggs into the clear bowl and begin to beat them. I add spinach leaves and cheese. Maeve has a face on her because she doesn't like eggs. I make tea because coffee causes me to heave. Jerome asks me about work and I answer with a curtness that he picks up on and finally he leaves.

Jenny wants to know why I was rude to her friend.

An ex-boyfriend does not a friend make.

I try to make it sound poetical so she won't know that I am envious of Jerome. His easy elegance and confidence that it's okay to remain friends with someone with whom you once lived, shared a life. Jenny sits with her knees under her beige jumper dress. She pulls the ends of her sleeves over her hands. I call the kids to eat. Maeve still has a face on her and Mikey and Joey want meat.

The day moves on and I watch Jenny with her tools, her face clammy with effort. I light the fire, even though it is early. There is an aroma of eggs in the room. Mikey and Joey and Maeve play rounders on the green. I do a bit of work and watch them through the window. I sit beside Jenny as she carves images of seaweed on to a piece of wood. This piece will be the big-deal part in a collection of carvings and drawings. She is inspired by the seaside. Running my palm over the carvings, I close my eyes and can feel bumps and scratches on the wood. Later on, the children come in from the green and they watch *The Simpsons*. We are all happy in this moment. I decide to run a bath for myself.

Setting myself up nicely, a towel within easy reach, I fill the bath and add a piece of seaweed, from the bucket beside the sink. Jenny's beach collections invade all our space. I test the water with my feet one at a time and am left as though wearing a pair of red socks, with the markings from the hot water. Omelette vomit floats in the toilet. I flush it away.

At night things move on as they always do, an extension of another day. Homework is not looked at on Sunday, but newspapers are read. Happy families. A vegetable soup is made, ready on the stove, and a selection of vegetables, peppers and carrots bide their time until they can be added to the roast once it has been given a blast at a high temperature. We talk about wintertime at dinner. I delight in the cold, just not when I'm out with the lads and the wind is fervent.

3. Jenny

March 1995

It was 1995, when I fell fast for Jenny. I first noticed her at the gallery on Lennox Street. My friend Austin had invited me; he had a couple of pieces in a group show. The room was full of the eagerness of young artists and their awkward confidence. The ceiling was high, but conversations made the room seem compressed, too many people trying to be the big shot. I was no different. I was trying to get noticed myself.

I wasn't an artist. I'd tried to be for a while, but I recognized early on that I simply didn't have enough natural talent, no matter how hard I worked. If I couldn't be a real artist, I figured that I could set my sights on something in the cultural domain. I had a few ideas but the problem was, I didn't know if any of them were feasible, and if I was to do anything I needed to make the appropriate connections. I couldn't work out how to crack into this world. Everyone else seemed to have a plan, or the semblance of a plan. I had nothing, only my wits.

She stood alone. She had a way of holding herself and you couldn't tell if she was nervous or not. Her hands clasped a tulip-shaped glass of red wine. I noticed her fingers. There was a certain grace in them. She wore a dress of crushed velvet. It was tight and I could see her thin frame through it. It delighted me. But I was frozen. Austin caught me staring at her.

She's pretty fine, he said.

Yeah, I said.

I remember how I tried to keep my voice level. I hoped that Austin knew this woman so he could introduce me, but at the same time I hoped he didn't know her. I wanted this discovery to be mine alone.

That's Jenny Mitchell; she's one of the artists. That's her work over there, Austin said.

He pointed to some canvases on the wall. Etchings and charcoal rubbings of what looked like the sea. Vibrant – I was drawn to them because that's what the sea always did to me.

Jenny Mitchell. Jesus, she's good.

Come on, he said.

And that's how I met her.

Austin had developed a swagger as he drifted over to Jenny and I followed him and tried not to be nervous. As soon as he introduced us, that feeling of unease and edgy tension seemed to lift. She smiled and her eyes creased at the sides when she laughed at something Austin said. He had a way with women and I was learning just from watching him in action. He went off in search of more drink and this gave me my opportunity to tell Jenny that I thought her art was beautiful.

It was the right thing to say because her work was just that. It was like a reflection of her own beauty and I told her this in a roundabout way. I mixed up the mention of her inner beauty with the wonder of the sea to make it sound more natural. I was drawing her in, and in truth I was some-what taken aback by her vulnerability when she mentioned that no one had bought any of her pieces, and yet little red dots were appearing, as if by magic, beside the other artists' work. I had a desire to hold her there and then and to tell her that everything was going to be fabulous.

I told her to give it time; it was early enough. I looked to my left wrist and stared at a blankness where there should have been a watch. It's early, I repeated, and said, any day now I will wear a watch.

I desperately wanted to appear interesting and I sensed that discussing the wearing of a wristwatch wasn't going to cut it. So I asked her all about herself; where she came from, her family, her favourite colour, the works. By the end of my first glass of wine, I was enjoying myself and had relaxed. Jenny had that way about her of making me feel at ease. I wondered why she had been alone earlier because she seemed so personable. People wandered over to her from time to time, mainly to congratulate her on her paintings, and she had kind words for all of them. When I asked her what was with the long face earlier on, she said that someone had let her down and hadn't shown up. I didn't make too much of a deal about it but I did worry that she might have been waiting for a bloke.

I was asking too many questions and I was relieved when Jenny changed the subject. She wanted to know how I knew Austin and I felt a slight pleasure telling her that he was an old college friend. I didn't actually imply that I was an artist myself, but I didn't give the impression, either, that I wasn't. I told her that I painted a bit when I got the chance and that I had a lot of other stuff going on, like being a barman at the Crown. I think I tried to make the place sound actually regal. I mentioned that I was currently looking for an editing job and I made my quest sound interesting. I had no problem throwing in the odd artistic anecdote, I was well read after all, and I secretly enjoyed supplying cultural references and Jenny, I sensed, might appreciate that.

It wasn't the time to start my rant about how unsuccessful I'd been with my artistic endeavour. Instead, I set about ensuring that we had plenty of glasses of red wine. I needed to get drunk, not badly drunk but enough. As the opening was drawing to an end, there was talk about moving on to another bar. I didn't give it too much heed because I wasn't sure if I was officially included in the invitation, and I was just about to make my excuses and leave when Jenny said that there was a group of them heading on to Hogans and she asked me if I wanted to go.

Try and stop me, I said and I kissed her gently on her cheek.

We went en masse down towards Lower George's Street and there was a lot of carry-on, artists spouting a whole load of drunken shite. I had to jostle for Jenny's attention on the way. It wasn't ideal but I put up with it. Everyone was smoking spliff and I felt that I had to join in, even though smoking it always made me puke, but I didn't let on.

Hogans was all bar. Sweat and stale perfume, aerosol deodorant and pouting lips, girls poured into tight sequined dresses, and there was an undercurrent of English voices with all the hen parties. People still smoked in bars, the last of the glory days. Jenny was still on the red wine and I wondered how her thin frame was capable of what it required to sufficiently break down the alcohol. I switched to beer. The music was loud and her artist friends were beginning to feed off one another's energy. At one stage Jenny went to the loo and when she came back she had a look on her face that suggested that she was no longer enjoying herself. I asked her what was wrong and she said that suddenly she'd felt a little bit sad and that it was most likely the wine talking and that I was to drop it. I did wonder if it had anything to do with what she had said earlier, about someone letting her down, but I didn't pursue it. Instead, I entertained her with stories of my surfing antics and my love of the sea and she seemed to come back to me.

You're lovely, I said.

I kissed her, this time on the lips and part of me was waiting for her to pull away from me but she didn't. Instead she kissed me back and some smart artist friend of hers said, get a room. I ignored him and asked Jenny to come home with me, and, to my surprise, she agreed. And she kissed me as we pushed our way through the heavy set of double doors streaked with condensation and out on to the street.

We laid into each other that first night. Not only with passion but with tenderness. She told me that she didn't normally sleep with guys she had just met. I believed her. If I hadn't, it would have broken the spell. My flat on Camden Lane was a mess but Jenny didn't seem to care. We drank all the drink I could find in my kitchen and, after that, she called it a night. She wouldn't stay over so I got her a taxi. It was only as the car was out of sight that I realized I hadn't asked Jenny for her number.

I wandered around in a daze for the next week. I went over it and over it. I even played out the sex in my mind again and again. Her touch. It seemed as if she was hungry for someone to kiss, to connect with. I thought about how I could meet up with her again, but I wanted it to seem casual. That's when I started to hunt out the gallery openings. My main source was *Event Guide* so I'd call up Austin and get him to come along with me. Sometimes Austin would bring me in under his wing – he had a few connections but I didn't want to crowd him.

I tried to put Jenny out of my mind while I began to hunt down interesting work. I'd done a business course after my stint in art college. This combined with my eye for the aesthetic seemed to be in my favour as I went from interview to interview. I quickly came to face the cold truth, that if I wanted to take on an interesting job then I was going to have to settle for a low salary. For the most part I didn't let this sad fact deter me. I kept at it. The day I turned down an entry-level job at Microsoft with decent enough pay for a rather vague administrative position in an arts centre brought it home to me. I started working for a magazine. It was meant to be a literary affair but I soon realized that they were a shower of cowboys. All they were interested in was selling advertising space in the magazine to subsidize our wages. It was more like a community newspaper than a publication of genuine merit. I soon got fed up chasing sponsorship, it felt personal, like I was somehow a charity case. To make matters worse, no decent writers were submitting to the magazine, so we had to write some of the work ourselves to fill the pages. I had to take on extra shifts at the Crown. The place was permanently jammed with suits stuffing toasted-cheese sandwiches down their throats mid-pints, and tourists looking for a taste of real Dublin. The music was always that bit louder than necessary but I had learnt quickly how to take orders from stricken and confused Spaniards asking for half-pints of Guinness. I had no bother working out what the suits wanted. They all drank Heineken.

I missed her.

Two months later on a Thursday night, to my astonishment and utter delight Jenny walked into the Crown. It was a great feeling to know that she had taken note of where I worked, and had acted on that knowledge. I remember clearly that it was Thursday because I could hear the peals of laughter from the old dears at the bingo club next door. Thursday was the big night. I often yearned to go inside myself of a Thursday for a peek, to see what all the bother was but I never got around to it. When Jenny stood before me, I knew then that I didn't merely want her in a physical sense, but that it would be more. It would be a deep love. When I was eight, playing football at the Mini World Cup, I had won a gold medal. I truly loved it, and I knew that in time I would love Jenny with something akin to that intensity.

This was the way my heart moved.

She said that she was hoping to catch me and I wanted to believe her, so I did. This wasn't just some chance encounter, it was meant to be. When she asked for a red wine, I fell into a momentary confusion as if I had forgotten that I was indeed a barman. I pointed out that we stocked Malbec and Cabernet. She chose the Malbec. I had an inclination to warn her that Malbec could be headache-inducing but I didn't want to come across as being bossy. Instead, I reached for a small bottle and unscrewed the black cap. As I waved away her money, I told her that she looked amazing and that I was really happy to see her.

She smiled at me and the effect of it did something to my heart and I felt strangely breathless for a moment. She took her wine from the bar and moved to a seat beside the window. I noticed how the light from the lamp outside shone in through the window pane and did something wonderful to her profile. She looked sublime. Her beauty was stark.

I began to make a show of gathering up some empty glasses. I went over to Jenny and started a bit of banter. It felt natural and her laughter at my jokes about the desperation of the clientele gave me a warm feeling inside. I was doing my best to hide my nervousness and my excitement, such that I found it difficult to make eye contact with her without images of our night together formulating in my mind.

Confidence was the first thing that struck me about the man who pushed through the door. To my horror he moved towards Jenny and kissed her on her cheek. I had to look away. I stood there with my hand in my pocket and she introduced him to me as Jerome and I distinctly remember that he didn't wait to hear my name. Instead he asked me to bring him a pint of Guinness.

I felt as if I had been firmly put in my place as I pulled Jerome's pint and there was a slight heaviness in my heart when I brought it over. Who was this guy and what the hell was Jenny doing with him? Jenny looked away as I put the pint on the table and she kept well out of the transaction with money, as though she was uncomfortable with it. I threw down a couple of beer mats. Jerome sat on a bar stool, his back held straight. He had removed his trenchcoat to reveal a fitted navy shirt. He wore a brown tie, it was thin and had a slightly woven effect. I had to admit he cut a fine shape of a man. As I turned my back on him to go to help Andy behind the bar, I could hear him speaking in a loud voice to Jenny.

What a day I've had. It was mental.

I didn't wait to hear any more. It wasn't easy but I kept my cool. I got busy wiping my beer-stained hands on my apron and tried to zone out the noise that was building up in the pub. I returned to my sanctuary behind the bar. People began to thicken around me. We picked up our pace, myself and Andy. Most of the crowd were coming in from the cultural organizations in Temple Bar. The suits became outnumbered. There was a certain pleasure in that. There was a buzz and I couldn't see Jenny because she was hidden by the wall of drinkers. I looked over in the direction of where they were sitting but I didn't think it would be appropriate if I went over to their table again. I hoped that I wasn't going to regret this decision, and I worried all the time that she might leave with Jerome without saying goodbye.

After an hour I looked up to find Jenny at the bar and she was smiling at me. She told me she was heading off and that it was great to see me again. I said the pleasure was all mine and I made her laugh as I used an American drawl. If God could see me, he would have noticed the way I was struggling. It was obvious that Jenny had chosen to come to the Crown hoping to see me again, she had even admitted it, but I still couldn't believe it and my emotions were on high alert. I desperately wanted to say the right thing and I was aware of the fact that there were other punters trying to catch my attention to get more drink. I was also acutely sensitive to the fact that she had come to the Crown with a man and I needed to clarify his relationship with her. I tried to be casual as I asked her if Jerome was her boyfriend and I also tried not to appear surprised when she told me that he was.

Even though it appeared to me, whether or not I had imagined it, that her voice had faltered slightly as she admitted she was romantically involved with this man, I was crushed and I could feel a heat on my cheeks. Perhaps it wasn't all roses in the garden with Jerome. That was my hope. All I could visualize was the way we had gone to my flat after Hogans that night, and had sex, how her skin had felt like silk to me and how I believed I had literally struck gold. The way she held my body after the act, how thirsty I felt, how I thought she was free – Jerome was nowhere to be seen at the opening on Lennox Street. The knowledge that Jenny wasn't available was daunting but I had always been impulsive, and I decided there and then, that you only live once in this world and I had nothing to lose by pursuing her. I didn't want to live with regret.

I pointed to a painting on the wall done by a local artist and I told her that Andy occasionally exhibited work by emerging artists. I called Andy over for confirmation and I introduced him to Jenny. I mentioned the opening on Lennox Street, where we had met, and how bloody good Jenny's work was. I said it was captivating and Andy said if that was true then he might consider hanging it. That was the way things operated in Dublin, it was all about who you knew and it was my good fortune that I knew Andy. Jenny's eyes lit up and she was all thanks.

I heard Jenny's name being called and Jerome appeared and said they had to go. He headed in the direction of the door and I was quick to notice that Jenny didn't appear particularly happy about having to leave with him. I took my opportunity and asked Jenny for her number and I whispered to her that I would love to see her again, even if we could just talk about art.

Tell your boyfriend it's business, I said.

She laughed and said that she would do just that.

She gave me her card. It was cream-coloured with a swoop of turquoise that I presumed signified the sea. Jenny Mitchell was in gold lettering and there was an icon of a shell over the 'i' in Mitchell. Now I could find her again. I flipped the card over and stuffed it in the back pocket of my jeans.

Andy looked over at me and gave me a wink.

We got back to work.

4. The Chase

May 1995

So it was official, Jenny had a boyfriend. I knew I was on dangerous ground but I didn't care, not really. I had to have her. She couldn't be happy with him, if she was she wouldn't have had sex with me the night I met her.

I didn't waste any time. I rang her the next day. When she answered my call, there was a caginess in her voice. I ignored it and filled the awkwardness by talking up her art, reassuring her, saying it was wonderful, how it had intrigued me. I reiterated that Andy was interested in showing it in the Crown. She seemed delighted with that and as she talked about the difficulties of securing a solo exhibition or even a group show regularly in any of the galleries in Dublin, I could hear her breathing quicken as she described what it took, how you had to push yourself, how you wouldn't get anywhere without a real drive. I told her that sometimes ambition could be a scary thing but she had to try to go along with it. I made a few self-deprecating remarks, to make her feel, I hoped, better about her prospects, how I couldn't really paint, for love or money, but despite that I still believed in myself. I said it was a matter of switching her mindset, if she believed she could achieve something, she would. I could sense her tone changing from negativity to a more positive one. Asking her out that night on a date seemed like the natural course of action, even though Jerome was on my mind.

This was a situation I could handle, perhaps things were

on the wane with him. I didn't get the sense of any hesitation when Jenny agreed to meet me at the bottom of Grafton Street, that very night. I wore black. My jeans were tight around my ankles but they looked the part. I splashed my face with a little aftershave. I could smell Hugo Boss as I left my flat and I jingled my keys in my pocket. When we walked by the Goths hanging outside the Central Bank, I felt tender towards them. They didn't have a plan either. Jenny didn't want to discuss Jerome with me, but I kept at it. Pointed questions. She seemed wary. The only information she volunteered was that he was a businessman. He owned something with his brother. She allowed me to hold her hand that night over the table in the Italian place on the square in Temple Bar. An empty wine bottle held a candle. I kept looking at it as the flame flickered and then looking at Jenny. Her eyes made me feel safe, like the sea on a fine day. The night sealed something. I wanted Jenny, but on account of Jerome I knew that I would have to wait for her. We didn't arrange to meet again, and that is how I left it. Jenny knew where she could find me if she wanted to.

How do you make someone fall in love with you? You use charm but there has to be depth to it. You have to say all the right things and they have to flow naturally from you. You have to appear as though you do not have an agenda because that is too obvious. I was ready to use everything I had to lure Jenny but I was waiting for the right moment. I had to make her come to me. I had to make her want to come to me, this was my strategy.

Weeks passed and still nothing, not a thing from Jenny and I was beginning to worry if I had come across as playing it too cool. I asked Andy for advice on the Jerome situation one night. We had finished our shift and had gone over to the Music Club in Temple Bar. The outside of the bar was covered with posters, techno stuff and some singer-songwriter who was making a big noise at the time and the usual jingly jangly groups that were like fodder for the masses. Andy knew the bouncers, so we didn't have to fork out. Dublin was like that back then – a city based on recognition.

The Music Club was a recent addition and it was still at that early stage of trying to define itself. It seemed to lack style to me, as if it had no thought-out agenda. The backdrop to the bar consisted of black sheets hammered to the walls. The bar manager looked like he wanted to be a television presenter. The other staff with their face piercings cleaned floors and polished glasses, all the while trying to get noticed.

We went into the venue and there was a DJ on the decks and the crowd were giving it everything, mesmerized. It was beautiful to look at – the trance. We hung around the back seats of the venue and enjoyed the music. It felt good. I felt normal again because I'd been spending far too much of my time worrying about Jenny and about Jerome. I told Andy that I was waiting for Jenny to come to me. Andy told me to relax about it.

She would come.

There was a scuffle in the middle of the dance floor. I could make out two girls having a go at each other. I'd had enough of drunk people for one night after working, so I told Andy that I was going to call it a night. He knocked back his drink and we left the club.

I lay in bed later slowly curling my hands into fists and then uncurling them, and I thought about what Andy had said to me about jealousy. I didn't have the right to be jealous. I'd only had Jenny that one time. She wasn't mine, not yet. What I was experiencing was envy.

5. She Came to Me

A couple of weeks later I was working at the Crown. It was pissing rain outside and the evening was moving along steadily. A few builders from the site beside the Stag's Head came in with a thirst on them. Myself and Andy knew them, so we had a bit of craic. There was a smell of gravy in the air from the lunchtime carvery. It was our lull before the office crowd bit in. I had my head in the glass dishwasher when I heard my name being called. I looked up. Jenny was standing there and she was a picture.

It was so good to see her. I tried not to let myself hope too much. But I couldn't control hope, no one can control hope, or expectation. It was like I had an inherent sense of our destiny and I attempted to play it cool as I asked her what she was doing in the pub.

She had something to tell me, she had left Jerome.

Joy, relief, giddiness. This was certainly good news. In fact it was so good that I didn't know how to suitably react, all I was capable of doing was smiling until my face hurt. She seemed upset. All I wanted to do in that instance was throw my arms around her, to take away her pain and to give her a small part of my happiness.

It mustn't have been easy, I said. I asked her how Jerome had taken it and she said, badly.

I could well imagine it – the hurt on his face, Jenny rejecting him like that. In a way I almost felt sorry for him, but maybe he knew it was on the cards, in any event his loss was my gain. She was here after all. I stacked some glasses and there was a silence between us. She seemed not to know what to do with herself after her announcement. She wore a boyfriend-style tweed coat and had a red scarf tied delicately around her neck. Red brought out her cheekbones. I had always believed that good things would come my way. Love was coming my way, and it was gripping me by the throat but I had to be careful with Jenny, she wasn't a piece of meat ready to be rolled out to the next hungry male that wanted her. Something had happened between us already, we had had that physical connection, just the one time but it had felt so right, so true, and now Jenny was here. This business of Jerome had been merely a barrier. And the barrier had been lifted and I had not controlled the lifting of it, Jenny had.

And I kept smiling. I asked her if she could call back in later, around closing time and we could go back to my place and have a chat or a drink or something. She said that she would love that, and I touched her hand gently and I said, that's brilliant, Jenny.

She headed off then and left me to my work.

There was always something to be done at the Crown even when it was quiet. That's what Andy had told me on day one, and he had made it pretty clear to me that he didn't care for any messing. I believed him. It was this understanding that kept our relationship on an even keel. We did the work, we never left customers waiting unnecessarily unless the customer happened to be a drunk suit acting the cunt. We had some fun.

The early evening moved into the late evening and the night drinkers came and all the time I thought about what had happened with Jenny earlier. Myself and Andy discussed it while we worked and it seemed to me that the possibilities of what could develop between Jenny and me were endless and I felt almost euphoric as last orders were taken and last orders were drunk, and the place became quiet once more.

There was a knock on the glass door and Andy answered it. Jenny came in and I hugged her and told her that we were almost ready. Andy offered her a drink while she waited on us cleaning up the last of the empties. I arranged the bottles of spirits that were lying on the bar. There was a particular way of aligning each bottle so that things wouldn't get away with us on any given busy night. Andy insisted that there was a place for everything. I kept to the rules. I was good like that. It was decent of Andy to give Jenny the red wine on the house and he made an attempt at chatting to her. She seemed incredibly shy in front of Andy, but I supposed that she was probably in shock after leaving Jerome. I moved quickly around the lounge putting on the finishing touches. I checked that the Open sign was flipped to Closed. I made little neat piles of beer mats on the bar beside the Guinness on draught. I remembered that it was Guinness that I had brought over to Jerome that night when he had been in with Jenny.

We went back to my flat and I cursed myself for not having a bottle of wine to offer her, and me working in a bar. Jenny said that she wasn't a big drinker generally, which I found surprising, considering our first meeting. She said that she had other methods of coping with stress. I did wonder what stress she was referring to. Was it what had happened with Jerome or was it her art? But I decided not to pursue it. She had been through enough for one day. Instead I sat beside her, my arm loose around her shoulder. We watched a late show about music and it felt great when she placed her head in the crook of my neck.

We took things slow that night, it was nothing like the first night we met. I was gentle, almost tentative with Jenny and it wasn't purely raw physical sex, it was more like an emotional connection was being made.

This was exactly what I wanted.

6. My Family

February 2017

I arrive home and I sigh because the pot that is supposed to support a plant at the front door holds instead a floral-patterned umbrella that I couldn't find earlier this morning on my way to work. My clothes are wet and my shoes squelch from my socks. I peer through the sitting-room window and I can see my children's junk on the sofa, laundry is in a pile and the whole mess signifies for me the end of yet another week. A weaker man would have lost his cool by now. I am determined not to become that man.

In a place far away from here I would probably be very happy. This is my mantra, my way of controlling my wishful thinking. It allows me to imagine my escape from the blot that is my work life. I am a failed artist, but more than that, I am living in a land filled with suits and I feel condemned. No number of after-work pints can fix it. It works for the rest of the gang, they enjoy the bollox talk about what an ogre Graham our boss is. It's an insecurity thing: we have collectively denounced him as being an asshole. There is something about him coming from the Midlands that makes him a nasty piece of work, at least that's what we think. I have consumed four pints and it has oiled my tongue slightly, taken the edge off things for now, but the problem is that once I've had four I need the fifth. The fifth is where it's at. But instead, I have a repeat episode of *Grand Designs* on the television, and my children's *Slam*

Attax wrestling collector cards and other shit all over the floor.

Did you have a good day? Jenny asks.

It was grand, I say. That's what I always say.

Her face has that look. I'm wondering if she's been at the pills again. I don't know what she takes but I understand it's got something to do with anxiety. She pops them to help her sleep. I don't like it, but there's not a whole lot I can do about it. She consumes other pills to help her stay awake. I don't like that either, but I keep that to myself. She's asleep when she ought to be awake and she's awake when she ought to be asleep. It's as if her body has lost its rhythm.

When she asks me what she should do about the pills, which she often does, I am at a loss.

Jenny makes fried eggs, and it seems unfair that I have had a stressful day at the office and that's all that's on offer. I am aware that she's trying really hard with her sculptures and her sketches, but the bottom line is she's not generating much of an income. I admit that I am disappointed. It's all down to me, all the pressure is mine, mine alone. She wears a long wraparound dress, a vintage rose velvet stitched along its edge. It suits her because it's Friday and I have consumed four pints. I reach for the wine on the counter and pour myself a glass.

Soft, I say. I tap her on her cheek. Make sure mine's runny. Where are the kids?

She doesn't answer me and the thing is that I know that they are likely to be out on the green – in the dark, playing hide and seek in the copse of trees at the far end. Jenny likes to parent from afar, I myself am more inclined to being a helicopter parent, but we have a rule that I will try not to be over-protective. The carrot and parsnip soup that I had for lunch is repeating on me.

*

I move to the trees on the green and I call the children. I am gentle at first, almost tentative; they hear me but they ignore me and I try very hard not to let a notch of irritation enter my voice. They continue to blank me. I end up shouting for them and I walk back towards the house, wound up. I am pumped. My neighbour is putting out his recycling bin and catches sight of me. I shouldn't sink to this level, but I do.

The egg on the plate has a greasy surface and Jenny has dotted it with black pepper and a piri-piri sauce for that smidgen of glamour. The egg is overdone but I know that I will eat it anyway. There are oven chips and baked beans. I will have a fluffy sensation on the roof of my mouth once I have consumed this family meal.

The children come into the kitchen and Maeve says, Daddy, you're back, as if I have not been only moments earlier calling them.

I rub Maeve's cheek and I psych Mikey and Joey up about the match on Sunday. An aroma of cabbage from yesterday's dinner hangs heavy in the kitchen. I feel nauseous. Jenny doesn't look at me during our meal. I find this incredibly sad, so I do the same. Kevin McCloud talks in his drawl, trying to help middle-class British people with their very grave problems of designing and building their unique dream homes. I sip on a bit of the wine and McCloud's nasal undulations make me cringe, but I pretend to enjoy it because I know that it will put Jenny into a better mood, and it keeps the children from annoying each other. I have a notion in my heart that I may be on the road to sex. Then again I may not be.

Jenny joins me with the wine once I have the children sent to bed. I think that it might loosen her up somewhat. I am wrong. A Friday night shouldn't be fraught with so much drama, surely?

It feels so wrong to be forcing yourself on to someone but that's kind of what I have to do. Sometimes. Far be it from me to attempt to be justifying my actions.

7. Orange Juice

We've run out of orange juice, Mikey says.

We told Mom to get some, she said she would, Joey says.

Well, she mustn't have been listening, Maeve says.

My children are like a chorus in a play. The orange juice play. I have a vicious thirst and the only thing that can quench it, I imagine, is fresh orange juice. I open the fridge door and instead, I pull out some processed orange juice from the Centra. I knock it back but it is not enough.

I look out my front window and see my neighbour's car jutting out of his driveway. He does this deliberately and he is precise. There is just enough of a protrusion to make it difficult for me to perform a three-point turn before parking my own car in my own drive. It gets under my skin. To think, that there was a time in my life when I believed that to have a driveway of one's own might be considered desirable and now even this desire is being frustrated.

Right, I'm off to Tesco, I say.

I'm still wearing my sports gear from my early morning run. I don't mind walking around the supermarket in Lycra. In my book, it gives other shoppers a sense of my fitness and it will save me changing again before the football.

Maeve asks if she can come with me.

I tell her, okay. I don't mind this, a bit of a chance for myself and Maeve to have a chat. Our conversations are few and far between at the moment. Mikey and Joey have their heads fixed to the television and I invite them to Tesco, mainly to witness their reaction. I shout out to Jenny that I am going to Tesco with Maeve, as if we are about to embark on a positively interesting expedition. The truth is I secretly enjoy these visits, but I don't let on to Jenny.

I ask Jenny if we need anything in the shop.

She is engrossed in her work and when she is like this, she completely blocks me out. It drives me up the wall, but I hide it. Instead I just shout milk and sausages to nobody in particular and these words thrown out into the air serve me sufficiently for now. I will brood over her behaviour later.

I drive to Tesco with Maeve even though we could easily walk the distance. Maeve is one of those children who is chatty when the mood takes her but mainly she is content with her own thoughts. She is in that reflective mood of hers today, and I am not getting a whole lot in the way of feedback from her when I ask about school and friends and the rest of it. I know only too well that she has inherited many of her behavioural traits from Jenny.

We drift in and out of the aisles and we buy junk cereals and I lose my normal strictness. I allow a few treats to go into the trolley and this lightness makes Maeve smile and for that I am grateful. I want this day to be a happy one.

I arrive home armed with the oranges, sausages and black pudding and the fry is officially on. I need to bolster our spirits for the game. Mikey and Joey still have the television on and the radio is on simultaneously and the whole thing is too much. They are playing tug-of-war with their football socks in an effort to stretch them out. I start to fry the sausages and pudding and that glorious smell is unmistakable. I begin to feel frustrated that I am attempting to make a decent breakfast, and that the lads aren't ready for football, and why the fuck has Jenny got her head stuck in some piece of art instead of helping me? It's almost as if she completely absolves herself from responsibility when she senses that she can get

33

away with it. I set the table and start to dish out the food, and still Jenny doesn't appear. I begin to shout, just a bit, about the importance of punctuality and Mikey's and Joey's water bottles for the game, how they should have them filled up by now. What have they been doing except sitting on their arses while myself and Maeve have been at the shops? I ask. There is talk of Mikey's laces on his football boots and how they have been tied. The triple knots make it too difficult for him to untie. He squeezes his feet into them, breaking down the backs of the heels.

We sit down to the fry and as always there's a frantic quality to the way Mikey and Joey eat. I mull over the very concept of real hunger and I wonder how they might survive if they were to properly experience it.

We are running late and I urge the boys to make sandwiches of the rest of their sausages and pudding so we can take them on the go. We make our way to the car and young ketchup-stained fingers touch old rough-textured safety belts. Maeve sits in the front seat and I wonder why my wife does not play the role of mother in our children's lives. Maeve is slowly taking over her position.

We arrive at Maxwell's car park. The rain is squally and the wind is something fierce. I open the driver's door and am treated to a blast. The boys' fingers already have that redness that can only get worse as the game progresses. I berate them about not wearing gloves and I throw my weight about, going on about why they are never prepared, and that they should have remembered to bring them. I tell them that I cannot be the only one to remember things and that they would forget their heads if they weren't attached to their bodies. As we make our way over to the pitch, the wind is at a crescendo and this feeling of wildness provides me with a sense of happiness. The threat of hailstones does something to my insides. It calms me and I recognize that I am not in control of nature. It is the closest that I can come to a religious experience.

I occasionally visit the church of St Alphonsus around the corner from our house on my way to the office. It's a way of sitting with my thoughts but mainly I enjoy the architecture. I am worried that the priest thinks that I am depressed or that I am in mourning, but I am neither of these two things. We don't go to Mass as a family mainly because it clashes with the football. Holy Communion is something that I ingest now only at a requiem mass. The days of going to weddings and christenings are over. Most of the friends that I've witnessed getting married over the last number of years have long since parted ways. Jenny and I may be the last ones standing. I feel a certain pride in that. I imagine that Jenny has similar feelings – or at least I hope she has.

Maurice is at the pitch and his spirits are high.

I'm out for the day, he tells me. After this, I'm off to watch the rugby. She's granted me this, Alison, she's a great girl at times. And we're going to hammer *Les Bleus*.

I cannot understand Maurice's love for the game of rugby. Heads stuck into arses in the depth of an Irish winter and the rest of it. Guys knocking back pints of Guinness and lager. Their women covered in excess foundation, the hue a touch too dark. Wrapped in knee-length cashmere coats to keep out the elements. Apart from anything else, the game as a whole is too violent for me. I find it difficult at times to drive past the National Rehabilitation Centre, on the way to the children's swimming lessons, without flinching in my seat, thinking of rugby injuries behind those closed doors. A grand old Saturday or Sunday morning out training with the

35

lads in a stadium. The sheer glory of the blue sky interspersed with soft cirrus. All crisp, the low morning sun. Perfect conditions and you are in this for the love of the game and then your world collapses around you. A spinal injury and the immediate knowledge that you may never feel again the things that you once felt. Your lover's embrace, the heat of a hot water bottle against your legs on a winter's night, being able to run. Mere memories.

We're up against a nasty bunch today. I can measure their enmity because their manager is already complaining about the referee being a couple of minutes late and his lads are becoming cold. We are all volunteers, and this is kids' football – I say this aloud and Maurice gives me a wink. The opposition's manager flaps his arms, rotates them as if he is a human helicopter about to take off, then he jumps up and down with small rapid leaps as if to prove his point about the cold. We start the warm-up and Maurice is as ever ready with a story for me.

Did you hear about that little girl in Bray, Des? he says.

What's that, Maurice? I line the lads up and get them ready placed one behind another to begin their target practice.

It was a bouncy castle that did it. Birthday party. A gust of wind, she fell and broke her neck.

And?

And kaput. No more. She's a goner.

What were the parents thinking of in this weather? I ask.

If I say so myself, he says. The weather hadn't anything to do with it. Pure negligence, that's all it was.

Maurice is forever at the notion of saying something himself. I am used to this by now but at times it can all be a bit much.

That's a tad heavy, I don't know about you, Maurice, but that story is a bit rough for a Sunday morning match. Will you lay off the sad songs?

Right you are there, Des. I'm not entirely to blame. It's Alison, she seems to have her finger on the pulse of misery and I don't know, I soak it up, despite myself. That's osmosis, right, Des? They're laying her out in her Communion dress. She made her Communion back there in the summer, the weather was grand then. Do you remember?

Jesus Christ, Maurice.

I flinch and I think of Maeve. It doesn't feel that long since she made her Communion. The big day out, the fuss, the bother, the money. I have an image of a beautiful angel masquerading as Maeve bouncing up in the air and then floating higher and higher until I can no longer make out her face. I look over to where Maeve is, leaning against the tall green fence, hunched over a book, her puffed jacket pulled up tight in against her neck. I think about her and the purple party dress hanging in her wardrobe at home. Jenny purchased it for her despite my concerns.

The referee arrives. I have a bit of banter with him and I thank him for making the effort to come out on such a manky morning. Mikey and Joey mention the possibility of getting a sausage roll at the end of the game and I nod with a certain ambiguity. I like to keep them wondering right up until the full-time whistle. It keeps them working at winning.

There's a bitterness to the elements and the other lads start their attack. It's an onslaught against us. They're mostly taller than our team and our boys look terrified, as though they're having difficulty connecting with their young bodies. They are clumsy and they cannot keep possession. I am at my wits' end, shouting and cursing at them to push on and to be strong and Maurice is at it too screaming murder. The referee suddenly blows his whistle and walks over to us and asks us to keep it down a bit, and to watch our language, that this is a friendly affair. I tell him that a league game is not a

37

friendly affair nor can it ever purport to be one. He says that the boys cannot hear themselves think on the pitch, let alone play at all, with us shouting at them. I am livid but I keep a cool exterior. I am fully convinced that the referee ought to have directed his warnings to the other manager who is giving it socks but I say nothing. At this moment an unleashed labrador darts across the pitch to whoops and cheers from most of the lads. Mikey and Joey, by contrast, look rigid: they are afraid of dogs. I blame myself. The fact that I was bitten by a dog as a child shouldn't be the thing that will define their relationships with dogs for the rest of their lives and no matter how many times I tell them this, they won't listen.

The referee manages to get rid of the dog and the half-time whistle isn't long in coming. The boys lash into the assorted selection of drinks. Maurice has bought Aldi-style Capri-Suns. The lads squirt each other with orange and apple juice as they attempt to pierce the minute silver foiled holes at the top of the drinks with weak straws that insist on bending. My hands are sticky from helping out. You get what you pay for. At least the lads are having a laugh.

Maurice, there's something bothering me.

What's that, Des?

It's, Jesus, something is happening to me, ah fucking forget it, forget I said anything.

You're not fucking sick are you, Des? Because Jesus Christ, Des, I wouldn't want anything bad happening to you. What would I do without you?

It's always yourself you're thinking of, Maurice. It's my back. It's not great.

All the time? Maurice asks.

It seems to get painful when I run.

You'd want to watch that. Take some pills, I don't know,

ibuprofen. I thought you were going to tell me that you were dying or something, Jesus Christ, you had me there. It's Sunday morning, let's liven things up. I want to tell him that there are other things bothering me. I want to tell him that that's rich after his story about the poor girl out in Bray. I begin to allude to the fact that it's not just my back that's been at me and that this isn't really the problem at all. That I have worries about Jenny, doubts about Jenny. I want to tell him that there are other things bothering me. Things to do with him, as a matter of fact, that he's encroaching on my position of power, getting a bit above his station for one. He's the guy who helps me out with the football. It doesn't fall on deaf ears that he's already dished out the instructions to the lads to start on their squat thrusts when I've my back turned to take a call.

Jenny.

I don't much feel like answering it, I have only just left her in the house. I don't pick up and I ignore the voicemail too. I've never timed how long it takes for the voicemail to ring to let me know that I have missed a call from Jenny. Sometime I intend to do just that. Maurice is on to me about the recent attacks on women down by the train station.

You should stop that talk now, Maurice. Anyone would think that it is yourself perpetrating all this. Jesus, don't tell me you've forgotten the case in England. You're like that lunatic who was constantly talking about those poor murdered little girls. Here, I better see what she wants.

Jenny's message isn't easy to follow. She's meeting Simon Thompson, the manager of Gallery One in Temple Bar. Jenny reckons that he is the greatest person to know in the field. I don't know whether to be happy or pissed off about this development. I gather quickly that there will be nothing in the way of lunch on offer for us when we get back to the house. I curse her: it is Sunday and I am looking forward to a bit of wind-down time. I rather fancy a couple of beers with Jenny in front of the fire, it's that type of a day. But that clearly is not going to happen now. I cannot help a trickle of jealousy from seeping into my mind.

The game restarts and we resume our normal shouts of encouragement without the expletives and it's almost as if our lads feed off our new clean energy. Mikey goes for a strike, it's on target and he scores. I go a bit overboard congratulating him but sometimes pride simply cannot be covered up. It's a beautiful thing to watch your own flesh and blood putting the ball into the back of the net. It is almost magical. There's a girls' team warming up beside us but the boys take no notice. They're all at that pure stage where their interest cannot be piqued. It's a wonderful place to be and for a moment I try to recall what that felt like, but I find it difficult to remember how I felt at any age.

I open my thermos flask and I hand Maurice a cup filled with scalding tea. He calls me his old flower. I try to concentrate on the game, but images of Jenny in a gallery space with Simon won't go away. I imagine him as elegant, fair, with an abundance of charm. It's what all men strive for. And I can't stop ruminating about why he would choose to call a meeting on a Sunday.

I snap out of it, one of my lads has been kicked in the face. I shout to the referee to do something. We get a penalty. A whoop of joy comes from the team.

Now, lads, listen up, I say. Maurice is dancing.

Lads, keep it together. Mikey, you're on. I presume that one or two of the lads might have a problem with this but I have no choice. Mikey is our best chance.

Crikey it's Mikey, the lads cheer.

I don't know why I worry about such issues. Mikey lines

the ball up. The keeper is fooled and we are well on our way to victory. Their false belief that the game is over causes the lads to begin to sit back and lose a bit of concentration. It's like watching Ireland trying to qualify for a major competition. They allow the other team to get back at them. I lose count after seven two and in the end we lose horribly. The full-time whistle goes and the boys are devastated. Nobody ever says it but I have a good mind to howl out that Dano shouldn't have let in all those soft goals. I am aware that it is up to me as a manager to change the goalie if he isn't up to the mark, but my problem is, I don't really have anyone else. I tell the boys not to worry and I throw about some bars of chocolate, little packets of Haribo jellies, even packets of crips, Meanies and Hunky Dorys. I grab at a packet of buffalo flavour Hunky Dorys myself and I lick the spicy meaty flavour with my tongue from each of the small ridges. Thank God for crisps.

Come on into the huddle, lads. I have a bit of a story for ye all to think about. It's coming into the season of Lent. That's Lent and not Length.

They groan about not being stupid.

So, lads, Lent is a time of sacrifice. What do you think, do you know about it?

A couple of the lads say that they've heard of it. None of them admits to paying it any heed in their family.

So, lads, well, it got me thinking. Lent is about sacrifice, yeah. So with that in mind, myself and Maurice here have decided that until such a time that Lent is over, we'll be giving up bringing crisps and crap.

I feel my control slipping. Dano, the fat kid, is not one bit happy.

How long is Lent exactly? he asks.

Forty days, I say.

And forty nights, Maurice adds.

But we don't have to give up anything at home, Dano says.

Well, let this be a new experience for you. It'll be a good thing for all of you lot. Less junk. You'll be able to run faster. I throw a bag of treat-size KitKats about. The lads are like scavengers – the lot of them.

Dad, do you have to be so religious with the team? Joey asks.

Yeah, Dad, if no one has to give things up at home, why does it have to affect our football matches? They're all at the weekend. We should be allowed to do whatever we want at the weekend. Don't you think Jesus would want us to have fun? Mikey asks.

I don't answer their questions and I wonder about the reason I take these notions upon myself to deny pleasure. Something inside me knows, or at least suspects, that this kind of denial, if taught early enough, will stand the lads in good stead. I don't want them to grow up thinking that they are entitled to anything and everything on a whim, I want them to learn about sacrifice and how, if they wait, good things will come to them, that they will be the better for it. Instead I tell the boys not to be smart and I instruct Maeve to collect the KitKat wrappers that are being taken on the arms of the wind.

I head over to the clubhouse after bringing in the nets with Maurice. Maeve buys hot chocolate for Mikey and Joey in the shop and they sit contentedly in the chairs by the door. The wind has died down somewhat and there is a heartening feeling in the way the sun shines through the clubhouse door.

I go to the jacks and stand at the wash hand basin. I tell myself to be brave, to grip this work situation by the balls. It's only a small thing, yet it feels immense. I tell myself that I should know better than to have let my guard down in front of Susan, Head of Personnel. Her easy tongue. I shouldn't go drinking with the office crowd – it's too dangerous. I cannot always be watching what I say. The stupidity of joining them in the Barge the Thursday before and drunkenly admitting to her I didn't complete my Business Degree but dropped out after two years. I think about my little white lie at the most peculiar times. Susan has promised not to tell Graham about it, but living with this thing hanging over my head isn't easy at the best of times.

I peer in the mirror and I notice my pallor. I am whiter than I should be, considering how much I expose myself to the elements. I walk into the toilet cubicle. There's one ad for the Samaritans on the inside of the door and another one advising us to consider our use of toilet paper in relation to saving the trees of the world. I vomit, making a weak sound, and am grateful to see bits of my earlier fry floating in the toilet bowl. There is a definite taste of acidity in my mouth and my throat burns with it.

8. She Fell for Me Through Dance

July 1995

Nineteen-ninety-five was filled with those beautiful summer nights that you could only dream of. It was what I liked to refer to as perfect concert weather. I wanted to impress Jenny with my sense of cultural appreciation so I brought her to a dance performance in the RHA gallery.

Fifteen dancers, moving with complete fluidity. I was captivated. The height of the ceiling made me feel as though I could achieve great things – I thought of the Renaissance masters in churches, capturing heaven.

The idea was that the audience followed the dancers around the gallery. The proximity of them was intense, so much so that at one point during the performance I actually had a desire to reach out and touch one of them. Jenny held my hand and whispered to me that it was wonderful to witness such powerful movement within the confines of the walls because she was used to visiting it as a gallery and experiencing its quietness and studying the pictures hanging in their innate stillness. She was struck by the comparison. All in a whisper. I squeezed her hand and I felt a pleasure travel down into my body from my stomach and into my legs.

There was an atmosphere in the room and it was erotic. What the dancers were engaged in, their bodily distortions done in complicated and extended strokes of physicality, seemed to evoke something in Jenny and her eyes met mine. I felt very much connected with her in that moment and I felt that our unity was becoming obvious to her and she appreciated the power of that unity. I could tell by the way she placed her hand on my back as one of the dancers moved so close to us I had to take a step backwards.

I had set up boundaries, boundaries that were deeply personal to me and they were lines that I'd drawn around myself. It wasn't intentional. It was as if somebody else had set those walls around me and all the time I wished for Jenny to break through them.

We went for a meal after the show. We talked about what we had witnessed with an abundance of freedom. I felt uninhibited and Jenny seemed to be completely relaxed after strangers' bodies being so close to ours. We could see the glitter on the girls' faces, the pores on the guys' faces. I had never been entirely comfortable with anyone in my personal space. Perhaps it was an over-reaction to my mother, who was extremely protective of me as a child. I remember the way she held on tight to my hand if there was a road in sight and my need to loosen her grip on me the older I became because it was a gesture that I began to find humiliating. And maturing was like that, a steady process of small realizations, tiny facts.

The restaurant had a feeling of elegance that came from its deliberate attempt to mix the old and the new furniture-wise, which was becoming a fashionable experience in Dublin dining. Jenny said she felt right at home.

She grew up in Bray, with its long promenade and the masses of stones on the beach. It was uncomfortable to walk on but she didn't mind that. I loved Bray myself, and growing up in Dun Laoghaire I spent a good deal of time out there with my old friend, Dean. I hung out in the arcades and then the Bray Head nightclub. I was surprised I hadn't met Jenny earlier on. Dun Laoghaire had its charm but Bray had something different going on. I enjoyed the games at the arcades and the smell from Henry & Rose, the fish and chip shop beside the DART station, the special aroma of cod being fried in hot oil. Nobody did fish the way it was done at Henry & Rose. The batter was crispy and the fish flaky with just the right amount of meatiness to it, so it didn't end up having a chicken consistency, which sometimes happened in other chippers.

She said that she wished she could dance.

I told her she could dance. I imagined her dancing, her body writhing in front of me, so close I could touch it.

I asked Jenny to tell me more about her family because I could feel myself going distant on her. I sometimes did that – got lost in my own thoughts and reflections.

Her mother was dead and her father had pretty much stopped talking to her when she had moved in with Jerome. He didn't like Jerome, he was too sure of himself, a trait that her father despised because it was the complete opposite of the way he was.

I talked to Jenny about opposites and about how my father was about things that were overtly dissimilar. Jenny as if teasing me asked me what the opposite of purple was and she said she had it in her head that it was a kind of off-white. It had something to do with Advent candles and although this didn't make any sense to me, I agreed with her. She was an artist after all and she could find colour opposites any way she pleased. I wanted to experience Advent with her. I wanted Christmas blessings with Jenny. I wanted to kiss her on the lips when the priest told us to offer each other a sign of peace.

Dad taught me other things like the difference between traction and retraction, about supply and demand and the subtleties of cloud formations and what they could mean. Some of the names rolled off my tongue but I had difficulty with others like cumulonimbus and stratocumulus and cirrocumulus. He taught me that for all the softness and innocence that could be found in nature, there was also a hardness, a vehemence, and this opposing strand was something that I should be aware of. If someone is kind to you, he once said, look underneath the surface, dig deep. Kindness is not free, it comes with a price.

There was a sense of contentment on Jenny's face as the desserts were presented – a chocolate brownie with walnuts for her and an orange cake for me. The cake was slightly bitter, perhaps the chef had over-grated the rind because it is underneath the pith wherein the bitterness lies. The tartness was overridden with a sweet orange liqueur that was delicious. We offered each other bites of each other's dessert and the sharing was deeply satisfying.

I sat back and looked at Jenny and I listened to her. I listened to someone like I never had before. There's hearing and there's listening and this was listening. It was only a matter of time before we met, this is what I believed. I heard every word she said, how she had found art. I said that there was art everywhere, you had to look for it. She admitted she was sad she had finished with art college because she felt there was so much more to learn and I assured her she could learn about these other things through living.

I was happy to listen to her the way I could listen to the grasshoppers seemingly singing, in Spain, under the intensity of the sun. I loved the way they could cease abruptly as if taking a breath. That was the last real holiday I remember with my brother and my parents. That sensation of enjoying the here and now of it. My mother told Dad to stop worrying about the shop, that Ciaráin, the manager, was well capable and that Dad should enjoy the time away. That was the first time I'd experienced the very notion of having to enjoy yourself, that this ability wasn't something innate.

It was almost as if Jenny was giving away too much of herself. I wanted to encourage her to keep talking so I kept myself locked in and I thought about the stoppage of the crickets, how I only noticed the peace and the quiet of my surroundings in the moment after they had ceased chattering. It was the way I felt after swimming in the sea. It was only afterwards, standing on the rough stones thinking that life cannot get any better, it was only then I could hear the sound of the waves crashing.

I wanted to become a father. That was the thought that struck me in the restaurant with Jenny that night, beautiful Jenny – scraping the last bit of her brownie and running her finger along the plate for the last dash of cream – I knew then that having children with her would complete me.

9. Contentment

August 1995

Jenny made me feel as if the sun shone on everything, warm and balmy and comfortable on my skin. I had better emotional leverage. Happiness was a word that I finally knew the true meaning of. I was there.

She got a tattoo of a ladybird on her left ankle. I thought the design was a little childish but I told her it was great, even though I worried about how it might age. There is something poignant, sad almost, about the maturity process and the way a tattoo moves with it and seems to fade in its own way, its earlier glory reduced to nothing, and it becomes a mere mark by which a loved one can identify you when you're dead. The tattoo fades away and becomes discoloured with it, I wasn't sure if I wanted that for Jenny. I didn't wish her to effectively ruin her beautiful blank canvas but I was careful not to appear negative. It was her body after all.

Everything about her mattered. I was putting so much energy into the relationship but I was careful not to come across too heavy, just enough.

She cut a fringe and dyed her hair jet black, without warning me. The first I knew of it was at the opening night of a club in the grounds of the film centre in Temple Bar. The place was full of noise, people squealing when they bumped into people that they knew and the satisfaction that they had been noticed. It was about being seen and in a way, it was pathetic.

I thought the new haircut was really becoming on her and that's what I told her. I managed to say the words without coming across as being disgruntled. I didn't want words to carry any dysfunctional weight. I was really pissed off that she had gone behind my back like that, it was I considered a pretty dramatic decision. But I didn't say that, instead I talked about glamour and initiative and I told her that she looked so good and she kissed me as I spoke. A couple of her old college friends were there so I didn't make a fuss.

Jenny had recently graduated from art college and she worked part-time in a café on George's Street. It had a great outdoor eating area, which was quite unusual in Dublin then – al fresco dining was generally a magnet for junkies to approach unsupervised belongings but this place wasn't like that. In any case Jenny didn't really care what she did, she had her eye on the prize – getting her art recognized.

She was a great one for a story and she told me about the café – pure entertainment listening to her. She mentioned a particular guy who came in and told her she was pretty, as he paid for his order. I didn't in any way want to go on about it, but I felt it was unnecessary her mentioning something like that. Two people, a fleeting throwaway comment about her beauty. I knew she was beautiful and that was enough. Suddenly I began to feel cheated, I wasn't so sure about this day job of hers, out in the public eye all day, in the summer – her vest top, becoming slightly sweaty under her armpits and if you were to go close to her you would find her secret Jenny scent emanating from those lovely armpits of hers and it would be faintly metallic and it would be a warm and comforting thing and I didn't want to share that with anybody, least of all a complete stranger. Her vest top – in tight to her frame so you could see the outline of her ribs and her nipples sticking out like two pubescent peaks, she didn't bother with a bra. It was only a part-time job but still and all.

The way I held Jenny's hand. It wasn't an over-extenuated grabbing of the hand, rather it was more of a delicate manoeuvre and Jenny seemed to take this in her stride, to like it and the enormity of that, of her allowing that familiarity to grow so concrete and the exhibition of that concreteness to others.

10. The Senior League

March 2017

Mikey and Joey insist on us as a family following the club's senior team playing the league games. And so that is how I spend my Friday nights now. Watching a hopeful bunch of nineteen-year-olds tear around a pretty poor pitch in the freezing cold. It gets bitter at the matches and the only respite is a cup of tea from a polystyrene cup with an ill-fitting lid, or a portion of curry chips. I often opt for the chips as there seems to me an inherent curried heat that offers a peculiarly comforting reward. I get myself a pint of beer too. Jenny insists on drinking wine which pisses me off as it's very overpriced at the clubhouse. However, if you consider the night as a whole, what with a few bars of Cadbury's for the kids, I suppose we might do worse.

I make friends easily enough at the club. I comfort myself that we are pretty much all in the same boat and I enjoy the chat as I hold my pint in my palms, calmly. Practically none of the other wives or girlfriends go along to the games. I prefer Jenny to join us. The way I see it, she needs a break from her art from time to time. It provides me with an opportunity to impart my football knowledge to her. I was a great player in my time but age has not been too kind to my skills. I recognize I am not as quick on the ball as I once was, and I also recognize that Lionel Messi I am not, but the coaching that I do with Maurice is a medium for me through which I can stay involved in the wonderful world of football.

Our boys run around the clubhouse high on chocolate and some cheap sweets called Millions. I swear each week that they are not permitted to spend their two-euro ration on such a heady combination but it's as if they lose their resolve once they reach the top of the queue at the tuck shop. In a way I understand, I would have done the same thing as a child myself if I had had a chance. We go into the clubhouse at half-time and I join the end of the queue of other like-minded freezing-cold dads. Jenny and Maeve find a seat by the door and Jenny removes her heavy wool coat. She looks well, wearing an olive green cashmere sweater that I'm fond of. Sitting there, with Maeve nibbling her chocolate and me looking over at them, we are the perfect family.

I come back to the table with a pint of Carlsberg and a small bottle of Merlot. Jenny tries to start a conversation with me about the first half of the match. In truth I am in no mood so I continue to stare ahead and ignore her comments. I want her here but when she starts needless talk and asks irritating questions I wish that I had left her at home. Sometimes it isn't easy to work out what I want, at all.

That cost almost six euro, that little shitty bottle of vin rouge.

Jenny says nothing, she rubs Maeve's hair and they both stare out the window of the clubhouse.

I kind of give out a little ha sound as I exhale my frustration about the price of the wine. A fucking league match in a fucking clubhouse, the wine should be subsidized, I give fucking-enough to the club. In fact if I'm to really think about it, I should by rights be getting a free pint on nights like these. A little token of gratitude for coaching the under-elevens would be most welcome. I'm sure Maurice feels the same. The pint isn't going down so well after the chips. I continue to neck it down regardless. I feel a headache coming on.

I drain the glass and I head to the toilet. I take a piss and as soon as I'm done I vomit in the toilet bowl. I grunt with the effort and my neck is clammy. I walk out of the cubicle to the sink. I press the cold tap and cup some water with my hands but it is difficult because it only releases a small amount of water at a time. I attempt to get more by pushing it down, the pressure being exerted by my elbows. In the end I use my right elbow to press the tap down and my left hand to catch the water. I take a few moments to dry my face and to gather myself. I resolve to go back out to Jenny and Maeve.

When I return to the table, Maeve seems sullen and I wonder if they've been arguing. I don't bother sitting down and I say that I'm going back outside to watch the second half of the game.

You're pale, Des, Jenny says.

It's the cold. I'll be grand when I get a bit more of it.

I lean in real close and I don't know why I say it but I do. I tell Jenny that her eyeshadow doesn't match what she is wearing as I believe eyeshadow should, and really and truly, it does nothing for her. I have my hand placed on the table while I am saying this and Jenny places her hand over mine. She asks me if I love my life. I respond that of course I love my life. She points out that she actually said wife. I say, oh yeah and the difference, if there is a difference, is smoothed over pretty effectively by me. Jenny pulls Maeve by the shoulder and gently gives her a hug. Maeve gives Jenny a smile signifying some secret knowledge between them. Jenny smiles back.

As I am making my way past the security man I spot Jerome Fagan coming out of the toilet with a boy who I assume to be his son. Jerome nods to me and I nod back. I intend to leave it at that but he comes over to me and I can't get away. It takes all of two seconds for him to ask after

Jenny. I tell him that Jenny is over at the table by the window with Maeve even though I'm sure he has already spotted her. Asking for her like this is in my estimation Jerome's way of asking permission from me to go over to Jenny. I tell Jerome that I'm going back outside to support the team. When I look back I see him at the bar ordering a drink and looking over at Jenny. Part of me wants to go back inside to make it known to Jerome that he cannot waltz about the place, seeking out my wife, but I fight it. Why he has chosen to join this club in the first place is beyond me.

I head over to our stand. There are shouts from managers telling their lads to turn and to face the opposition like fucking men and what about the defence? I stand on the wooden step that is loose. Our side score a goal and because it is so unexpected the way the game is going I actually miss the ball going into the net. All I'm aware of are the supporters and how they are shouting well done to the lads and Mikey and Joey are banging their fists joyfully on the metal barricades and in the rush I feel happy. I can just about make out Maeve in the bar, her face pressed against the glass and I give her the thumbs up. She waves back at me. I cannot see Jenny.

We get back and it is late enough that the kids agree to go to bed without a story. What I really crave now is an opportunity to watch bullshit TV. With one swift flick of the remote control I am presented with something called *Robot Wars*. There's a lot of jargon going on, which is exactly what is pleasing about this kind of programming. Aftershock buffeted by the strike. Crucial movement is the fight, clenching movement is the battle. Aftershock, sabretooth, terrorize team jellyfish. Grown men, shattered grown men working on designing a robot. Gemma from team jellyfish earnestly

55

dressed in an aquamarine overall talks with passion, it has to be said, about the difficulties in repairing a small fragment of the team's robot that has quite simply fallen apart. The presenter is wearing a jumpsuit, I guess that she's meant to look robot-like. It's absolutely absurd but I'm gripped. Is there going to be a jellyfish sting in the tail? This is unconventional behaviour in a robot. This is like a step up from an earlier addiction to all that wonderful, time-pressed pit action in Formula 1. Lego creatures with wheels.

I feel like going upstairs to prod Mikey and Joey awake and haul them downstairs and give them a taste of this. Perhaps they can create one of these robots and as a family we can make a shitload of money. Jenny sighs at the programme but I tell her to be quiet and to go back to her book.

I watch *Robot Wars* to the bitter end, armed with a couple of cans of Pražský. The cool beer slipping down my oesophagus makes me feel that bit mellower. I am getting into my zone. My money worries which have been getting me down lately don't seem as pertinent as before. I haven't told Jenny that I have extended our Credit Union loan – it's in my name even though she did put a fair whack of her own personal savings into it, in order to bolster my fund in the early days. I didn't want to appear completely broke to the powers that be. But I needed the extra so I could take out a loan to get the rest of the house deposit together. My wages haven't gone up in ages and no matter how much moaning I do to Graham it doesn't make any difference. He won't give me a rise.

After a while the beer runs out and I decide to open up a bottle of wine that I've been saving for a special night. This is now a special night. I pour a small glass for Jenny which she accepts but I can kind of tell that she doesn't really want it but is taking it for the sake of it.

That was brilliant, I say.

Jenny nods over at me. I'm assuming that it wasn't brilliant for her and that she's humouring me. Humour away, I don't give a fiddlers.

Can we watch *Location, Location, Location*? I have it recorded, she asks.

I tell her that she certainly cannot put it on, that I'd rather watch paint dry. It's a fucking repeat of a repeat of a repeat, now repeat after me. I don't know where this mean streak of mine has come from. I suppress it when I can but she's not watching those two clowns trying to buy property for losers and telling terrible jokes. There has to be a better way to live.

After a bit of an argument, we settle on a late-night show about the history of punk music. She's sulking a bit, but so be it, it's better to have the room soaked with music than watch people who are incapable of making a decision becoming more and more indecisive. In my view this is the whole problem of choice, that people have to make a choice.

11. God

April 2017

I often feel that God is coming at me. Perhaps fear does that to you. Perhaps having children creates a fear of the unknown. What if they grow up disappointed?

Saturday morning – I prop up my pillow and I take Jenny's satin cushion and place it at the back of my neck. I kick the cushion with the terrible peach paisley design and the lace trim off the bed. Jenny purchased it in a charity shop. She buys an awful lot of tat, used unloved stuff from other people's lives, and she's always trying to be retro, it's like a disease with her. The cushion reminds me of the insipid carpet from my old flat on Camden Lane. I wonder if Jenny was trying to be ironic when she chose it. I lie back in bed. I wish she would come to me. To place her cool palm on my forehead and to bring me a cup of tea, for I often bring her tea in bed and this might be as good time as any for a little payback.

Jenny, I shout downstairs but she doesn't hear me because she has the radio on – mainstream stuff from Lyric FM. I wish she would put on some decent sounds. Jenny, I call her name again. There is no response. I get out of bed. I'm wearing grey boxer shorts and an old black T-shirt. I rub the surface of my bedside locker, a layer of dust is on my finger. I find my grey velvet dressing-gown on a chair under a pile of clothes. I resolve to clean up later.

Resolutions are difficult, more so having the interest to follow through with them. This is why Lent is a good time for me; it forces me to make these promises. For the first time since childhood I kick-started the season by getting a light smattering of ashes on my forehead. I am tempted to put a pair of socks on my feet but an image of the crazy man I spotted on the beach has stayed with me. He wore gold flip-flops. Gold flip-flops over white-towelling socks. I am aware of the fact that Jenny does not enjoy seeing me wearing socks with bare legs and sometimes I do it out of spite. For now I refrain.

I walk downstairs and go into the kitchen. Jenny is frowning and trying to take a slice of toast out of the toaster with a steak knife.

Jesus Christ, what are you doing? You'll electrocute yourself. I'm serious, it's dangerous. A woman died doing just that a couple of years ago in Donnybrook.

She has her back to me and I place my arms around her and she stays in my embrace but for a split second. She holds the steak knife aloft as if she's caught in a horror film. It's like she can't relax or something. I shrug and walk into the downstairs bathroom to take a piss. Hot urine streams out of me in a giant gush. I always piss like this in the morning.

I go back up to the bedroom and consider having a wank. Jenny brings me tea and I thank her for it, even though it is lukewarm. She hands me the paper, which I am truly grateful for. She kisses me lightly on my cheek and her thin lips are cool on my bed skin.

She leaves me feeling slightly ashamed for going off the edge again about her meeting with Simon Thompson back in February.

I can picture her clearly now. How she came home and the children were acting all needy with her – as they always do, when she's spent more than a couple of hours away from the house. Earnest faces – the list of games played on the green, the new football, how Maeve had thumped Mikey on the back because he wouldn't pass the ball. How Maeve had hurt her arm doing a handstand. I could see that Jenny wasn't one bit interested in the children. Her eyes seemed glossy with hope. Simon, it seemed, had provided her with this hope. I felt nervous for her as she told me that Simon had said that her recent work was good enough to include in a group show he was organizing. I asked her about the other artists. She reeled off their names. I hadn't heard of any of them but Jenny kept using words like young, exciting, innovative and brave. I wanted then very much to tell her how brave she was but I was inclined to believe that she might not take my observation seriously. Either way, she seemed to be floating, and each time the children asked her something, she talked over them, without apology, and continued to quote Simon.

I can hear Jenny moving about downstairs in the kitchen. The sound of her cowboy boots clicking on the wooden floor is unmistakably Jenny's and her pacing about annoys me. This is what familiarity does to you. I stretch out my legs, flex my toes and stare up through the skylight at the sky. It seems mesmeric. Jenny bids me farewell as she closes the front door. I respond, but not with much vigour, and I doubt very much she has heard me. I close my eyes and the heat of the sun through the skylight feels heavenly on my cheekbones and I allow myself to fully relax and to drift into a half sleep.

I come to with a start and grapple for my phone in the duvet. It's noon and I have been semi-asleep for almost an hour. I think a bit more about Simon Thompson and I consider his motivation. Is Jenny realistically too old at this stage to make it? Has she not missed her opportunity? Indeed, these very questions are ones that I have posed to her in the past number of weeks. I'm not being unnecessarily cruel, after all I do appreciate her work, but I do wonder if it is too little too late.

I get dressed and go downstairs. Mikey and Joey are out on the green messing about with a football and I put on some chillax music. I make proper tea and sit in Jenny's chair and wait for something to happen, some divine inspiration or something. It isn't long before I take it upon myself to go out and clean the car. I grab the red basin and a sponge from under the sink. As soon as I start soaping the car I curse myself – Mikey and Joey move away from their game to get in on the action. After a lot of mucking about and my temper frayed, I finally tell them to very kindly fuck off back to their game, because if anything, they're causing me more work. I sit down on the kerb to try and relax. The sunlight shining quickly draws out the streaks on the surface of the car windows and I am at a loss as to how to eradicate all these marks. It does cross my mind that there are real problems of war and other such heavy and loaded issues going on in the world. But still the imperfection irks me.

I go back into the house and sort through Jenny's art supplies laid out on her desk. I like to do this when she is out. Jenny and her friend have gone into town, each hoping to get their hair cut in some way that will make them seem more alluring. I don't believe that Jenny needs to make herself any more attractive to anybody except me.

I select a gouge; a type of chisel with a curved blade – designed to remove large layers of wood, smoothly. I run my hand over its handle and it feels cool to my touch. I place it beside a slightly smaller instrument with a flat cross-section. I take hold of a rasp, which gives the wood a very smooth surface. There are bottles of linseed oil and walnut oil to gently treat the woods. Varnish is too strong and can leave an unwelcome glossy effect that looks like the sheer finish of a toffee apple.

I start to read the paper. The home section is my first

choice and immediately the juxtaposition of our messy house with other people's organized havens starts to annoy me. I read enviously about other people's harmonious existences. I wonder why I am reading this. From time to time Mikey or Joey appears in front of me, begging me to go outside, to sort out an argument between them. My default response is to tell them to work it out between themselves as I was brought up to do as a child. This tactic gets me only so far, and after a while, I come to the conclusion that I may as well go back on to the green to act the referee. I look in the mirror in the hall and I realize that a beard doesn't suit me and I resolve to shave it off this very afternoon.

After a while I come back in. Maeve is lounging around the sitting room, reading a book. Her shorts seem just a little short for such a day with a chill in the air. I tell her about the dangers of complacency as it is still only April. She duly ignores my concerns and I wonder what kind of a teenager she will become.

She tells me that she is hungry and I agree to go and get some croissants. She gives me that smile, that look of triumph, and I know that I am easily won over, and that I am supposed to be watching their sugar intake and that Jenny thinks that they eat too much crap and she'll go mad. I don't care about this today. Where is she now, I ask myself? Wandering about town. Having a little well-deserved break from her work, her work that is incomeless. I wonder in that moment what it is that I deserve.

I go back out to the green and attempt to round up Mikey and Joey. C'mon, lads, let's get a couple of croissants.

They are busy with the other kids on the green, and so I leave them while I head across the road to the Centra. Mikey says that he'll see me but Joey has his back to me and that is that. I relax a bit when I think about our local Centra and what it offers to me. I can pretty much buy whatever I need there. It has a fine wine selection and I feel it in my bones that the quality of fruit on offer is often every bit as good, if not better, than the selection in any supermarket. These things matter to me.

Tomek works behind the counter. From Poland, he's a large and pleasant type and I'm forever trying to gauge what age he is. I've asked him before, but he won't tell me, and I feel as though he is deliberately misunderstanding my question. I'm not sure exactly what this information will do for me. Perhaps it may serve to ground him. Right now he is the tall Polish man, working in the local shop. I'm curious to know his reasons for choosing to come to Ireland. Was it a search for a life of security and optimism? I wonder about his family, his house, a dog, a favourite scarf, a favourite brother, a favourite food. I have heard that they eat pretty gruesome stuff in Poland, you'd have to be made of steel to even contemplate one of their so-called delicacies.

I nod to Tomek and head to the fridge to choose rashers. I opt for streaky maple cured, even though I know that I will either overcook them and the rinds will be a blackened mess, or I will undercook them, and they will be too chewy and I will feel the bacon bristles on my lips as I try to make light of the situation.

Tomek often speaks to me of Killiney beach, he likes to walk there. We exchange stories about the people who frequent it and Tomek says that it reminds him of Poland. I buy rashers and croissants and we bid each other goodbye until the next weekend. I feel slightly guilty as I make my way back to the house after telling Tomek that I have always wanted to go to Poland. I have no major desire to go to Poland, I don't know why I said it.

12. Some Place Special

October 1995

My special place. A place that would become in time a haven for us – the way Dun Laoghaire prom is for old people, as they walk to and fro, connecting with the same ground, over and over. I wanted a magical location for us – a place that would evoke in us a special feeling, always. I chose Killiney beach. I suppose it was sentimental.

Even though I knew it had ended badly with Jerome, somehow I needed the specifics. Jenny was reluctant to talk about it and she implied that I was abnormal because I wanted this information.

I said it is a fact that stagnant water carries mosquitoes on its surface.

We sat together on the bright blue wooden bench at the end of the ramp that led on to the beach. The bench was well-worn, paint peeling, and I thought of previous stories exchanged. The history of break-ups and new romances was absorbed in its knots and twists. I felt a sense of peace in that moment. Our togetherness, the powder blue sky. The delicious warmth of the early autumn sun, sweet like fresh mango. Seagulls, I counted five, formed an exquisite pattern as they flew close to the surface of the water. A flock of turnstones scattered on the stones, busily going about their business. Stones that were grey and white and dull green. Stones that were thousands of years old containing fossils, the indentations of tiny bird footprints. And the ochre bricks that were tossed and mauled by the sea amongst the others.

Killiney beach was my favourite place in the whole world. The sheer vastness of the bay, totally underused for as long as I could remember. Perhaps it was the gravelly quality of the beach or the fairly inaccessible car park, I didn't know and I didn't mind. I figured there was more of it, just for me.

Jenny said that somehow she had never been there before and I said that some day I wanted to live beside it and I'd take anywhere within walking distance.

I removed my black Converse boots and rolled up the ends of my jeans. I made my way to the twinkling water's edge and gingerly placed my feet in the sea. Jenny followed me down, her maxi skirt swayed on her hips as she walked. I loved the way she moved, it was so elegant.

I cupped some water in my hands and I threw it at Jenny. She laughed and for a moment she seemed very young to me, and vulnerable. I came out of the water and I brought Jenny into my arms and held her really tight. This was what it was supposed to be like – natural surroundings and an exciting feeling, a sense that this was going somewhere.

And I told her she was so beautiful.

She laughed and broke free from my embrace and she ran on along the beach towards the broken fences by the steps which led up on to the top road. I ran after her and caught her. We were standing in an area where the sea had exposed a great rift of sand. Behind it, enormous pieces of driftwood, moved by the ferocity of the waves, lay stranded together with lumps of concrete pipes and granite boulders. It made for striking beach furniture.

It must have been some storm, I said. It's hard to imagine the sea has the strength to move concrete around like that. It's been crazy the autumn we've had, look at the state of the place.

I tossed a crumpled tin of Linden Village into the bin at the steps. I said that it was mad what comes out of the water and that I often thought about bodies being washed up.

I said that every single time I came here, I wondered why I didn't do it more often. There was something about the place that was sheer magic. Like a postcard.

Jenny said she liked my passion, and that it was a great trait to possess. I was hoping that she was going to tell me that she was mad about me, that's what I wanted. With her talk of passion, I thought that she might be taking the piss and that bothered me.

I said that it was making me feel a bit old talking about the appreciation of nature and I suggested that we go and get pissed or see a film or something.

With the nature trail out of our hair, we bought train tickets and sat on the sick green tartan seats. I mentally compared our train system to other ones that I had been on: U-Bahn, S-Bahn, Métro, Underground. People put their feet on seats in Ireland – supposedly for a laugh, but it pissed me off. There was a smell in the carriage, that distinctive metallic whiff. A woman sat in the seat in front of us and it was obvious to us that she was a member of our nomadic people and the air was hot and sweet and sickly. I turned away.

Jenny looked out the window for the journey back into town. The waft of the algal bloom reached us when the doors opened at Dun Laoghaire but it really came to a head at Booterstown.

The wind whipped in through the doors and it felt fresh as I pointed out our little bird sanctuary to Jenny.

The smell was powerful and I told her it was because of the algae and that actually it wasn't that bad and I said that if she got a whiff in high summer, she'd know all about it.

We got off the train at Tara Street and we headed into

Temple Bar. I suggested Rosario's, a place I'd been to before. It was cheap enough and we ordered pasta covered with arrabbiata sauce. I'd had it once before and, at the time, it had seemed almost extravagant. The second time round it seemed more like acidic tinned tomatoes on top of a bit of spaghetti. The token dried Parmesan made me think about cats and how they release a smell I found repulsive.

I ordered a carafe of house red and I noticed that the waiter was getting a little frisky with Jenny with his fake Italian accent. I knew by looking at him that he was probably from Artane or somewhere. Part of me felt proud of this fact, that the girl that I was with was making such an impact. Rosario's – there was something shit cool about the place, despite the waiter, and I recognized faces from around town, and I nodded at one or two of them.

It was the perfect end to a perfect day. The sea air had done us a world of good and things were stronger between us than before. We had found our place and I was looking forward to revisiting it over and over with Jenny, now that she was firmly in my life.

13. Celebration

Our relationship grew tighter and stronger and although it had only been a year, I felt that Jenny had been in my life forever. It was her twenty-first birthday and that had to be celebrated and I was going to do it in style.

Even though I believed that we had each other and it should be enough, I knew that on some level Jenny was still at that stage where it was important for her to be surrounded by other people to mark special occasions, otherwise they weren't sufficiently meaningful. She had been looking forward to her birthday, talking it up for some weeks beforehand, and I felt a compulsion to do a ring around and invite some of the old college friends to join us, mainly to impress her. I figured that I should get to know them better.

I went ahead without Jenny's knowledge and booked Pizza Stop because I knew that she liked the informal atmosphere of the place. The evening was going well. Garlic bread, scattered with shavings of Parmesan, and bruschetta lay on a platter in the middle of the table which was covered in a red and white checked oilcloth. I had ordered the starter with the intention that the act of sharing food might open up the conversation. It worked. There was a lot of talk of music and people taking on shit jobs in order to pay the rent. The conversation was such that I found to my pleasure, with my job at the magazine and in the Crown, I had a fair bit to offer. Some of the crowd laughed at the things I told them about the ins and outs of running a magazine. I tried to make it sound bohemian or glamorous but I think for the most part I put them off. However, I felt that my contribution was as good as the next. I was at that stage in life, young – where you felt that anything was possible. Despite having lost my brother Brian, I had a false belief in my own immortality, it was as simple as that.

There was a lot of over-hyped banter and I could sense us all beginning to relax with the wine. It was the second least expensive on the menu. Everyone was dressed in a way that was supposed to look careless – as if they hadn't put much effort into their choice of clothes for the night, but I knew better. I had waited the guts of an hour for Jenny in her flat earlier when she was getting dolled up. By the time she emerged from her bedroom I'd drunk two cans of beer.

When we were ordering desserts I handed her a small package. She placed it on the table, unopened. She seemed more concerned with filling her glass with more red wine than she did with my gift. I leaned over her and asked her if she was going to open it. She said that she would later and I felt hot – like someone had slapped me. The waitress arrived with the tiramisu. Jenny's portion had a lit sparkler in the middle. We sang a drunken 'Happy Birthday', some other customers joined in, and in that moment I felt pleased that I had gone to the trouble of letting the waitress know when I had booked the table that it was Jenny's birthday. As the sound of our voices tapered off Jenny looked to me and she was beaming.

I asked her again to open her present.

She unwrapped the box and took out the necklace.

I couldn't believe it – instead of putting it on, she looked at it for a second and then she placed it back in the box and put the box into her handbag. I had spent a considerable amount of time choosing it and I wanted some affirmation.

She said it was perfect but she was afraid that she might lose it and that she would wear it when she got home. In a playful tone, I suggested that there was actually more chance of her losing it from her handbag than from around her neck, but she insisted the catch might not be strong enough. I found that I couldn't help myself pulling it back out of her bag and insisting on putting it on her neck.

See the catch is grand, I said.

There was a silence at our table. We could hear the talk from other diners in the pizza place and the background music seemed to be louder than it was before. My ears felt like they were going to pop and I took up my wine and knocked it back. One of her girlfriends started a conversation about the likelihood of her ever succeeding in getting a career in publishing. I told her to fuck off and to stop talking about work. It was Jenny's birthday and the only thing that we should be talking about is where we were going next. I was getting pumped up. Nobody spoke and I felt their eyes on me, greedy like witnesses to a car crash. Jenny had her hand held over the silver necklace as though she was protecting it. I asked her if she liked it, and she nodded.

It was expensive, I said. You can tell by the quality of the catch, and I looked away. I was the smooth guy.

I called the waitress over and asked for the bill. Conversation resumed, but it was quieter in nature than before and there was a shift in the energy. Jenny and Angela went to the loo. When they came back I was busy splitting the bill between the ten of us. I figured that it was twenty quid a head including the tip. Angela suggested that Jenny shouldn't be included in the bill because it was her birthday. I told her that in principle I didn't agree and that if anything Jenny was getting off lightly. If Jenny was Spanish she would have had to pay for the lot of us, as was the custom in Spain.

Nobody seemed to have thought any further ahead than the restaurant. Some of her friends started to back off when I suggested going on to Sound House on the Quays. Maybe I hadn't made a good impression. I didn't care. I figured that if Jenny and I were going that it would be enough but Jenny insisted that they all join us. And they did.

The club was the same as it always was. It had that quality that was hard to put your finger on, but something about the crude set-up of the place worked. It was organic. I bumped into Austin and I was pleased because I hadn't seen him properly since I'd started going out with Jenny. The thing that I liked most about Austin was that you didn't have to make conversation just for the sake of it. It had always been like that. We stood with our backs to the bar and took things in. I was drinking beer and it wasn't resting easy in my stomach after the wine and the pizza. In between gulps of beer I found myself swallowing my saliva. I realized after a bit that I was going to be sick.

I made it to the toilet and vomited. It was mainly straight beer but in the yellowy froth slices of pepperoni and lumps of green pepper were clearly distinguishable. I took my head out of the toilet and sat on the floor of the cubicle. It was astonishing how quickly I felt the better for it.

But when I went back to the dance area I didn't feel great again and decided that I had to leave. Jenny pretended not to hear me when I told her it was time to go. I grabbed her elbow. She said that it was her birthday and that I needed to relax and that she intended to stay out late, with her friends. As late as she wanted.

You do that, I said.

I didn't mean to come across as being abrupt, and I apologized, and that seemed to be that.

She repeated what we both knew by heart by then, that it

was her birthday. She said that she would come over to my flat after the club. I felt as though I had no alternative but to agree and I truly wanted her to have a good time, it was her birthday after all.

I left then and I headed on into the dark of the night. The boardwalk along the Liffey was at conceptual phase back then. As I walked I imagined how on earth it might work in a city full of heroin addicts and drunks. Dublin City Council was talking about our city and Paris in the same sentence, about flower boxes and a riverside café culture. The whole thing was preposterous. It would never happen. I was headed to Rick's for a burger. I figured that it might actually settle my stomach.

The place was jointed but I decided to wait anyway. I was very annoyed with Jenny for not leaving with me. For making me look like an idiot, all needy. I wasn't sure if I particularly liked any of her friends but it struck me in the strip-light that that wasn't the point. It was as much to do with pride as anything else.

14. The Picnic

April 2017

Even though the real hurt of the winter is over, I promise myself not to become complacent. I am well aware of how surprisingly cool spring can be. The garden is still in shreds; little bits of plastic that have been blown about during the winter storms continue to decorate the sparse bushes.

Jenny wears her old jeans that are ripped at the knee and splashed with oils and paint. She is using pencils and charcoal and she is sketching out a figure. She frowns as she works. I stand behind her and I touch her shoulder lightly. There is a photo of a man wearing a white dress beside her canvas.

I ask her who he is.

She tells me that he's a Brother from the order who live in the large house beside the beach. They pray in groups at the edge of the water. She often gets up early at weekends to watch them. It would be nice if she was as attentive to my needs in the early hours of the weekend, it would be nice if she could touch me at the weekend. I wonder if Jenny is attracted to things that are unattainable.

I am preparing a picnic for my family. I boil conchiglie because the kids love the shell shape of the pasta. The day is mild and unassuming despite the large black cloud in the sky that I can discern out of my kitchen window dangling against the purple of the Dublin Mountains.

I was thinking of Glendalough, I say.

She nods and I take that as a sign of approval. She begins to help me get the food together, slicing tomatoes with a delicacy and adding them to a bowl containing lettuce and capers. She cuts great wedges of fruit cake and won't hear of it when I suggest smearing each slice with a great lump of butter.

Sporadically I have an inclination to go somewhere with some spiritual significance. This is why Glendalough comes to mind. It is in my estimation the epitome of grace in nature. I often think that it is a place that illuminates the true meaning of the majestic in a religious sense. I'd often go there as a child and walk by the lake but never swim because we were warned that it was perilous. St Kevin seemed to speak directly to me there. I was genuinely religious as a small boy and I could enjoy the meditative quietness of the surroundings. I imagined the monks and St Kevin praying with his arms outstretched. I visualized him, as the story goes, waiting tirelessly for the bird's egg that had been laid on his palm to hatch. I thought of St Kevin wandering about studying ornate manuscripts. It was all so magical to me. I have tried to explain my fascination with the place to Jenny before but it seems like we could be going anywhere for all she cares about it.

Joey and Mikey are beginning to niggle at each other. A full fight is brewing, this is something that happens with children when they are faced with the prospect of being cooped up in a car with each other for any more than ten minutes. I reckon that we should be within the grounds of Glendalough within an hour and a half and I ask them to stop and to think of my patience. I often describe my patience as something that is wearing thin or fit to explode and I am aware in my heart that I shouldn't bother expressing my frustration to them because it doesn't get me anywhere and if anything it

74

frustrates all of us. I think that they get at each other because they cannot help themselves, because they recognize that Jenny and I are trying to hang on to some semblance of love and it isn't easy. My mother told me that she didn't have it particularly smooth with my father and she told me that I oughtn't to be unrealistic in terms of my expectations. I wonder if my kids can pick up on my disappointment.

I am a nature man myself, the landscape in all its variety evokes significant pleasure in me. I tell Jenny often that we have such a beautiful country and we should appreciate it. It starts to rain, it pisses down. I rather enjoy the rain myself, it dispels bad feelings as well as old streaks of urine, dog fouling and sick and other detritus found in gutters across the country. Jenny complains about the rain. I find her negativity difficult to accept and I decide to ignore her observations on precipitation.

Mikey wouldn't eat his Coco Pops this morning, she says.

I keep my eyes on the road. It seems like a small thing. As a father I should probably be grateful that a child of mine is resolutely refusing to eat a cereal which I know in my heart to be extremely non-nutritious, but I am not happy. What worries me is the fact that he won't eat any cereal at all. Frosties, which I imagine to be a dream for most children, are left to go into a soggy, autistic-beige pulpy mess. I have resorted to boiling Mikey an egg in the mornings, timing it so it's still runny, ochre yellow. He has been happy with this but lately I've noticed that he's not finishing it off and the yolk of the egg is allowed to dribble out on the plate and I have to use a scrubber, with a certain tenacity, to remove the stains.

We head towards Kilmacanogue, passing Avoca Hand-weavers on our right. I tense up when I notice Jenny casting her eyes to the red and white sign of Avoca advertising a new lunch special in the Avoca Café. The Avoca Café is set in a large open-plan greenhouse and it's painful, filled with women wearing far too much makeup combined with taupe clothes, on a child-free brunch. In short, it gives me a pain in my hole. I drive on a couple of hundred yards and I pull into the petrol station on our left. It's hot in the car despite the rain and Jenny won't talk to me and I don't understand why. I tell the kids that I'll get a couple of packets of Tayto when I'm paying for the fuel. They won't hear of it. They have to come into the shop with me to choose the crisps for themselves. This is so irritating that I want to smash their faces.

In the petrol station, I head straight to the Banklink to withdraw some funds. I like to deal in cash, I am better able to keep track of my spending. My mother was terrible with money and in the end it killed her because she could never relax. Maeve is pretty in an ankle-length floral dress that she picked out herself in Penneys. Mikey and Joey are in their football gear, as they always are. I don't mind this, it saves us doing unnecessary laundry. I notice the way Maeve appears to others. Soft. I don't know why I was so angry with her for coming into the station. She is a mother hen to her younger brothers as she lists the pros and cons of the different variety of crisps to them. I often believe that those two have absolutely no idea how lucky they are to have Maeve as a sister because it seems to me that she does truly love them. I grab a coffee for Jenny and we head back to the car.

Jenny has a face on her and she takes a sip of coffee too quickly from the plastic lid and she curses because the coffee burns her tongue. She flicks through the weekend supplement of the *Irish Times*.

That's a rag, I tell her. I don't know why I have to denounce her for reading this part of the paper. It's just that it annoys me pretty intensely that she never bothers with any decent sections of the newspaper. She keeps well away from anything at all that might pertain to the domestic political sphere or world news. She ignores anything to do with the Middle East because I think she finds the whole thing too confusing. I admit that it isn't easy working out exactly what is going on over there but at least I make the effort.

It seems casual the way she drops Jerome's name there, in the forecourt as she blows on her hot coffee. Jerome, it seems, has asked her out to have a drink with him. An image of Jenny and Jerome cosy as fuck in some bar causes me to start the car at an entirely unsuitable speed. The kids talk about whiplash and I tell them in an angry voice that whiplash only applies in a situation when you stop very suddenly, not take off. I don't know if I'm correct with this theory as I've never really done any research on the topic but I'm in no mood now for doubting myself. I begin to drive at speed and Jenny asks me to slow down as I'm frightening the children. I know that she is right but something in my physical makeup prevents me from being sensible. It's almost as if the car is driving itself and the control that I normally have has vanished. I am a navigational dummy. Jenny is shouting at me now and I sense that the kids are becoming a bit uneasy so I attempt to distract them.

St Kevin is a very significant saint. I drown out Jenny's voice. My voice has a frantic level that I'm not partial to, it's verging on the hysterical. I begin to direct my audience using my teacher's tone. It's never too early for small ears to be filled with knowledge. I have gained many an interesting fact from my father and I want to pass this information on to my offspring. I believe in early intervention, that it may in fact help them to become better people when they outgrow their childhood innocence.

St Kevin is boring, they say as a chorus.

He's not boring, he's a saint.

The groaning competes with the radio. I commence my directive about what constitutes a saint and why this is worth knowing. I move on to the subject of canonization and I think it is at this point that I lose them. Jenny stares out the passenger window like the queen being brought out on a day trip. I try not to think about Jerome's motivation. His arms around her as he kisses her on both cheeks when she meets him in the bar. The awkward laugh emitted from his fucking mouth when he asks Jenny what she would like to drink and he discovers that things haven't changed from the time when they were together and that she's still quite fond of the wine. How he'll try not to look too pleased about their previous intimacy. How he'll try to keep his eyes from looking at her body, he'll smell her perfume. It's the same all the same, she still wears Quorum aftershave, she always has. There's something sexy about its scent on a woman's body. And Jerome will know all this too because he has been there.

I gather together the five euro for the car park.

The lake of Glendalough stands eerily, the backdrop to our day. The conditions immediately begin to change as they often do here. The steady drifts of stratus appear to move down the mountainous terrain until their reflection seems to be touching the lake. The long ridge is proud, a magnificent background to the icy depths of the water. There's a group of teenagers messing about with the life ring, pulling at the long rope. I watch them for a few minutes and I say nothing. When they start trying to use the ring as a lasso, I can't leave it so I go over to them. I go on about how a stolen life ring is a stolen life. I tell them to put the ring back. I talk about social conscience and I ask what their parents would think. They tell me that their parents wouldn't mind.

The weather looks like it is turning for the worse. Jenny beckons me over and tells me that she is going to set up the picnic, in case it lashes. She wants me to stay at the table and leave the boys alone. But, I cannot let it go. I tell her to set up the picnic, if she feels so inclined, and I head back over to the lake. Mikey and Joey trail behind me.

I notice that one of the lads has a delicate look about him, as though he's not completely right in the head. He flexes his hands, exercising them. He mutters something under his breath. A low soft sound. I tell him to speak up, if he has anything to contribute we had better hear it and that I'm all ears. The lake has a soft ripple as if the presence of the clouds is pulling at the surface of the water. I speak calmly and I tell the boy to put the ring back and something about my tone is enough to make him wind up the rope, and I suppose I have picked out the most vulnerable one. When he is finished, I walk away with Mikey and Joey. They ask me why I chose that one particular boy to put the ring back. I tell them I picked him because he was the closest to it.

I don't tell them that I feed off weakness.

The picnic is successful enough in terms of variety although I will not be sorry if I never see another morsel of pasta in this life again. I swear to God it makes me constipated but the kids can't seem to get enough of the stuff. We sit at our regular picnic table and I have a pain at the lower part of my back from the hardness of the bench. The sky has turned almost black and my fingertips are freezing and yet I put on a brave face. I am well aware that I will not get away with using the cold as a reason not to have a kickabout. The boys are already putting on goalie gloves and trying to do squat thrusts on the uneven grass. Jenny sips coffee from a thermos flask and she looks around at the trees and the mounds of grass as if she is seeking some answers. A group of tourists are sitting by the circle of stones in the expanse. From here I can hear American accents and I can feel myself flinch.

Mikey and Joey start at me. I tell them to get warmed up and that I'll join them once I have a cup of tea. I pour some milky-sugared tea from yet another thermos and sit back. I often think that there is something wonderful about eating out in the open. Things seem more exciting than they actually are, apart maybe from the congealed pasta shells. I don't like to put pressure on myself to relax because in a way I feel that this defeats the purpose of relaxation as a concept but at times I don't have a choice. There are two things that are really bothering me, one is this drink business with Jerome and the other is the fact that the skirting boards in the kitchen back home are manky dirty. I realize that Jenny can meet whoever she likes but I don't have to be happy about it. Jenny as if seeing dark thunder in my eyes tells me that while I'm playing football with the boys, herself and Maeve are going to take a walk by the lake.

I watch them set off and as if nature knows what Jenny intends the April sunlight bravely appears, bringing a whole different outlook to the valley. It feels more like a place of hope and even though I'm not particularly fond of Americans I'm glad for them that they won't be subjected to an afternoon of rain. I know in my heart that Jenny prefers to take these little walks of hers alone. They are for her a chance to smoke without me looking on with disgust. Her filthy habit. Sometimes she tells me that she'll give them up but generally her intonation isn't right and I know that she's lying. That's another thing that I suppose bothers me, if she can lie about smoking she can lie about her feelings for Jerome. I am getting carried away and I know it. I know it in my bones, the way my heart starts to race and I try to keep away from these negative thoughts. I think of how I have read that red is the colour of depression and that for some depression is really a fear of losing love. I am not depressed.

We play about and we mark goals with jumpers and ano-raks. We make the goals large, then we decrease them in size just to make things a bit more complicated, more challen-ging. I make obstacle courses from cups and plates and the two thermos flasks. I can hold the boys' attention if I do the obstacle course too. They're not content to allow me to sit back once I've set everything up. It's all about my partici-pation. I go along with them because I figure that's what any good father should do. After a while I become tired and I tell the boys that I'm going to sit down and have a tea break. I attempt to read the sports section of the paper but Mikey and Joey start arguing about who has won and I tell them to shut up, to give me a small bit of peace, but they won't let up. I tell them that if they shut up I will bring them over to the shop and buy them an ice cream. They stop arguing for maybe a minute and then in despair I tell them that the ice cream idea is off. It's fucking over, I shout at them and there in the valley I feel like I'm going mad.

I'm shouting with increased vehemence and I'm telling the boys that they're ungrateful. They, in their innocence, point out that they have in fact nothing to be grateful for, seeing as I have let them down on the ice cream front. I am at a loss because, in a way, I know they're right. I stop in the middle of my rant and the boys ask me what's wrong with me. Mikey asks me if I'm having a stroke but Joey assures him that this isn't likely as I'm quite a fit dad for my age, compared to his school friends' fathers. I reckon he's on to something here, there's no shortage of potato-heads at the school gates and that's no lie. But they're beginning to argue too much amongst themselves. I'm all for debating in gen-eral but there is something about Glendalough that in my mind demands peace. To be incessantly talking seems wrong somehow and I ask them to desist as I cannot think. It is in this moment of unexpected silence and clarity that I realize that Jenny and Maeve have not returned and that they have been gone almost two hours.

There is no denying that once I make this observation I'm worried. I'm well aware that my level of distress could be deemed excessive. I don't see it in the same light, there is no such thing as worrying too much about the people that you love, there is nothing over-indulgent about this. I try to calm myself down by saying that Jenny and Maeve are together and they are on their way back and then I look up to where I last glimpsed them at the lake and they are nowhere to be seen. I rationalize that they have most likely taken the board-walk trail around by the lake, and yet if that is the case they should be back by now. I think about looking for them but I don't want to leave this spot in case they come back. I pace about and Mikey and Joey whinge and ask me to play more football, that it will take my mind off things and it will help their mother and sister to hurry up. I start to line the ball up to take a shot against Joey and I can feel my heart and it's as if it is hammering against my chest and just as I am about to kick the ball I spot Jenny and Maeve coming towards us. I think about the heart and about the fact that it's essentially a muscle and how it needs to be regularly exercised.

Where were you for fuck's sake? I ask Jenny.

I try to keep calm but my voice is husky and gravelly and that's the way it goes when I'm angry. Jenny is gushing about how the walk has cleared her head, has really given her the inspiration that she has been missing. I tell her that I'm glad she feels this way but the reality is, it shouldn't really take two hours to find a little semblance of hope or indeed of clarity in what is essentially a nature reserve. She wants to know why I can't be happy for her. I tell her that I'll be happy for her when she starts making a bit of money. This is her

cue to talk about her upcoming group show in Gallery One
and how she might well be on the cusp of something here,
something big and it takes only a split second to talk about
Simon Thompson.

We've had enough of everything here today. Enough
milky tea, enough pasta. I have lost my desire to explore. I
cannot be bothered to go over to St Kevin's Tower as I was
hoping to because Jenny has taken so long walking with
Maeve. The truth is that we may as well have spent the day
in Maxwell's Park over at the football pitch. I make a show
of lashing everything into the boot of the car. Jenny sits back
in the passenger seat in expectation of a relaxing journey. I
drive home too quickly which isn't like me because I'm normally a fussy driver. The kids are tired and they are at each
other in that prickly way that only siblings can be. It's a special familial test. Brian and I would have been at the same
malarkey when we were kids. But I'm in no mood for it.

When we get home it's almost bedtime. Upstairs in Maeve's
room I can hear Jenny reading to the kids. I move in and out
of their bedrooms putting away clean clothes from the hot
press and toys and magazines that have been discarded on
the floor. I can hear their contentment as they hold their talk
in, it's the one time when they are quiet and contented. I am
glad that they like stories about wizardry because it keeps
them safe in the arms of innocence for that bit longer. People
allow their children to move away from childhood too soon
in my estimation.

I sit at Jenny's desk and I rub my fingers along it, feeling
the marks in the metal. They are like minute scars that are
left after someone has repeatedly cut themselves. Her desk is
part of her. There are photos stuck to the wall. Happy shots
of the children. Others – of objects that no doubt she has

found interesting for one reason or another, over time. There is one of herself and the children that I remember taking in Connemara. Huddled together after a long day of swimming in Dog's Bay avoiding seaweed and magenta jellyfish, Maeve's purple lips and Mikey and Joey posing for the camera but you can see that they are shivering behind their smiles. Not a single image of me. I scour the walls, nothing.

I open one of Jenny's art books and I read about artists who had affairs with their subjects like Hockney and a couple of other names that I haven't heard of before. I look closely at a painting by Munch called *Jealousy* that he painted in 1895. The haunted eyes of Stanisław Przybyszewski catch me off guard. They are arresting. I learn that Przybyszewski was a Polish writer and a friend of Munch's. His wife modelled for Munch and Munch had an affair with her. Munch, it seems, was obsessed with jealousy and came back to the theme again and again in his paintings. There is something in Przybyszewski's eyes that I recognize in myself.

I get up from Jenny's desk, it is time for a cup of tea.

15. Group Show

May 2017

I am aware that Jenny holds Simon Thompson from Gallery One in high regard. He's been at the centre of the Dublin art scene for over twenty years. And right now she's putting a lot of her faith in him. I hope she's not expecting miracles. I know that he's promising her this break but there's nothing worse than blatant desperation. There's an article about him in the newspaper in the weekend supplement. Jenny is doing that irritating thing she does of insisting on reading something that she finds interesting aloud.

Simon Thompson, owner of Gallery One, speaks of twenty years in business, she reads.

I tell Jenny that I am well aware of this fact because she never stops going on about how great he is. I wonder how he can still have the same enthusiasm. On the other hand maybe I'm just frightened because I'm becoming increasingly aware of how quickly the years are going. I think about the longevity of some of my connections and it makes me feel old.

I'm making pasta for the kids – fusilli and I'm stirring in a cheese sauce that doesn't look that appetizing but I persist with it. Jenny stops reading and I stop stirring my sauce. This is probably a good thing as it is beginning to stick anyhow. This often happens when I attempt to create a full-blown meal from what is essentially a roux. Jenny puts the paper down on the kitchen table and goes to her desk. She starts to dot small amounts of oils on to her battered artist's palette. Orange and black and red. I sense that she's going to paint an angry sea, a furious sea caught out in its rage just before sunrise. Because this truly is the most beautiful time of all in which to witness the promise of the brilliance of the sun and the savagery of the water.

Is that it? I ask her.

She tells me that I don't seem particularly interested in the article. And that it's okay, it's only to do with the upcoming group show and that it doesn't matter to her at all that her name is in the paper. Imagine her name underneath all the other artists? All I can think of is sweet Jesus Christ. I tell her that I have been listening but that it's not easy to listen and to make lunch at the same time.

Hang on, your name is last? I ask her.

She says, so what, it doesn't mean anything. I assure her that being listed last is probably as good as being first in its own peculiar way. I ask her about the other artists in the show. She grabs the paper again and finds the article. I can hear the pleasure in her voice and it wavers when it gets to her name. I have only heard of one of the other artists before. I'm not sure what to make of this ambiguity.

She tells me that she is meeting with Simon later this evening to talk about the show and to make arrangements for when they can move her work from our house to the gallery. I really don't see the need to turn what is essentially a business meeting into something social. I mention this to Jenny and the fact that I'm not happy about it. She paints quickly, her eyes have an intensity about them.

I call the kids in from the green. Nobody wants the fusilli because there is a smell in the kitchen essentially of burnt sauce. I tell them about real hunger. They've heard it all before. The kids have no option now but to eat the pasta. Jenny yells from her desk that she isn't hungry. I have a good mind to tell her that she ought to lead by example. The pasta is blandness coated with the acridity of disaster. I begin to shout at the kids now, telling them that they're ungrateful fucking brats. It's not their fault, I know that, anyone can see it. I look to Jenny and it's almost as if she cannot see the trouble that I'm in. I swear under my breath to Jesus and I feel faintly remorseful that I am resorting to this kind of carry-on but I want her to help me out here. The kids stab the twirled lumps of pasta with their forks and shove them into their mouths with resignation, then they head back out on to the green. I cannot look at them as they pass by me, and I am at a loss as to how to clean the burnt sauce from the bottom of the pot.

Saturday is a day for getting things sorted out around the house but because I am so pissed off about lunch I decide to head out for a run. I put on my black Lycra shorts and my new Lycra top that has a special mesh flap at the back of the neck for added ventilation. I haven't tried it out yet but a very young sales assistant in 53 Degrees North has assured me that I will not regret my decision to purchase this. I try not to focus too much on the fact that it has set me back almost a hundred euro. I have to be worth such extravagance. If you don't love yourself then how can you expect anyone else to love you? And looking good helps.

I walk into the room in my gear to tell Jenny that I am going for a run. She has her head down and she has what looks like a small knife in her grip. She is scraping bits of paint away from a canvas and then wiping the paint on to an old sheet scrap. There's a certain strength there in her arms. I call her name again. I wonder how is it that Jenny cannot hear me despite the fact that I am standing right beside her. I tap my finger on her desk and she looks at me.

I jump lightly from one foot to another as if I'm giving her a taster of how I will perform.

She tells me she has a hcadache.

I'm not sure exactly what this means. I know that it is meant to signify more than the fact that Jenny is suffering from a sore head. There's more to it than that. There has to be. I ask her straight out if she's taking her medications these days. Her answer is loose as it always is. It isn't easy being evasive and in a way I admire her for her ability.

Without telling Jenny what I am about to do I go upstairs to the bathroom and I turn on the light. I select a scissors and take hold of my beard with my left hand. I give it a good pull as though I am removing a grey pubic hair. I breathe. I fog the mirror up and I can't see my face. It has disappeared behind my breath. The bathroom feels ghostly now, as if something bad is about to happen. I think of the open packet of smoked salmon downstairs in the fridge. There is roughly half left. If we don't eat it for dinner tonight I will have to throw it out. I cannot risk poisoning my family, it simply isn't worth a saving of approximately eight euro and ninety-nine cent.

I lean in closer now to the mirror and I use my right Lycra elbow to rub my breath mark away. There is a faint squeak. I wonder if Jenny will be having dinner with us before she goes to meet Simon, I presume she will be, and I mentally count her in for the smoked salmon. I start to trim my beard, carefully at first and then with a touch more abandon and then I'm pretty much hacking away at it. I cut a bit too close at my chin and I worry that this might be a problem when I begin to close shave. I take out my razor and I finish the job off. Apart from the red tender area of my chin the rest of my face is there all right. It's as if my personality has changed. I have gone from a bearded individual to a soft man. I touch my face. I think of the seal that I often see in the water at Killiney. I am not an old man yet and yet I like reassurances.

I wash the sink, pushing any small trimmings of hair down the plughole with my fingers. I breathe the soft fumes of splattered urine on the bathroom floor. I open the window and the welcome air comes inside and with it comes a positivity.

I go downstairs and I walk over to Jenny to say goodbye. She asks me if I haven't gone yet.

I close the door and it is all behind me now. I wave goodbye to the kids on the green. Mikey sees me and smiles, my heart is uplifted. I set my machine to zero. My new contraption to count my strides. It fits neatly into a small pocket of the arm of my new top.

This is a small blessing.

16. Slap

June 1996

Cold as a stone fresh from the sea. Cold feet, flip-flops, cold on the balls of feet. Lingering cold, smooth press silken finish on the stone.

We were on Killiney beach and it was one of those rare humid days that you felt inclined to take immediate advantage of, and the mist that accompanied the humidity only served to further your anticipation that it would pan out to be a good day.

She wore a deep red comb decorated with black lace in her hair. A black flower in the centre set it off. You could tell that the weather was getting better in the main because there were more empty beer cans strewn about the bin at the end of the ramp. Jenny bit her thumbnail, then grazed slowly on her other fingernails. I asked her to stop, that she would ruin them.

She continued chewing her nails. I mentioned that I might have to purchase that dreadful substance that my mother made me lash on my nails when I was a kid. The taste was something that I couldn't forget.

Jenny mentioned casually that she had arranged to meet Angela for dinner, later on. I was thrown a bit by this as I'd more or less assumed that we would be doing something together. I asked her where they were planning to meet and she was quite vague about the precise location but mentioned Dame Street.

I fingered the sand. I held up a dark grey stone and ran my

thumb over it, smoothing it, polishing it. I licked the stone, enjoying its saltiness, and then I watched as it dried – quickly with the afternoon sun and my breath exhalations. All the time her eyes. A vacancy there that I hadn't noticed before. It is difficult to notice a vacancy, like noticing nothing. I thought about how this was a double negative. I was drawn to noticing such things in the magazine submissions and there was a lot of that carry-on, people trying to appear cleverer than they actually were.

I said it was grand that she was meeting Angela, but things felt a long way away from being grand and I tried not to show it. I stabbed at an empty can of Tuborg that was lying on a lump of excrement that I hadn't noticed before, and I cursed all dog owners and addicts because it wasn't entirely clear if it was dog shit or human shit. I looked up at the cliff face. The wild valerian, *Centranthus ruber*, was beginning to come into bloom. Pinks, cool whites, deep crimson. I was looking forward to the appearance of the clumps of ragwort, *Senecio cineraria*, that were a real sign of high summer.

But I had taken quite a bit of trouble over a picnic. News of her plan for later on wasn't washing well with me. I had bought decent ham from the deli off Camden Street and I had chosen the bread carefully – it was nutty with caraway seeds. I had bought paprika Kettle chips too. I had splurged on two bottles of lychee fruit-flavoured sparkling water that I had spotted in the Asia Market. All for nothing.

A feeling overcame me, call it an inward sense. It wasn't a new emotion and I felt the natural inclination to quell it. Before I'd even met Jenny I'd had a longing that I carried around with me, unthwarted and unrealized. But it was there on the stones searching for an absolute understanding about the vast bay that I came to the realization, I was going to have to watch myself.

Jenny unpicked her red comb and let her long hair swing down loosely. It was silky and in beautiful condition. Her fringe made her seem more girlish and young.

When she remarked casually that she needed a bit more freedom from me, I was taken aback, I couldn't see exactly how it was I was impeding her freedom. I had told her to go meet her friend.

And that is when she started going on about Jerome. How he had made her feel suffocated, how he was all-encompassing. How seventy per cent of the time she was unhappy. His tendency towards being possessive of her, constantly suggesting that she didn't love him as much as he loved her. She said that you couldn't quantify love and asked me what constituted the concept of love? I told her I didn't know.

But I did know that in order for my happiness to be fulfilled, I required Jenny to love me with the same intensity that I loved her. I realized then that I had to keep the conversation light, so I changed the subject and began to ask her about her work, encouraging her to talk about it. She explained she felt that she was really only in the developmental stage of things and still had a long way to go. I was surprised by her lack of confidence, especially after being in the group show in Lennox Street, and how well things seemed to have gone for her over the last year. I encouraged her to talk about textiles, mediums and contrasts. I was enjoying myself getting an insight into her artistic mind because, even though she felt that she was only setting out, she had talent. It was attractive in Jenny – this ability to speak succinctly about her art. It seemed to bring out her passion and she made me feel as though the beach had been filled with colour, once again.

I leaned over to Jenny, there on the sand, and I grasped her two hands together in my palms, as if she was a child shivering on a cold day. Her beautiful artist's hands. She looked away over to Killiney Hill. A grey mist hung heavily on the vast slope.

I assured her that if she had agreed to go out with Angela then that is exactly what she should do. I told her how relaxed I was about two girls going out alone. I said I was mature about stuff like that and I couldn't understand why some guys might have a problem with it. Nonetheless I advised her not to walk by the block of flats near Stephen's Green on her way back to Camden Lane. She held a lock of hair between her thumb and her forefinger and swivelled it in ripple-like movements. It was a habit that I had learnt to enjoy watching her perform.

But underneath it all, I was worried about who she would meet aside from Angela and I said words to that effect.

Next thing, you'll be telling me that Jerome is joining you, I said.

I almost laughed when she said there was in fact a significant chance that Jerome might well be there – herself and Angela were planning on catching up with an old crowd and they had a number of friends in common with Jerome. I felt a very slight nauseous spittle develop in the back of my throat when I heard this but I acted like it meant nothing. I was being analysed and I felt that I had to go along with whatever Jenny was offering me. It was a test.

The beach began to feel oppressive. The small car park by the tunnel was empty except for a lone metallic silver car. I focused on the deep red of the litter bins and the brighter red lifebuoys. Dalkey Island and its splendour seemed to be trying its best to distract me but right then I had eyes only for car parks and litter bins; such was the sense of an uncomfortable feeling overtaking me.

Jealousy. I had learnt all about jealousy from Othello and I understood the significance of how dangerous it could become. I knew that girls didn't want to be with someone who showed signs of being aggressively jealous, so I attempted to act like nothing on earth mattered more in that precise moment, other than the fact that Jenny was going to have a great night out with Angela. But in my head I knew that something had shifted. My thoughts had moved from envy, that I would miss out on a nice dinner and a good night out, to jealousy that Jerome would be around and that he might charm Jenny back to him. I couldn't lose her, not now.

I made a play at picking up a few stones for distraction. I chose stones for colour and for texture and I came across one that I knew was much older than the rest. It had minute fossil flecks across its width and a golden shimmer that made it look as though it was rusted. It was exquisite. I chose another. It was pale coral with a silver glittery finish which reminded me of a Bourjois eyeshadow that Jenny often wore.

I apologized to Jenny for over-reacting and said I was going for a swim and she should join me. In spite of the fact she wasn't partial to the cold of the Irish Sea, I insisted. She turned away from me and began to change and I spoke some more about the varieties of stone. She didn't say anything. Her bikini was cerise pink and more suited to a holiday in Spain but it was still lovely on her. The colour reminded me of a nail polish that my mother used to wear, when I was young. She would hold me as we crossed the road together, her nails digging sharply into the palms of my hands as if she never wanted to let me go.

Jenny hadn't brought flip-flops with her and it hadn't occurred to me to warn her to do so. She didn't flinch as she grappled with walking barefoot, over the stones. I was worried that she might step on something sharp, possibly a syringe – it was well known that junkies frequented that part of the beach, on account of its peace. I imagined there might be something attractive about shooting up with the sounds of the surf in the background.

I ran on ahead of Jenny and quickly dived into the greedy depths of the water. I called her to join me. She was hesitant and after I did a couple of strokes of the crawl I swam towards the edge and attempted to take her by the hand. She told me to stop. I splashed her. I claimed the water wasn't that cold and she should make a run for it and not allow herself time to think about it. She hugged herself and looked to the yellow buoy out beyond. I was getting to a cold zone and standing about wasn't helping. You needed to keep moving, that was the whole trick. And I was getting pissed off, I wanted her to stop arsing around and take the plunge. I realized that it wasn't going to happen like that so I came out of the water and physically pulled her in.

She began to scream, like a child, and I told her to stop, but she wouldn't listen to me. I figured she was hysterical so I slapped her face. I laughed the slap off, even though I could tell she was deeply shocked. I told her to stay down in the water and to swim ten strokes of front crawl because it was the stroke that had always managed to control my breathing — that had always calmed me. Jenny managed a couple of strokes and then she ran back towards the white towel she had left scrunched in a ball on the stones.

I followed her out of the water and towelled myself down. I put my shorts on and sat on the ramp and looked out to sea, briefly. I stabbed at an empty Budweiser can that lay on the beach. I gathered a handful of pebbles and threw one at the can. It made a satisfying ping. I continued to throw pebbles at it and Jenny lit a Camel Light. She had waited for me to become distracted so she could take advantage. I explained I had slapped her to calm her down and that she was using that as an excuse to smoke.

I despised the petty quality to my voice but it came with

the territory. Jenny seemed to have trouble registering me. She continued to smoke and I felt at a loss. I didn't feel happy just sitting there, the two of us with this awkwardness between us and I decided to change tack.

Jesus Christ, Jenny, I'm so sorry, I said.

It wasn't my intention, I assured her, to come across all heavy but the fact was she had been out of control, in the water, and I had done what I thought was right. I promised I wouldn't slap her again – ever. She cast her eyes out to sea, away from me.

I talked about the incredible power of the sea and how I was in awe of it – how it could take a life, with no mercy. The sea is the boss, I said. That was my defence for slapping her. I counted the red bell-shaped markers for the lobster pots – three, and the buoys – three, and I thought about how and why I was peculiarly addicted to the place. I knew Killiney Bay like some people know love.

I looked out to the vastness of aquamarine, the sea a menacing monster to some, to others the perfect playground, to some a way of exiting their painful lives. I thought about the endless possibilities. I fixed my eyes on the lobster pot markers out at sea.

It wasn't the right time to tell her I worshipped her. How could she believe anything I said after the slapping incident? It couldn't make sense to her – it hardly did to me.

The blouse Jenny wore was slightly see-through, which I particularly liked, and it accentuated her thin shape. I reached out and ran my fingers along her clavicle – it was exquisitely delicate.

I averted my eyes from Jenny and I was drawn once again to the sea.

17. Jerome

September 1996

It was a Saturday afternoon and it was gloomy in the main. I needed a bit of exercise, my fitted shirt that I wore to the Crown was straining on me a bit. I asked Jenny if she would join me but apparently she was going to get a bit of work done. I was disappointed but I said nothing – giving each other space was important.

I went alone to the pool and I swam sixty lengths, up and down thirty times. I mixed up my strokes, but it was front crawl in the main, and I counted them as I went along. By the time I was finished I was relaxed and my lungs felt exercised.

We were going out for a meal and a couple of drinks. I had money. I wanted Jenny on my arm because that's what I wanted. We walked on into town and the buses belched out their toxic fumes at the end of George's Street and still my mood was light. And the push of people at the bus stop outside the Oxfam shop didn't put me off either. There was no particular reason to choose Devan's; close to the Crown, nothing more than I was used to it, and its puke-filled gutters at the end of the night were simply something that you had to content yourself with. You were in this until the end, and there was a certain charm in that before you went for a kebab.

We had a couple there and then we moved on and found a bar on Capel Street, where we discovered a group of Poles slamming small glasses of vodka on the bar and then lashing them down their necks. We knocked back two very strong vodkas and the warmth of the vodka slipping down my throat did something to me and I became repetitive. I wanted to know why Jenny wouldn't come swimming with me, earlier. I felt as if she wasn't as keen to do things with me as before. I accused her of pulling away from me. And she said that I was being ridiculous and wasn't she there with me now. I felt like I was watching a drunk starting an argument outside the pub, just for the sake of it. And I had a growing sense of detachment.

I used my breath to try and calm myself down. I was out of control and being unreasonable but I had a habit of turning the minutiae into something of gravity. This surge in energy was coming from the alcohol in my blood and while I was aware of that fact I didn't seem to be able to fully grasp that the energy was becoming negative. I wasn't showing my best side. I brought my drink to my lips. The vodka burnt my throat something fine. I was brazen, and in love, and I had a funny way of showing it.

We went on to Sound House, because that is what the vodka told me to do. And I was easily led when it came to spirits. The club was set in the basement of the Multimedia Centre on the Quays. By day it functioned as a gallery space for up-and-coming artists. There was a faint smell of sewage in the place. I didn't care, the music was good. The room was painted a deep red and there was a mottled effect on the walls. I placed my hand against one to steady myself and I felt moisture. It was almost as if the wall itself was sweating. I looked around and I saw swaying bodies and tight dresses and I was delirious. I moved without effort on the dance floor and then the vodka started to wear off a bit, so I got a couple of beers for myself and Jenny and she seemed pretty content. I sucked the beer from the neck of the bottle and it felt cool and sweet on my lips. Jenny started to dance and she was all legs, then she moved away from me. She latched on to a group of guys and she began to ignore me. I danced, lost in my own world for a bit, and I kept my bottle of beer held low in my hands. I stopped dancing then, and I stood at the side wall and watched Jenny sway. She laughed and I enjoyed watching her being happy in that moment. She caught my eye and I beckoned her to join me.

She came over to me and pressed herself against my chest and she lifted her head up to kiss me. She was a little shaky on her feet and I had to put my hand on a giant-sized ashtray to balance myself.

I kissed her and it was almost as if we had forgotten where we were for an instant. The beat of the music was heavy and I felt a sort of hammering in my chest and I wanted more of her. Her eyes were closed when she was kissing me and there was a look about her of earnestness and she felt very warm to me. But something was bothering me and I broke out of the embrace momentarily.

Jenny wanted to know what was wrong with me and I said there was nothing wrong. But she pressed me and I didn't like to be pressed so I admitted that I was pissed off with her for taking so long to extricate herself from the guys on the dance floor. It was embarrassing, I said.

I said, there's dancing and there's *dancing*, Jenny.

She told me to relax and said she was going to get a beer and she asked me if I wanted another one.

I held my bottle of beer up to the light. I was almost finished it so I said, sure.

I waited for her to come back with the drinks and after a while I got fed up so I headed over to the bar myself. I saw

Jenny standing with her back to me. She was talking to some guy and she was laughing and flicking her hair with her fingers. She was talking to a bloke, no big deal. I called her name. She didn't respond. I called her again and they both turned to me.

I would recognize Jerome Fagan anywhere, even though I'd only met him the one time at the Crown.

The roof of my mouth felt dry despite all the booze I'd consumed. Jerome fucking Fagan, what were the chances? I tried to pass it off. Dublin was such a small shitty place then. It wasn't Jenny's fault that she'd run into her ex at the bar. It was her fault, however, that she'd stayed talking to him for ages when she could have been with me. I started to walk away. I turned around and for a split second I thought that perhaps Jenny wasn't going to come with me. She said something to Jerome and then she came with me. I stopped and turned to her and I kissed her heavily on her lips, and I sensed that Jerome witnessed this kiss. That was what I desired.

She laughed and I felt better for it and everything was back on track. We were having a blast. We stayed on for a while: dancing and talking as best we could over the noise, and I kept Jenny away from the bar for the duration by insisting that she had bought one drink for me and that it was one too many. She was my girlfriend and it was my job to look after her. Meeting Jerome like that had put a bad taste in my mouth and after a couple more tunes I suggested that we leave. The place was beginning to wreck my head and I felt suddenly focused on getting Jenny home.

When we were getting ready to leave the club, there was a layer of sweat on my torso, and Jenny's lipstick needed a touch-up because I had kissed her heavily on her lips and they appeared to be bruised. Jenny was annoying me because she couldn't find her ticket for the cloakroom, and she kept trying to remember the number and describing her jacket to the girl working the cloakroom. She even described it as 'a thing of great beauty' and the girl was losing her patience. I stepped in and managed to convince her to have another look. She found it and handed it to me and alluded to the fact that perhaps Jenny had had a little too much to drink. This observation didn't wash well with my Jenny and she began to cause a bit of a scene. I managed to convince her to drop it and she agreed, though with reluctance.

Out on to the street we stumbled vaguely like the rest of the clubbers. They shouted a bit. Heads nodded in agreement with each other about how fucking great the club was, and Jenny and I stood near them but we weren't part of the group. We were on our own, and she started to pull out cigarettes from her bag. I didn't like her smoking but I said nothing. We stood like that for a couple of minutes. I watched Jenny smoke. Despite the fact that I didn't approve of her smoking, I was drawn to the delicate movements in her fingers as she brought the cigarette to her lips. She inhaled as though the very act of inhalation was an offering as something almost religious, or sexual. I had an acute sense of the depth of my feelings for her at that particular moment. The street lamps emitted a glow against the coldness of the night air. Jenny huddled her body into her over-sized tweed jacket and I said, let's get chips.

She agreed and we headed up Aungier Street to hunt for chips. I found a greasy spoon near the top of the street and ordered two singles. While I was waiting for the chips, Jenny decided that she wanted nothing less than a batter burger. I felt a mixture of embarrassment for her and an unwarranted anger. I couldn't understand why she opted for a batter burger when she could have a spice burger. In the end I did what any gentleman would do and I got Jenny what she wanted. We were content in that kind of greasy way with our late-night feed. We went outside clutching our brown paper bags. But the contentment didn't last. I was pissed and it seemed to make sense at that moment to have a go at Jenny, she was fair game. I was angry, too, that I was subjected to mayonnaise on my chips because I hadn't thought to ask the girl with the spotty skin behind the counter for tomato sauce. Her acned face had been merely inches away, and through the steam and grease of the chipper I had seen, not only large bottles of ketchup lined up, but bowls of sachets as well.

I wasn't good with things festering and I started on about Jerome. What a fucking coincidence it indeed was meeting him like that at the club. I had to know if she had spotted him first or was it the other way round?

I felt the need to point out that there was a significance to be drawn from such a distinction. But I wasn't in any state to say what that significance might be.

I began a rant about Jerome wanting her back and that she had been encouraging him, talking to him. I said he was an over-confident prick and that I could tell that immediately from the first time I saw him. The way he swanned into the Crown that night. Jesus Christ, anyone would have thought that he owned the bloody place the way he was going on. And his clothes, I shouted, his clothes, what was he wearing?

We were becoming louder and I knew well that I was losing the run of myself. I was too drunk to make any proper sense, and people were beginning to look over to us as if they were monitoring my reactions. I started to experience a sense of desperation that I wouldn't be able to close down the argument. That often happened to me, that inability.

And then I said that she was obviously still into him.

She tried to explain that Jerome was keen to remain friends with her and I laughed in a way that could only be deemed hysterical.

I didn't care and I told her not only that, but that I didn't fucking care. I didn't know what I was saying. My tongue was thick and heavy and my mouth was filled with chips, and bits of potato spat out of me. I didn't fully realize what was happening to me.

I had always prided myself on my impeccable treatment of women, I was never unkind. I was brought up to be like that. I didn't know what snapped in me. It was caused by a combination of things. My irritation that we had met Jerome. My feelings of drunken, irritable and unfulfilled lust for Jenny, and the fact that a group of lads were standing nearby giving me the distinct impression that they were saying something derogatory about her. I put my fingers to my chin and I licked the garlic mayonnaise off them and there was a salty aftertaste in my mouth. I went over to the lads and I asked them straight up what they were at, slagging my girlfriend. One of the guys gave me a push and a smack in the face. I could taste more saline in my mouth and I recognized that the metallic saltiness of blood and the fake garlic of the mayonnaise were indistinguishable.

I became deeply confused with myself. Sure, I had started a bit of an argument with Jenny about Jerome and I wasn't doing myself any favours by getting involved with the lads, but how in the name of God had it come to this?

I dropped my chips on the footpath and I got stuck in. I pushed in against the lad and I could feel his arms around my chest, and it was as if he was giving me an embrace. My head felt heavy and I had it bent in, lowered into his chest. I was glad then that I had learnt to box as a teenager. I wasn't going to use my skills proper on the street, but showing that I knew my moves was enough of a deterrent, or so I thought. I stayed in that position for a second or two, my head in his chest as though we were lovers. He brusquely pulled my head away from him and I stood up. I faced him directly. I gave him a good nudge in the shoulder and I said to Jenny that we had to get out of there. I pulled her by the arm, she didn't seem keen to come with me but I didn't leave her with a choice.

I was dead chuffed with myself that I had stood up for Jenny. What if they really had being saying inappropriate things about her? I had sorted them out pretty quick.

We walked the distance to my flat. It wasn't that far away but with the drink and the aggro it felt like a long while. Jenny kept trying to make light of the argument. I was trying not to sulk but it wasn't easy. I mustered up some small talk about spice burgers in Ireland and I told her a story about a regular at the Crown. The nutcase who would come in on a Wednesday and tell us how after twenty-five years of marriage he had only just come to the conclusion that his wife was dull.

We were pissed. We walked up the three steps to the house. I found myself having a bit of difficulty opening the front door. It wasn't a bad place as places go, but the weeds growing out of the cement in front of the basement did something to me. It gave the whole place an air of neglect when it could have been something special. The inability of the landlord to bring the house up to its potential annoyed me. I finally opened the door and I immediately started going on about the carpet in the hall as I always did.

And as always, Jenny said she liked it because it was retro and I said that she was only saying that because she was a bloody artist. And in my drunken state I wondered how my horrendous shit-brown carpet could be pleasing to the eye.

I checked the brown-veneered shelving unit in the hall for post.

Fucking bank statements, I said. I don't need to know how many times in the one night I've hit the drink-link. It would wear you thin.

Out, it would wear you out, she said.

Her comment irked me somewhat but I didn't let on. I sometimes did that. Put the wrong word into a sentence. Andy had pointed it out to me before and Matt at the magazine had mentioned it too. But when Matt had drawn it to my attention, the fact that it was said in a literary context, at the time I believed it to be a compliment.

Jenny went to the loo, which was on a separate lower level to my flat. I went on up to the flat and let myself in. The place wasn't in that bad a state. I moved some free newspapers off the couch and shoved them in beside the microwave in the kitchen. I walked over to my music system and gave myself a moment to admire my choice of separates. I put on the Stone Roses. I cleared a couple of mugs from the coffee table and I shimmied my eyes over the bed in my room. I had a brief sniff of the duvet. Jenny came in all shy as if it was the first time she had been in the place.

She stood in the kitchen and she was looking at the coffee percolator, I guessed in an effort not to make eye contact with me, to hold on to the tension for a bit, after our earlier argument. The half pot of cold coffee from that morning was on the hot plate. The filter bag was full of old ground coffee covered with traces of bubbles. I started to prepare some baked beans and toast for us. I needed soakage because I had left half my bag of chips on the footpath. I realized in that instant that the radio was still on. Late-night come-down music competed with the Stone Roses from the stereo. I turned off the radio, opened the fridge, and scoured the shelves for booze. My movements seemed to ease the bad feeling that was between us.

I asked her if she wanted a beer and she said that she had drunk enough and would love a cup of tea.

I couldn't be bothered with making tea at such a late hour. I opened a bottle of beer and I began to pull Jenny to me. I started to kiss her but she didn't seem terribly forthcoming.

I apologized for arguing with her earlier on, I apologized about losing the head with her about Jerome. I apologized for having a go at the lads at the chipper. I was defending her, I assured her. I didn't like the way they were talking about her. I spoke of my bravery.

I reached out to touch her face.

She moved away from me slightly and said to forget the tea, that she would have a beer after all.

I wasn't keen on getting her a drink. I had lost my taste for my own beer at that stage but I went to the fridge and pulled out a bottle of Corona.

Things weren't going the way that I had envisaged. The whole night seemed all of a sudden to have become interminable what with the Polish bar, Sound House, Jerome, the chipper. Jenny perched herself on the high stool at the counter and smoked a cigarette. The smoke seemed potent in the flat.

We were both wrecked and I suggested that we hit the sack.

It was annoying me that she ignored my suggestion in the way that a girl would if she hadn't exactly made up her mind if she wanted to have sex with you and I was running out of ideas. We had been together for well over a year. I didn't need the stress of small talk to get her into bed. I wanted sex, nothing more. I wanted post-argument sex, heated and slightly brutal. But Jenny was holding out on me so I had no option but to revert to recounting more of my stories in an attempt to amuse her and to bring some fun back into the night. I felt like a bold child, trying to make amends. But Jenny could be tough to crack.

I was becoming increasingly agitated. So I suggested going to bed, again. I was all smiles as I tried to coax her into the bedroom. But she wasn't having any of it. I couldn't understand why she had bothered coming home with me in the first place if it was going to be like that. It was late and the mood was lost and she said she was going to hit the road. I was fuming inside as I walked her out on to the road and I left her there by herself to flag down a taxi, I was damned if I was going to wait for one. This was my way of punishing her for not being forthcoming.

I went back into the flat determined to drink more beer. I was annoyed with myself for spending a rake of money and not really having a great night to show for it. I was annoyed with myself for freaking out about Jerome. I sat down and reached underneath the sofa for my wooden box. It was precious to me, bought in a shop that sold hemp and crystal paraphernalia in Temple Bar, and I felt that there was something magical about it. I ran my hand over the lid admiring the intricacies of its aboriginal strokes. The box was for my treasures. Whenever I drank I would go immediately for the photo. I ran my forefinger over it carefully as I had done many times before so as not to smudge the finish. My poor dead older brother Brian, killed in a car accident just weeks shy of his twenty-second birthday. Multiple fingerprints were discernible on it and they were emphasized by the way I held it under the light. Brian was wearing his favourite jacket, his black biker, and I knew that he had his leather bracelets underneath the cuffs that he wore proudly, like a Spaniard. I put the photo down in the precise place that I kept it. And I cried easy drunk tears. My face was wet and I rubbed my cheeks with the backs of my hands.

18. The Run

May 2017

You can run so much freer without a beard. I feel as though someone has slapped me across the face and made me wake up. But all in a good way. I have never before realized how much facial hair can slow you down. I am alive, a mermaid swishing her tail. I am like my faithful seal swimming underwater and then finally lifting its head to the sky.

I am drawn straight to the beach. I can smell the salt on the air as I'm making my way towards it. It's early enough in the day to still see the damage of the previous night's drinking in the village. Empty pint glasses are balanced precariously on walls, cigarette butts are gathered in flowerbeds. I run on, past the dirt, and the smell of the salt beckons me and I feel a silkiness on my face and I wish that my new top was sleeveless because I want to feel this saltiness all over my arms and all over my body. I want something touching my body all over. I don't have a musical device in my ear because this impedes my immediate enjoyment of my environment. It distils the twitter of the birds, the arguments between drunks left over on the beach from the night before. It is important to drink in the atmosphere of our lives.

I start off with a jog, keeping it nice and soft, rhythmic. I think about Jenny and Simon and what kind of shit he'll be feeding her later on. My patella feels a little warm after a bit. I worry about the build-up of lactic acid as I run. I am no expert but I am accustomed to hearing other runners talking about their knee issues so I can only surmise that this too is my problem. There is something sinister about the way small defects creep up on your body. The air is warm and there is pleasure to be found in that. The heat moves my mind away from my knee worry and I wonder if I make a pasta salad tonight will that ensure that with the smoked salmon I will have enough for everyone for dinner. The tide is out and the sand is compacted and this leads to excellent conditions for running. I couldn't have it any better. I thank God for small rewards. I move now with a little more pace and my knee seems to settle down a bit. I still have a sense of warmth deep in my kneecap but I think I am capable of shifting my mental attention to another part of my body. I can do this.

I move on down to where the workmen are doing up the dilapidated Tea Rooms. They haul great pieces of wood up the ramp. There is the sound of foreign voices and some chart music plays from a radio. I hope that they are building a restaurant. How nice it might be to go to the beach for dinner, it would be like living somewhere exotic. I imagine myself sitting in the place looking out the window with rain lashing down, pelting against the glass. I imagine that the sea would be fired up and I think that I would still be happy. I head down into White Rock, the smaller cove off the main beach, and I wave at some of the swimmers that I know there. I don't stop to talk though because I don't wish to lose my momentum. In order to run up the steps that lead to the iron bridge that goes over the DART line I have to go at them in one fell swoop.

I think about blackberries and I look forward to September this year when they will emerge from their briars and fill the air with their delicious smell. I like to eat blackberries straight from the bushes despite all the talk of the danger of worms. Everything in this world has a right to life. I get to the Vico Road and I stop for a breather and look over the small stone wall built along the footpath behind which people throw their bags of rubbish from their cars. There is nothing of particular value to be seen. I cross the road and head up towards the Obelisk at the top of Killiney Hill. I feel like my legs have a strength of their own and this is the thought that is carrying me. I am sweating profusely and I'm not entirely sure if the top that I purchased in good faith is worth its price tag. I climb the last of the steps and I come out into the open area in front of the Obelisk. A smaller monument to my left has a set of steps at its base and I sit on one of the steps and stare out to sea. Dalkey Island seems to call to me and I want to go there, I want to go there very much but I am in my heart afraid of the current that surrounds the island. I am afraid that the sea will be too powerful and that it will catch me in its arms and throw me out on to the sand days later as if I am a worthless migrant fallen from an unseaworthy vessel. This is my fear. I close my eyes and then my body swerves forward and the tiredness that I have been fighting with for most of the morning is now finally catching up with me and I am powerless. I shake the sleep from my frame and I stand up and I do a couple of easy enough stretches. I hold my right foot with my hand and I push it into the back of my arse and I hold it there nice and firm counting to thirty. I do the same with my other foot. I move on down off the hill and something has clicked in with me.

I arrive back to the house and I feel changed, as though something has shifted. Jenny looks up briefly from what she is doing. There are flecks of paint along the insides of her long arms and they are mainly orange, and black, and yellow. She looks at me but she doesn't say anything about my beardless face. I check to see if there is hot water and then I go upstairs to shower.

The evening isn't long about settling in and I start executing my plans for the smoked salmon and the pasta salad.

Jenny picks at her food and in the end I tell her not to bother with it at all, that she's putting us all off. The kids don't seem that perturbed that there is more pasta on the menu. I tell Jenny that I like the dress that she is wearing. It's a coral pink and it's a colour that brings out her sallow skin. I recall purchasing it for her in Rome in a small boutique. It wasn't a particularly expensive place and the attention that the girl in the shop gave us seemed well at odds with the amount that we were going to spend. Perhaps kindness is more peculiar to a city that seems to be filled with warmth and beauty. Jenny seems pleased that I have mentioned the dress and this is all it takes, it seems, for her to come back to me. Joey gets ice cream from the freezer and Maeve brings over a cake that she has made while I have been out running.

Later on when Jenny leaves to meet Simon I go to her desk. I can hear the shrieks of laughter from Mikey and Joey as they mess about in their room. I can hear Maeve asking them to keep it down, that she's trying to sleep, and then I hear Maeve laughing. Their humour is infectious. I sit at Jenny's desk and I study a book that she likes on David Hockney. There is a splodge of oil on the cover of the book. An opened bottle of linseed oil is close to the wooden sculpture of a turnstone that she has been working on for ages, as if she has recently added one more coat to protect the delicacy of the wood. Beside the turnstone is a sketch of the Brother from the monastery close to the beach. The Brother is on his knees, praying, and he is concentrating on the sea. He is oblivious to the fact that he is being watched. Jenny has created an intimate scene, a sense of a religious privacy. We know very little about this religious order other than the fact that they dress in long white garments and they appear to be happy but moderately so. And it is this lack of knowledge that is so intriguing.

I know that this drawing has been difficult for her to do and I know that Simon is excited to be including it in the group show. Each part of the body is outlined carefully and great care has been given over to create a haunting, yet peaceful image. I know all these things because Jenny has been tirelessly outlining her artistic process to me over time and with a particular vigour over the last couple of months. It's almost as if a sense of desperation has overcome her in the intensity with which she has gone about her work. I know all this as I pick up a Stanley knife that she has carelessly left in the empty gherkin jar with all her pencils. And I don't know if I am punishing her for being so incredibly careless as to leave such a dangerous implement lying around where there are inquisitive children living or whether I'm punishing her for being out with Simon. My heart can play funny tricks on me.

I slash the face of the Brother and a sense of peace comes to me. It's as if I have stolen his serenity and I don't know how I feel about what I have done and I know that I will most certainly blame the kids. Maeve has been cutting things on Jenny's desk, I'll say that she cut the drawing as it was underneath her paper. I will give out to Jenny for leaving dangerous things lying around and I will tell her that Maeve almost reached out for the Stanley knife earlier only I intervened. I place the knife back in the gherkin jar. The label says fifty per cent free. I am the only person in this family who likes gherkins. Mikey and Joey believe them to be evil cucumbers in disguise. Sometimes it is difficult to persuade children otherwise when they get a notion into their heads. I get a damp cloth and I wipe away any marks of oil and paint on the desk.

When Jenny comes home I tell her what has happened. That Maeve was cutting out a stencil on her desk and accidentally damaged the drawing. I can tell from her demeanour that she has had one drink too many, one little bottle of vino over what is the ideal amount for her because her teeth are black. The dress that was looking so fine on her earlier on as we struggled through the pasta salad and the smoked salmon now seems to be sucking the life from her pallor. She is messy in this later light and I tell her not to worry too much about it, that she can use the other pieces. She's only one piece short. I tell her that in my opinion it wasn't her best in any case.

It is only later as we lie in bed, our bodies not touching each other, that I want to hold her – to tell her the truth, but instead I turn away. We are separate beings. I drift asleep. It is close to dawn when I begin to wake and I know that she has been crying because even though my eyes are not fully opened I can feel her eyes on mine. And yet she says nothing and the melancholic blood of the wine is still there, potent in the bedroom, her breath.

19. Party

June 2017

I arrive home from work to find Jenny in the kitchen staring out the window into the back garden. Her shoulders are hunched as if she is protecting herself from attack. I don't know when exactly she started allowing her posture to slip.

I call her and she ignores me at first, the dishwasher is on and the clink and spray is quite noisy. I place my hands on her shoulders. She turns around to face me. Her skin seems thinner than it normally is on her face.

You scared me, Des, she says.

I wonder who in the name of God does she expect to appear in the kitchen. I'm not in the habit of frightening my wife. I explain to her that we are going out, that we need this. She mentions that she has a loin of pork roasting in the oven and I press my forefinger gently to her lips. They feel strangely hot and I imagine that lips should normally be cool. I tell her not to worry about the pork and that I have a babysitter booked.

She goes upstairs to get ready and I call the kids in from the green. They are not one bit happy about it so I bribe them with tortilla chips. I climb the stairs to see how Jenny looks and while I am about it I go into the bathroom and I douse myself in Hugo Boss. I am reeking. The doorbell sounds and I don't have time to check on Jenny. I go back downstairs and open the door to Caroline, the babysitter. She seems nervous and I tell her that she has very little to do really beyond watching TV and eating biscuits. It's the first time I've used Caroline and we haven't discussed rates, so I get to the point straight away. I make it clear that I am unwilling to fork out eleven euro an hour for her to have the privilege of eating me out of biscuits and I manage to get her to agree on eight. I feel slightly mean doing this to her, but she has a choice, she can always go home. As we are leaving I can tell that she's not happy about it so I say, see you later, in a singsong voice.

We take the DART and we talk on the way to Blackrock. I tell Jenny that she looks good because she does. Her dress is a cobalt blue and she wears it cinched into her waist with a leather belt that I bought her in Top Shop about ten years ago. Jenny looks after her stuff well. She wants to know about the party. It's Dean's party I tell her and that it's in his new house he has recently moved into with his girlfriend. She wants to know who'll be there. I don't like to give too much away because I've noticed lately that she has become a little introverted and she doesn't find it as easy to socialize as she once did. This is a development that in itself pleases me because I don't really see the need for her to be so involved with other people. I believe that her family should be enough so I just tell her the usual crowd, Dean and the lads. Dean is my oldest friend from childhood. We did everything together in the early days, smoke and drank and sniffed out girls. He was adept on the girl front and he taught me a trick or two over the years. I was a quick learner.

It's a good idea for us to get out. You look good, Jen.

I flex my fingers and think for a moment that things aren't so bad. I've a lot to be thankful for in this life really, my children, Jenny.

Jenny doesn't look at me on the DART, instead she watches the familiar floating by. Even though it's a typical Irish June the evening has developed that unexpected build-up of heat you'd get in Spain. The Irish are always caught out around this time of year. Young men struggle in their grey flannel suits, sweat from the morning and the afternoon lying dried out in the armholes of their shirts. Some of them take a sniff when they think that they cannot be seen. I don't risk this type of behaviour myself although I am tempted to at times.

Jenny tells me that Maeve is worried at the moment because a boy in her class likes her. I explain to her that I spent my schooldays probably making life a misery for the girls that I fancied, but that I never meant anything by it. It's what young boys do. I assure her that it's all harmless, that I am much more afraid of social media and all its dangerous implications than I am of normal social interaction between boys and girls. I also make it clear to Jenny that she ought to be acting primarily as a mother to Maeve and less of a friend. Jenny explains that she treats Maeve as a friend so she can get information out of her. I admit that I am baffled. I move on to telling her how well Mikey is doing in goals and that it would be a nice gesture if she were to come and watch him play in a match some day. Jenny talks about her art, how she cannot sacrifice art time for football. She gets herself so worked up about it that the conversation about Mikey is lost.

We get off the DART at Blackrock station and my mood is upbeat. The evening has got that glorious feeling, the afternoon sun having done its job. It puts a lightness into everyone's steps. Jenny appears nimble, I feel veritably light-footed. Responsibilities are jettisoned. It is right that we are out, here together, the two of us. Every couple needs time away from their children, it is only natural.

We make our way on to the main street. I suggest a pint before the party. It is probably a bad thing to be inside on such a wonderful evening and I am deeply torn, and I conclude that despite the pleasant evening and the immediacy of the sea that engulfs your senses as soon as you step out of the carriage at Blackrock, I rather fancy a drink. We head into Jack O'Rourke's, an old favourite haunt of mine, and immediately the prospect of the evening ahead feels exciting. It is seldom that we find ourselves alone like this, a night out, the prospect of a decent party, sex perhaps when we return later. I push Jenny into getting a pint of Guinness because, I figure, it's better value than those little bottles of wines she's partial to. There's not a whole lot to offer her in the way of decent wine by the glass in any case in O'Rourke's. It's not that kind of place, I assure her. Despite the heat Jenny drinks the Guinness. I don't enjoy mine much as the creamy top is turning a dirty slush colour as I am drinking it and I feel strangely bereft.

We drain our glasses and head away from the village with its exclusive boutiques and the salty air. The paths become more meandering and you get the sense of tranquil urbanity that is particular to Blackrock. That's why Dean chose to live out this way, so he divulged, plus it's close to Seapoint swimming point. This fact alone would be sufficient for me to choose to come and live here.

We find the estate and my romantic notion of having it all, the tranquillity, the urban, is immediately crushed. This is the pits, this is where you don't want to end up. The estate's called the Meadows and it's pretty clear that some forward-thinking developer basically destroyed a lovely wild expanse of land to make way for a whole load of semis. It's a fairly regular set-up, a decent place to bring up kids but beyond that not much else. An ennui is palpable. Everyone's garden is practically the same, the boundaries delineated by the glossy oval-lime greens of *Griselinia littoralis*. The areas designated to each family hardly warrant such divisions but despite that the *Griselinia* provides privacy all year round, a coveted thing in such close confines. The suburban popularity of the species is down to its rapid growth and its low maintenance and that is what great family men desire. Despite my scorn for Dean and what he's bought into, I have a heaviness in my heart, in the bottom of my stomach. I understand that I'm not much better because my own garden hedge, I realize, is composed of exactly the same species.

I am one of these people.

I too am a great family man.

We take our time trying to find the house because I haven't been here before. I have forgotten the number and I'm becoming confused because each road in the estate is replicated again and again. We turn into a cul-de-sac and Jenny points to a peach house at the end. There's a couple of people out in the front garden chatting and now we can hear the pumping music.

We make our way over. The party is in full swing. Dean makes a great show of helping Jenny out of her biker jacket. I've a mind to make a wisecrack with him about Jenny being too old for such a jacket but I hold back, it wouldn't be fair. Jenny doesn't like Dean. It's on account of something I told her about him and a girl that went down years ago. It happened after a night at the Alternative, a nightclub that we persisted in frequenting in the Old Bray Head despite the fact that it was a complete dump. We had been drinking vodka before we hit the joint. There was a girl there that I was into. I'd noticed her a few times before. She was one of those Gothic types that I was partial to at the time and I snogged her on the dance floor during a slow set. That was the kind of behaviour that we were accustomed to.

After the club we all went back to Dean's gaff. His parents were away and we had the run of the place, drink was the main attraction. Dean's father was in sales and his garage was full of cheap Riesling that he'd give as gifts to customers at Christmas. It was easy enough to help ourselves to a couple of bottles, they were never missed. The trouble was white wine wasn't a great come-down drink by any means, if anything it disagreed with us and we could become slightly aggressive with it. The girl came back to the house with us. I was kissing her hard in the kitchen and the Mock Turtles were belting out of the stereo. The room was a cigarette haze and my eyes were sore with it almost as much as they could become with the chlorine burning me when I swam in the local pool.

There were a couple of other available girls back at the house but Dean the fucker had his eyes on mine. At one stage he asked her to dance with him. I think she agreed because it was his house and perhaps she felt as though she couldn't refuse him, as if she was caught up in a weird hostage situation over which she had no control. She was fairly drunk, we all were. She was set in close against Dean, he cradled her head with his hand. I was uncomfortable with it but I tried not to show it. After a couple of minutes, she screamed and extricated herself from Dean. We all stood around as she informed us that Dean had given her a hickey. I looked at her neck, a big sweltering red mark was there all right but I laughed and tried to make light of it. I could see that she was close to tears so I told Dean that he was a prick but yet I insisted that she shouldn't have made such a big deal of it.

Jenny acts as if Dean and I were engaged in some Dionysian, mental situation. Something out of control. I have tried to tell her that it was nothing like that but she won't believe me.

When we go into the house I push a bottle of red wine into Dean's hands. He thanks me without looking at it, I have to tell him that it wasn't cheap. He puts it to one side and keeps talking to Jenny, asking about her art. She seems pleased by his interest but too bloody quickly she starts to mention the problems that she's having with it. How she finds it difficult to get any work done on account of the kids, they're still so young. It's not what somebody who is hosting a party wishes to hear. Dean is zoning out. He's only asking about her art to be polite, he doesn't care about Jenny, about anything that she's trying to pursue. Her dreams. He's humouring her and it's sad to witness. I think she realizes in that moment that she has taken Dean's questions too seriously and she might well have looked a bit cooler if she had just said that things were going fine. I think she knows that she has embarrassed us both.

The night goes on and I keep drinking, beer that I find in the fridge, beer that I find behind a sack of potatoes in a kitchen press. The wine that Dean ignored earlier on looks fair game to me and I go in search of a corkscrew. Jenny advises me that it's kind of rude to drink it, after all we have brought it as a present. I tell her to shut her mouth. I'm not sure how many, but certainly a few people in the kitchen hear me when I say it and they look over as much as to say that my behaviour isn't on. I want very much to know in this instance what drives one person to judge another person. I am only telling Jenny what I believe to be true which is this, that I am going to open this bottle of wine and that Dean will not notice.

The warm buzz of the party is beginning to wear off a bit. Jenny's words have pissed me off and the wine seems astringent on my tongue after all the beer. I fear that it may give me heartburn and a grievous headache in the morning but seeing as I've opened it I have no option but to keep drinking. I'm getting hungry as well and the only food I can find is a couple of cold-wrinkled cocktail sausages on a greasy baking tray in the kitchen. They're tasty enough but I need more. Dean and his girlfriend are dancing in the kitchen and the music is becoming louder and Jenny mentions Caroline the babysitter and that we have to consider getting back to her.

I feel condemned. To be told in not so many words by your wife that it is in fact time for you to go home is difficult to hear, not to mind digest. The reality of the situation, however, is that she is correct and ultimately if we do not get our arses out of here soon, we are going to have to fork out a small fortune to the babysitter.

On the way home in the taxi, I finger Jenny. I don't imagine that the taxi driver sees me. He takes his money from my hands with no complaints.

I pay Caroline, rounding it down to thirty euro. It's half two in the morning. She leaves the house quickly, I don't offer to walk her home.

Jenny is already in bed when I go upstairs. I start to pull at her, the way I see it, this might be the perfect end to a great night. I think about what I have done to her drawing, I think about admitting it, think of her looking at me, I think of her fears. I don't feel a great physical reciprocation from my Jenny but in truth that lack of enthusiasm has never strictly bothered me before as such.

20. How About Paris?

September 1996

Dublin was becoming all glamour as though it was on the cusp of something remarkable, it had hit its groove. Coffee places were becoming fashionable. It was a long way from the old Coffee Inn or the International Bar, where the coffee was percolated and stale. Suddenly you could get espressos and lattes, and internet cafés became cutting edge. We were swept along with the excitement of juice bars, and we began to view noodle bars, where you could get sushi and chicken ramen as the new norm.

Decent clothes shops opened and you didn't mind carrying a paper bag with the Makullas logo on it down Grafton Street because it was understood that if you shopped there you were a certain type of person.

And the night scene that Dublin offered was something. We could go out clubbing and before we set off we could go to eateries on Dame Street where the food was affordable but good and where they served red wine in small glasses, and without asking, the waiters would bring a basket of bread and dipping sauces, olive oil and vinegar to the table, and jugs of water and it was the fact that you didn't have to ask for any of it that made the gesture seem so cosmopolitan. Yes, Dublin was on the up and we were part of it.

Jenny secured a lease in a small artist studio on Strand Street, behind the Quays. She worked there when she didn't have a shift at the coffee shop. Part of me was jealous of her, the fact that she had this space but I said nothing.

I badly wanted her to move in with me but I didn't want to rush her. I'd fucked up badly with the night out, bumping into Jerome in the club and the slapping incident on the beach, and I really wanted to make it up to her. She told me that her father wasn't pleased when she'd moved in with Jerome, that once she lived with the first guy she'd fall into a habit of casually living with all future boyfriends.

The slippery slope, I said, the slippery boyfriend slope.

Jenny laughed and told me not to take things too seriously. I grasped her hand and I yearned to hold it for always and that is the way it was. I wanted everything to be this good, to remain this strong. I thought it was worthwhile mentioning that I didn't believe in backtracking as a general rule, it was a theory that was burnishing in my mind, there were lots of things simmering in my brain. I went along with her laughter. I began to fix a salad, lettuce and ripe vine tomatoes and chorizo – fried until its juice was released on to the pan – a handful of feta cheese, diced into cubes. I put on the Orb and I opened a bottle of Malbec and for Malbec it wasn't half bad. I could feel a twinge on the right-hand side of my head, an ever so slight pressure being relieved, like a valve, a tiny ping, a small blood vessel popping.

We sat on the couch to eat, the wine perched on the coffee table. I felt privileged to have a coffee table but it wasn't something that I would have actually admitted to anyone. I had no ashtray on the table because I didn't want Jenny to feel as if she could light up casually in the flat.

I wanted to make delicious meals for Jenny every evening. I wanted to fix calamari and not worry about the aroma of seafood in the flat. I wanted to make vongole and other things involving rocket and Pecorino cheese or Parmesan.

I wanted the ladybird tattoo on her delicate ankle to be the first thing I saw jutting out from the bed sheets in the mornings. I wanted to lie close by her at night, her body cool, always cool – it was like she had bad circulation, but I didn't mind the coolness, I could warm her up. I wanted a reason to pick up flowers for under a fiver from the girl outside Neary's on a Friday evening. I would choose purple tulips. I wanted a reason to buy flowers. I didn't think men could buy flowers just for themselves. I needed her things about the place – nail varnish and her sketchbooks and pots of paint. I wanted her collection, her myriad of stones and pebbles and postcards from the gallery shops that she collected for the pleasure of it.

I didn't want Jenny to cower from love. I told her that I would bring her to Paris, the city that was so beautiful from dawn until night. The Pont Neuf – we could sit under it on a bench and we could touch our fingers casually almost, and it would feel tangible, our love.

I suggested winter, that way we wouldn't have to wait so long to go. I told her we could drink coffee close to the Panthéon. I remembered there were a few decent brasseries there. Jenny wanted to know about the booksellers, along the river. I told her that despite all the tourists, they were friendly and you could take your time browsing.

And I told her that it was along the Seine where I had bought my book about African art. She knew the book I was referring to because I kept it on the coffee table in the flat. She had leafed through it but I felt like she hadn't given it enough attention, less than half the amount I would. That was the beauty of opposites. Not everything had to have a perfect symmetry and I wondered if that was a tautology.

We broke off from enjoying the meal to have sex. We were loving in decadence. Later on, I felt faintly embarrassed.

There was something about her vulnerability which seemed to reflect my own, the human body is so personal. I told her that I felt as though my heart was about to explode with happiness but I was wary of getting ahead of myself. I wasn't a character in *Revolutionary Road*. I wasn't Frank Wheeler. Jenny wasn't April.

You give so much of yourself away in the beginning, so much that at times it doesn't seem right or fair. You are so close to the human truth and that is the way it was with Jenny. She was my truth. Even her name – I discovered the Celtic meaning of it was white wave and I wondered if that had anything at all to do with the pictures of the sea she had painted that I first saw in Lennox Street.

21. He Is Still Part of Her

October 1996

Jenny was twelve when her mother died and afterwards she withdrew into herself, as though she didn't need people. Somewhere deep inside herself she became used to her loneliness but when she met Jerome that changed.

She was in art college at the time, taking a coffee break, in a deli somewhere off Thomas Street, and Jerome breezed in and struck up a conversation with her. She wasn't lonely any more.

She told me how loneliness is such a terrible thing. I couldn't agree with her more and I described the loneliness that ate into my conscience once Brian had made off with himself out of this earth and left me with an ache that never fully lifted.

Jerome, she said, saw an alluring picture in her, one of complexity. It seemed a bit lame to me that he had compared her to a piece of art while setting out to seduce her. And seduce her he did, magnificently. Jenny had a way of talking around her relationship with Jerome instead of imparting any real information. It was driving me insane. I wanted more. I wanted to know his qualities without really wanting to know about them. Sure, he was a good-looking guy, I clearly recognized that fact when I saw him the first time. But there had to be more. What was it about him that allowed her to show her vulnerable side, to be loved? She had been living with him for a year before we met at Lennox Street.

Jenny assured me that she had never been unfaithful to Jerome before me, that was something, and I felt peculiarly honoured but it was a fact that I had already sensed. I asked her to sum him up, to describe him in one sentence, and she said he was kind and I thought to myself that that wasn't a bad attribute, not one bit. And she told me that he made her laugh and that a part of her would always remember their laughter, the good times.

But he couldn't have been as kind to her as I was. He showered her with affection initially but then his affection became too much for her and she began to feel suffocated by it, by him. Over time he admitted to her that he wasn't comfortable with her having a life outside of himself. He didn't want her going out with her own friends, and I told her that I would never be like that with her. She was young, I said, she could explore life, she could see her friends, I wouldn't treat her like a possession.

And the laughter between them, she admitted, faded away like the last of the bright evenings as summer draws to a close. She must have loved him and she admitted that she had, certainly at one point, but that it is entirely possible to choose the wrong person to love.

I had gone one step further than Jerome. I hadn't merely instigated a relationship that was pleasurable from the get go, it was deeper, it had to be. I often took Jenny to clubs and as she danced the rhythm that she kept was a kind of power for her and I enjoyed immensely watching her. Those nights were so good. We drank a fair bit and Dublin seemed all the more interesting for it. You never really knew for sure where the night would lead. For a while I felt as happy as I had been, when Brian was alive and we would go along to our local pub and our local club and chase local girls.

It seemed there was no end to what was on, openings and

fringe festivals and comedy in the International Bar. Jerome couldn't have given her that much. I knew that it was unhealthy to talk about past relationships and I tried to act as if her personal history didn't matter to me, but it did.

I revelled in the very notion of our togetherness. I tried not to focus on the past. What mattered was the future. I was careful around her. Jerome had become too possessive over time, Jenny didn't want that from me and I assured her that I wouldn't let that happen. I wouldn't let my own insecurity get to me. I thought about love and realized that you cannot make somebody love you, you cannot make somebody need you, it has to come from them, they have to want to love you, they have to want to need you.

But I could lead her in the right direction. I could, for example, imply that she wouldn't be in such a favourable place without me. I could plant a seed of doubt in her mind, I could entrap her. Then I could chip at her. Chip tiny fragments of her away, the way she tapped wood with her chisel, the determination on her face.

22. Chicken Fillet Roll

June 2017

I hear a humming. I look up and see a small aircraft in the sky. It hangs low and then magically careens overhead and performs a somersault, a silver darting in the sky. I am a child again mesmerized, this is what awe feels like.

Does it hurt here, Joey? I press one hand under Joey's small foot and I hold the ankle with my other hand. The ankle bone seems tender because he winces when I rub it.

Can I get a chicken fillet roll from the Centra when we get home? Joey asks me.

I'll think about it, I say.

I never eat chicken these days. It is nothing more than rubbery meat filled with hormones. I cannot even look at it in the butchers, all those battery birds reared within increasingly shorter time periods to satisfy growing consumer demand. I used to eat chicken though, used to dip chicken wings into succulent sauces, licking chicken juice from my chin and from my fingers. Everything was grand, until one day I looked into the bowl where I had put the wings after I had managed to tear off the flesh from each one with deliberation. I had a tiny string of chicken meat stuck in between my teeth as I was doing my calculations. I had eaten sixteen wings and there were still some left on my plate. I was personally involved in the devouring of eight chickens and I had yet to complete my meal. Something happened in that moment, it was like a perspective shift, a revelation and it was important. I was a grotesque person. And I made up my mind to make that change, I would never eat chicken again, willingly.

Joey will do anything to score himself a chicken fillet roll from the Centra. Nothing can put him off. I have even made him sit through an entire programme on the manufacturing process of these chicken fillets. Basically a chicken fillet of this quality consists of the chicken carcass, a couple of spices and a glue-like substance, all processed into a grotesque paste. It is then shaped into a rubber breast. There is no chicken meat involved. I will allow that it is difficult for a child to really understand this concept.

Joey says that I'm hurting his foot. His tears are waiting in the wings to come out, his stored-up upset gives his eyes a glossiness. I tell him that he should have watched where he was going, I feel mean saying this but that he's got to learn these basic things. I warn him about being less clunky on his feet. I tell him to study Mikey, who never has accidents. My opinion expressed, the frustration that I feel is more settled now. Joey allows his tears to flow as if in response to the comparisons that I have made about him and his brother. Someone else might be fooled, but not me, I know that the real reason he's crying is because I am refusing to promise him a chicken fillet roll.

We're in town and it's supposed to be a day out and now Joey's gone and wrecked his foot. I want to tell him that he's a clumsy fucking fool. The city is full of Spanish and Italian students, being summer, and it seems as if these warm-blooded youths have ensconced themselves in our city for the foreseeable future. There's nothing bad about this, if anything it lends a little colour.

I feel the gentle warmth of the sun on my face and in particular just underneath my eyes. It could be a result of tiredness too and not simply the heat. The chatter from the students is constant. A tourist drags his Samsonite luggage along the cobbled path. I close my eyes and for a moment I am somewhere else completely. I am in a place of pure heat with the pleasurable innate knowledge that tomorrow and the day after that and all the foreseeable days will be drenched in sunshine too, and my body jerks forward as if I am a street drunk. But I'm not a drunk caught out in the early summer sunshine, I am somebody who is thinking about being in Spain. I could almost fall asleep.

I ask Joey if he is capable of hobbling to a café that I have spotted a few doors down. He maintains that he can and Mikey and Maeve give a cheer. He stretches one of his arms up to my shoulder and the other up to Maeve's. He uses our body frames as human crutches. He wants a whole load of attention on account of his accident. I feel strangely compelled not to provide him with it. Perhaps I am just feeling too tired.

The coffee shop is full of sounds. Murmuring voices, heat, coughs, jazz, the angst-squeaks of children. Cool baristas exchange gossip, conversations about their good nights out. Music. High rifts of conversations flake as they become more ghostly, or move again with increased intent, mightier now, veering away going their own distances, developing their own themes. There are dangerous flirtations being played out between customers, between the waitress and a customer, between a barista and a customer. There are croissant flakes on the display table left over from the breakfast rush. Saint Etienne is playing in the background and it is this that makes me feel old. Old yet happy. I am part of something interesting.

I order tea for myself and a longish piece of twisted pastry which has been dipped in chocolate at either end and sprinkled with pistachio nuts. The children take forever working out what they want. I don't blame them, the choice is over-whelming. There are flaked almond croissants and Gur cake on a pink plate beside an artificial poinsettia which looks completely out of place. Unrecognizable cakes spill out of baskets set in the window. An overloading of icing and holes pressed into the dough. The 'Sorry We're Closed' sign is on the inside of the door and it has sticky finger marks all over it but this unhygienic detail doesn't put us off.

I have mistakenly left my black Lowe Alpine rucksack on the floor beside a dresser filled with a selection of mis-matched cups and saucers. A girl trips over it, she curses at me but when she realizes that Joey, Mikey and Maeve are in my care, she softens and asks what happened to Joey's foot. I allow her to buy him a gingerbread man seeing as she's offering. Women never fail to go soft on a man caught in the act of fatherhood.

An Arista Coffee Roasting Company sign is suctioned on to the window. I look at the floorboards with a certain amount of pity as they are composed of fake plywood. The circles of sourdough are stacked neatly facing outwards, each one has a beautiful imprint from a special basket called a banneton which is used to let the pungent dough rise. I know this because I like to make my own bread when I can, the pleasure to be found in such an activity is immeas-urable. There are Goodness Grains on sale here, I presume it's a kind of porridge. I rather like the idea of porridge being good.

The girl behind the till is very beautiful, young, I notice. Her pale fingers tremble slightly as she handles the rings of sourdough, as she tidies crumbs away, as she cleans the dis-play counter that holds a selection of goods filled with cream. I see Joey avert his eyes from the cream, as the very act of even looking at it causes him to become nauseous. When the girl has finished arranging the breads she places a device that looks like a meat thermometer into a bowl of coleslaw presumably to monitor if it is still edible. I know the dangers of coleslaw. I have been poisoned by it before and it is not a pleasant experience. It crosses my mind to tell her that if she is in any doubt at all about the safety of the coleslaw, that perhaps she should cut her losses and discard it, that way she can sleep in peace. I notice that her nail varnish is black and that this is not what I am expecting. I imagine her nails would be better painted a gentler hue, possibly a purple or a salmon pink.

Metallic tongs like miniature fish slices are on a table so customers can help themselves to whatever they want. Maeve still hasn't made up her mind about what she would like. I don't really mind that now because I am slightly mesmerized by the girl behind the till. It is more than the fact that she is beautiful, it is more. I re-tell Maeve the story about the woman who stuck her hand into the toaster in Donnybrook and died. It's an old favourite.

Rocky Roads are two euro and fifty cent. Mikey is well used to comparing prices when it comes to cakes. This is the only way he can fully understand the value of money. He is getting awfully excited; I tell him to calm down as we are not about to get into a price war in a bakery. He finds fifty cent on the floor and I swear he is delirious. A Christmas decoration is still in the window and this provides me with a sense of sorrow. It reminds me of my vile neighbour and how he likes to leave his artificial Christmas tree up until March most years. I know that this in itself is insufficient reason to dislike somebody with something akin to intensity that I do, but I admit that I cannot help it. Keogh's crisps are arranged in old-lady wicker baskets. I think that I may be somehow related to this family of crisp manufacturers and if my mother was correct it may be a loose connection at best that might go back more than one generation, and with this information in mind, it seems on the face of it rather a pointless exercise to trace because deep down I wonder how this information may change my life.

23. Daffodils

July 2017

I haven't bought Jenny flowers in almost two years and then it was daffodils.

It is not as though you reach a point where you want to cup your hands over your ears and shut everyone out. There are many different ways to listen to children. I give what I can. More and more Jenny retreats into her work. Sometimes I think her confidence issues are fabricated. Sometimes I wonder if it's all a façade, that really she thinks she's brilliant. I have read somewhere that confidence comes from love. I love Jenny. Self-love is another kind of love. People with self-love have hobbies and Jenny has a hobby so it makes perfect sense to me that she in fact loves herself. This hobby is occupying her tremendously. I try not to appear worried that it is taking over her life, that she doesn't have enough time for us. I try not to worry about Jerome.

I find love in places where you wouldn't expect to find love. In the boys' sweaty football socks and their football training tops. The pleasure I take in placing them in the washing machine is testimony to that love, but before I do, I bring them close to my face and I drink in their smell, the specific aroma that can only come from young boys. Young boys who attempt things like bicycle kicks on the pitch and skidding on their knees in victory charges and doing the worm. I can hear their laughter and their joy.

And Jenny's ability to make us laugh as a unit when we

need it. And the way she often kisses me on my cheek when we are together in the kitchen, while she rinses her brushes and I am boiling pasta, or potatoes. Sometimes she touches my arm gently with her palm after we have all shared a family joke even if it isn't particularly funny.

You've got to act sometimes, children need to grow up happy; this is what I tell Jenny.

And the smile she gives away, unabashed as the children sing along to songs like 'We Are Family' and Jenny tells me that she never had this, this proper family. The premature absence of a maternal hand for her, her father that we see occasionally but who doesn't appear to have any real interest in us, the children, we know that. There isn't any doubt in Jenny's mind that her father tried his best. Tried to be a combination parent, a bit of both. It is one thing to be a good father, it is another matter altogether to be both a good father and a good mother.

I can feel Jenny's pain. At least my mother had met Jenny, had the opportunity to know my family. Although she is gone now, at least she had that chance. Sometimes I think this makes me the better parent. Things have a way of turning out after turning inside out on you and you are trying to right yourself. You are disorientated, the sea spits you back on to the shore.

I fear sharks coming to Irish waters on account of Joey's questions and I think about jellyfish and the belief that I cannot be stung twice. I was stung once as a young boy. I can enter the water safe in the knowledge that I've had my share of pain from their poisonous tentacles but I cannot have the same confidence about sharks.

And when I fear love I think not only of Jenny but of my children and although these thoughts bring me joy, they too bring worries about carbon footprints, and excess.

137

24. Paris Enfin

November 1996

Paris was a glorious time for us. Jenny bought clothes in a second-hand shop near the Pompidou Centre and she was amazed, being an artist, by Beaubourg with its structural pipes exposed and the whole inside-outside-ness of it. Groups of Spanish students sat in packs in the square and they clapped and sang and it reminded me of growing up when they gathered on the green outside our house, and I could catch words like bastante and entonces and mira and tenia and polvo. We took the escalator to the top floor and looked out over the city and all the while, I held Jenny's hand.

There was no such thing then as Airbnb and we stayed in a mediocre family-run hotel. It was clean. This was the most important thing. Breakfast wasn't included in the price but I didn't mind that. I made it clear to Jenny, gently, that we would have so much more fun buying our bread and crois-sants from the bakery in the morning than eating cornflakes in a hotel. We could picnic by the Seine. It wasn't like the Liffey where you would be sharing your space with junkies who thought they were athletes, such was the extent of their leisurewear.

It was much colder than it would have been in Dublin. And when we walked by the river we longed to jump on to a Métro to warm up a bit but I explained to Jenny that we would have to stick it out, that you couldn't really get to know a city unless you pounded its pavements.

We went to a bar one evening and all the chairs were lined up outside in rows. It was like being at the cinema, looking at passers-by. There was a definite voyeuristic satisfaction and every now and then I looked to Jenny to see what she was making of it and she sipped on her demi and she smiled at me. I asked her what she would like to do the following day and she suggested Notre-Dame and I agreed to it even though I wanted to go to Père Lachaise. I had a penchant for visiting sites outside the norm.

The next night we drank Pernod at a place beside our hotel. It was so casual, as if the barman had opened up his house and essentially transformed it into a bar in the centre of Paris. The city was relaxed in terms of licensing, I told Jenny, compared to Dublin and this was all part of the charm. I thought of the large pubs that were all the rage in Dublin with their high ceilings, exaggerating the noise, and I compared it to what myself and Jenny were experiencing, the quiet bar, the two of us, the lone barman. I was happier in a place like this.

There was something about being in Paris with Jenny. It wasn't just the romance, it wasn't like that. It was more about her, the way she came alive, she was vibrant and it felt like she had reached a higher level of contentment within herself. She talked about her work and how she was finding a new level with it and how things she had locked away seemed to be coming to the fore. She told me that before her mother died she had encouraged her to pursue her artistic dream. Her father had implied that she was wasting her time going along that path and she admitted that sometimes, she felt as though possibly he was right. I wanted to tell her to shut up. I told her I was glad she hadn't listened to her father. She held my hand. We were at a part of the bridge by the Seine where there were thousands of locks attached to it, each one representing two people, one relationship one lock. I liked the idea of being locked together in love. Jenny suggested that we buy a lock of our own and attach it to the bridge to represent our love and in that moment I was beyond happy.

We went to the Louvre one afternoon and it was cool and airy but not cold like outside and Jenny couldn't get enough of the place. After a while I suggested that we take a break, there was only so much art you could absorb, but she wouldn't listen, she wanted to keep going, so I told her I would wait for her outside. There was a bar there with outdoor heaters. I ordered a crisp beer. Even though the demi was expensive it tasted so good, clean and delicious. There was only so much art I could take in one day. I started to read a bit of *Orlando* because I had brought it along with me but I found it hard to concentrate so I watched other tourists. When Jenny finally re-emerged I listened to her with happiness as she told me how she felt completely illuminated and I thought how she was lighting up my life.

It was in Paris that Jenny talked to me a little bit more about Jerome. Jerome was essentially a good person, that was her starting point. It wasn't particularly what I wanted to hear but I listened more acutely when she told me again that he had been quite controlling of her at times. She told me that one of the things she liked about me was that I wasn't like that, that I was more relaxed. It was true, I didn't ask her where she went in the evenings when I was working in the Crown, who she was with, what she had eaten, how much she had drunk, but now I felt like she was interviewing me properly for the role of her boyfriend even though I already was her boyfriend, and had been for over a year, warning me about the things that she didn't like. And in that moment I began to worry about where she did go in the evenings when I was working in the pub. I worried about who she was with, what she had eaten, what she had drunk, but I said she had nothing to worry about, I was relaxed, I trusted her, I said, and the smile on her face, the smile.

The sex between us was satisfying, not because we were in Paris, together, but because we were eating a lot and sipping on wine and Pernod and the sex was lazy and comfortable and Jenny talked to me afterwards as we lay in the white cotton sheets. I could love her and we could have sex but it was more than two unconnected events or emotions, it was more. Jenny would lie across my chest after the act and I would feel her hair on my bare skin and it felt like she had surrendered herself to me, totally, but it wasn't a surrender in the sense that we'd been through any kind of battle. It was more a realization that she had allowed herself to be mine forever.

It was our last full day and evening in the city. We were going to the late-night opening at Musée d'Orsay. Jenny told me that Jerome did this once to her, took her away for a few days, the way I had done. I was sick and yet I wanted to hear more. It was London – admittedly a great city but I felt Paris had the upper hand. Jerome hadn't let her get involved with the itinerary, he had planned everything down to the last meticulous detail. He had brought her to galleries and museums but she knew he didn't care much for what they contained. It was orchestrated, as if he planned these visits to amuse her. She felt suffocated, like she couldn't be herself. She realized that it was possible to be lonely even when you are not alone. When she told Jerome how she felt, he acted as though she had done something wrong, that somehow she had punctured the pleasure from their trip. They went to the same bar in the evenings and it would instil cabin fever in her and she said nothing. Jerome insisted on paying for everything and then made her feel bad about it later on. It was like he was calculating her cost in his life. She told me about the first time Jerome met her father. He brought a bottle of wine. Halfway through the meal, Jerome had absolutely insisted on trying the wine he had brought even though there was another one open. I told Jenny I would never do anything like that.

Jenny told me stories about Jerome because I looked for them. How he bought her gifts, beautiful items, she even described a necklace he had given her as a Christmas present as exquisite. He bought her flowers frequently, apparently, and I didn't want to believe it. Jewellery – a History of Ireland ring, a silver charm bracelet that he would fill with charms over time. What a perfect arrangement, I said; inside I was seething – such presumption. I wish I'd thought of it. She was wearing the charm bracelet and she shook it in front of me as if I had asked for proof. There was a heart, a ballerina figure, a cross, all of them lovely, especially the cross. She touched it as she told me that Jerome had hurt her the night he gave her that very charm. She played with it and I noticed how long her fingers were and how elegant.

That was the night I came to you, she said.

There were tears in her eyes. I felt myself well up. To think that Jerome had done such a thing and that she hadn't mentioned it before.

I reached for the basket of bread and I grabbed a slice and dipped it into the sauce beside my pork chops and I ate rather greedily because I didn't know what else to do, I couldn't think of anything better to say than that I was glad she had come to me. It was pathetic. I took a sip of my wine. I held her hands and I curled my fingers into them and I said that I would never hurt her.

That's when I realized I would have to meet Jenny's father and make a good impression. And that's when I asked Jenny if she would move in with me and I felt such utter joy when she said that she would. Oh Paris, how could I ever thank you enough?

We finished our meal and the last swig of the wine gave me a warmth in my body and I suggested that we make a move if we were going to Musée d'Orsay. Jenny's eyes seemed to brighten. I thought in that moment how the eyes are incapable of lying and I said again that I was glad she had come to me.

The talk about Jerome was in the past, as though Jenny had shed a skin like a snake does in the sun. She was my beautiful creature and she was all mine and I felt it in my blood. I felt an excitement, like the feeling in the final countdown to an exam, the last minutes before an interview, that focus that you have to call into force, the need to run and the urge to fight that need. And the way you talk yourself up, your rehearsed spiel, in the warm office filled with sunlight which will not look as good on grey winter mornings once you have secured the position. An anecdote that you mention casually that shows your ability to work in a team. The memory of a past job in the office beside the Italian deli on the Quays where you first thought to purchase brioche and the way you felt nervous ordering it with a latte to go, acting like brioche was something you were accustomed to, how you kept your voice constant when you asked for a couple of the small almond fingers, dusted with icing sugar, as an afterthought.

And those were the times.

25. Christmas Eve

December 1996

I put so much energy and hope into searching for the perfect gift for Jenny, our second Christmas together, in the end buying a photo frame from one of those household shops that were appearing in the city full of novelty tat that we didn't know we didn't need.

The frame itself was pretty unexceptional but what made it special was the shot I placed in it, of Jenny working at her desk, in the studio – a mesmerizing Jenny amidst her tools and her ideas and her paper. The youth of her face.

When I gave it to her she ran her hand along its surface and I mentioned that the wood was ash and she seemed impressed by that. We spoke of the poignancy of Christmas and how it makes you think about the people that you have lost. She talked about her mother and I told her more about Brian, his terrible head injury. I talked about contusions, about the exact condition the drunk driver had left him in, how Brian's skull had been pushed into his brain.

Her kiss was different this time. It wasn't like our first Christmas together when we were in some kind of a frenzy, when a sense of urgency overcame us and we wouldn't linger for the sake of lingering. This felt slower, better, more relaxed. Perhaps the connection through loss created an intimacy.

Jenny missed her mother. She spoke of the energy of her as she strove every year to make Christmas in their house the best day of the year. And it was, up until Jenny was twelve and she lost her and it marked the end of Christmas as being the perfect time. Many of the memories that she held dear were diluting that little bit more, year by year. Memories that are so vital you are sure you will recall them forever but you find you cannot catch them and keep them and that is a terrifying fact.

I felt for her. Her father had tried to continue where her mother left off. He read her favourite Christmas stories even when she became too old really to be read to, but he wanted to keep the tradition alive. But it wasn't the same, his voice wasn't the same, the joy of Christmas was forever extinguished for Jenny's father after his wife died and that realization was in his intonation, and Jenny heard it. You cannot bring somebody back, and Christmas is the worst time to try and do it, everyone knows that. Every year since, Jenny celebrated Christmas with her father, just the two of them, but it wasn't a celebration in the true sense of the word, it was a day that they got through and at the end of the day, her father would say, that it was another Christmas over and Jenny never knew how to respond.

I said that Christmas wasn't the best time of the year in my family either and the loss of Brian was felt acutely, and I told her that my mother still laid a place at the table for Brian and that neither my father nor I could bring it upon ourselves to say how that made us feel. We didn't have the words and even if we had the words we didn't know how to use them.

26. Living Together

January 1997

My flat on Camden Lane had always seemed a good place to live. When Jenny moved in, it was perfect. A new year a new beginning. I was full of an enthusiasm to decorate. I painted the walls a heritage stone colour. I framed a couple of old album covers and Jenny covered the rest of the living space wall with her stuff. It was her living mood board – cut-outs from *Circa* art magazine, postcards from the Gallery of Photography and from IMMA and the Temple Bar Gallery and Studios, a photo of us from her twenty-first birthday that I'd asked Angela to take. In the shot Jenny's lips were covered in a deep red stain that I particularly liked.

I told Jenny not to worry about money. She had her grant, I had my work. She gave up the coffee shop gig, it wasn't practical and secretly I was glad of it. I told her I would look after her, I was there for her. She seemed so happy and she told me that she loved me and I believed her and I believed that it would be enough.

We held each other at night and relished the excitement of the moonlight coming in through our bedroom window and all the while her body beside mine. The feel of her, our closeness.

I found an old table outside the Green Building in Temple Bar and enquired about it at the restaurant next door and discovered that they were doing up the kitchen and didn't need it any more. The owner said it was mine if I could organize its removal. I had a friend with a van and he came over and we hauled it to the flat.

I love it, she told me when she came home that day, and I saw her brush it carefully with her hands and it seemed so right, to bring something from an old space to a new space, another place where different acts could be performed on the same sheet of metal. From cracked eggs to turpentine, there was a certain beauty in the surface's resilience to mixed chemicals and harsh products. I imagined the kitchen porters scrubbing it down at midnight, after last orders had been taken from under hot lights, and it had reached that time of the night when the chefs and the waiters could tone down a bit on their bad language and their abuse and sit back at the end of the kitchen near the wash-up area and have the talk, and suck on their cigarettes, with the back doors opened fully out into the darkness of the night. The table washed and clean and ready for another day. The sharpness of the metal was like something from an operating theatre and I could hear the clink of the instruments as they were laid out on it, the surgeon's scalpel and clamp and tweezers and saw.

The table was perfect for Jenny's work and she decorated it with empty jam jars and other jars, filled with buttons and feathers and craft glue and ribbons and marbles and cigarette lighters. In one jar there was a lone silver Zippo lighter that was a gift from Jerome and every time I looked at it I wanted to throw it away.

Above Jenny's desk she had pinned to the wall, feathers and flyers to the Magic Roundabout and Carl Cox and Strictly Handbag, a spell on a sheet of her expensive handmade paper. It came from a book she had about witches' spells. The idea was to anoint the door jamb in your home with an essential oil. You could choose from frankincense, cypress, cinnamon, clover or dragon's blood. You had to walk through the door and close it behind you. I performed the spell with Jenny one night when I was drunk and I remember waving around a piece of rosemary and threatening to light it.

Her work was going quite well and we often talked about it in the evenings. We sipped Jacob's Creek or Corona with a wedge of lime pushed down into the neck of the bottle. She spoke of the possibility of a collaboration. I told her to be careful about sharing her work. I couldn't stand the idea of a shred of Jenny's brilliance being overshadowed. I was worried that she didn't have the strength in her to keep pushing herself forward and I urged her to be strong. I didn't feel strong, I just said it because I wanted so badly for her to believe in herself. I used an analogy of tennis players and how they go out on to the court to win Grand Slams and do whatever it takes and it is ultimately everything to do with psychology, and nothing more.

But I also assured her that life wasn't all about work and her career. Some day I wanted a family and it seemed like the right time to bring this up. I was quite taken aback when Jenny said that the very notion of a foetus siphoning nutrition through the umbilical cord, sucking every available bit of goodness from her body, was terrifying and how the force of that might impact her work. Her outburst seemed terribly dramatic. I said that things happen for a reason and not to worry too much about the future. All that mattered was the here and now.

Later in bed, I turned off the bedside light and we lay in the dark. I wanted everything to be perfect. Jenny spoke of her ambitions and her dreams. She spoke of the sea and how she missed growing up beside it. She could wake up in the morning and head down to the promenade and she would brush her hair on the beach and the flyaway strands were taken with the breeze.

We all end up back into the earth, she said.

I wrapped my arms around her back and pushed my forehead in against her neck where I felt safe and warm and all good. I didn't like talk of morbidity and death and I told her this in the bedroom darkness.

I lay snuggled into her. She spoke of the astringent pungency of dried-out urine in the gutters on the streets of the capital, when it wouldn't rain for a while and the feeling of relief after a downpour, how the air would feel lighter and everything would feel refreshed and I said wasn't that a good thing? She said that other cities didn't smell nearly as putrid as Dublin did in summer, that you couldn't smell stale blood and puke and dried-up booze and Chinese takeaway puke and urine, and she said the Irish had to be dirtier than other people, in other cities.

I told her if we moved away from town then she would be giving up the studio, everything. If we relocated to Bray, for example, then artistically she would be on her own and hadn't she only been talking about collaboration. The only cultural activity out in Bray was a tiny arts centre where you had to pay to exhibit your work. Jenny was above that.

I remember when I stopped talking. How I made up my mind to cease being the person who always controls the narrative. I was the listener, I wanted to be the listener. I wanted my ears to be filled with her thoughts.

27. Work Trip Blues

July 2017

I'm trying, really trying to keep my hand in with the job and it is deeply frustrating. I tell Graham that I'll go away with the work crowd for a team-building event even though I don't want to go. He tells me that I don't have a choice. My work is boring enough as it stands but to be subjected to this thing down in Cork is deeply upsetting. Subjected to headache-inducing activities that even a decent hotel by the water will not compensate for. No amount of comfort can help me be okay with flip charts and ice breakers. I have had to endure ice breakers before when I joined the Dram Soc back in college. People acting out roles and asking each other what they believed in and what their hopes were and the whole lot embarrassed me to the point where I found it difficult to speak, let alone engage properly. I imagine that this kind of activity is more suited to an American well used to self-promotion.

Modesty can be so disabling.

When I tell Jenny that I will be away for a couple of days with work, for a moment I glimpse in her a happiness that wasn't there before. I suppose we could do with a break from each other because things aren't going so well between us since Dean's party, last month. Jenny has accused me of attacking her in bed after the party. I have told her that quite possibly it was the drink talking and perhaps she should be a bit more careful with the things that she's saying and in case she's forgotten, we are husband and wife, after all. I suppose that it might be a good thing for me to get away from the kids for a night or two because the school holidays are in full swing now and the lack of structure in their day is making them go crazy. I blame Jenny. When I am at work she allows them the run of the place during the day. They can watch as much television as they like because she doesn't seem to have any inclination to entertain them, she is too busy with her art and her chisels and her implements. I have a good mind sometimes to throw the lot into the bin, to destroy them. It doesn't hurt to conjure up plans, if anything it's good for the imagination.

The heat of summer is building slowly as it tends to in Ireland and you can feel it on your skin, mainly in the mornings, but it has that peculiar Irish habit of subsiding considerably as the day progresses so you have to take what you can get when you can. The children are often disappointed by the inconsistency in the weather. I tell them that the weather cannot be considered a proper mark of disappointment and further, that the surprises that the weather brings with it can only be a positive thing. There is nothing worse in this life than predictability.

As the days drift nearer to my departure date, Jenny acts like she's increasingly annoyed, not by my imminent leaving in the sense that she will miss me, but more that she's irate about the amount of work she will have to do about the place by herself. The dinner on the evening before I leave is fraught with tension. Mikey and Joey are fighting about who shall get the last sausage and to make light of the situation I decide to raffle it.

A number between one and twenty, I say. I whisper twelve into Maeve's ear and she smiles her knowing smile at me. The boys argue about who is going to go first and I suggest

Mikey as he was born five minutes before Joey. Joey says that it isn't fair as he didn't have a choice when he was born and I look over to Jenny for help but she is just sitting there with her head inclined towards her desk. The raffle is over in a matter of minutes, Mikey guesses correctly on his second turn and then I go and suggest that he split the sausage in two. Jenny says that this is what I should have done in the first place and I thank her for her words of wisdom even though they have come too late. We sit at the table in silence, broken only by Maeve, who brings over a cake that she has baked. I look at the Victoria sponge, it has been slathered with a deep purple icing that looks like something you would see in the Vatican. 'Goodbye Daddy' is just about discernible in a dark green icing and I feel tears well up. She goes to so much effort. When Maeve is cutting the cake Jenny goes to her desk and begins moving things about. I ask her to wait, at least until Maeve has finished dishing out the cake, but Jenny asks for her slice to be brought over to her while she works. I feel terrible for Maeve.

I walk over to Jenny's desk to see what she is working on. There are small piles of curled wood where she has been sharpening her pencils with vigour. I open her sketchpad. The head of the Brother over and over. I wonder if she is punishing me. I think of Picasso's early childhood sketches, and the variety. The sense of deliberation. She asks me to put the sketchpad down, that she's working with it. She bends herself at the desk as if she doesn't realize or care that we're not designed as human beings to sit like that, that we cannot bend our backs even though we think we can. Hasn't she ever heard of the Alexander technique?

I pick up a piece of paper from the desk. Jenny's artist's statement is impressive. I've never seen this before. There's so much here that I don't know about her. I realize now that

I thought I knew everything. But that, I figure, is the arrogance of marriage. I feel slightly ashamed that she has never told me that she used to volunteer for a homeless organization, distributing sandwiches and coffee in the middle of the night to poor beat-up souls huddled in lanes and squatting on bridges. I'm ashamed that I don't really know the artists that have influenced her, that she can play the piano. I have never heard her play. She has never mentioned wanting a piano. And the eloquence of the language, her exquisite use of words. Her professionalism. And the guilt I feel now is acute. I have ruined something.

28. Work Trip

I get away from the house on an empty stomach. I wheel an overnight bag down Military Road with all the importance of a good hard-working family man out to breathe in the toxic fumes of enterprise with an enthusiasm that I do not feel. This isn't the first time that I have been subjected to this kind of thing and I should view it as a positive sign that the company still deem it worthwhile to include me in such activities. It means that I'm still at an age where I have much to offer them as an employee. For a while I have worried that like Jenny, I might have missed the boat. I might be coming to that dangerous and unknown stage where I could be overlooked for a younger, hungrier type. Perspective is all about confidence and nothing more.

July can often come with a coolness that I always find surprising. To feel cool at a time when sallow people in other countries are enjoying the constant pleasantries of high summer is deeply unsettling. And yet I wouldn't have it any other way. I know in my heart that it will rain and I am prepared.

Because I'm now officially on a mini-break I treat myself to a croissant and a coffee from Café Feliz at the DART station. That's happy café in Spanish. I have my doubts as to the merit of direct language translations. The woman who runs the place refuses to add extra hot water to my coffee when I ask her to. She says that it will ruin the flavour. I let it go and head to the platform. As I am sipping the coffee I have a good mind to go back inside to tell her that the flavour as it stands is no great shakes, but I resist it. I don't want to fall out with her, I have to walk by her every morning.

It is only when I'm on the DART that I remember that I don't drink coffee because it makes me ill. I take the train to Connolly station and then I take the Luas. There's a heroin addict on his mobile phone moaning loudly to his girlfriend about the weather. He wants to move to Torremolinos and if she doesn't want to go with him then she can go and fuck off and mind the kids, that he'll go by himself. But first of all he has to get to James's Street hospital to get the plaster taken off his fucking arm. I look out the window and I see people waiting. They're not doing much else while they're waiting, as if there isn't enough time to settle down and do anything in case whatever it is that they're waiting for arrives. My mouth is still bitter from the coffee and the croissant has left a layer of fat on the roof of my mouth which I try to scrape away with my tongue. I think of Jenny, her tongue.

It's soft at the tip but the back is lumpy. I like to kiss her right back there at the back of her throat. She doesn't like me doing it, she says that she feels as though I am choking her. I think that's what makes me want to push my tongue. But it's not something you could readily admit. I have an image of last night, of how she reluctantly had sex with me on account of the work trip. I feel good that I have ejected the store of sperm that has been wilting in my body of late, it has for the most part nowhere to go. I wonder about sperm. I wonder about it a lot. I wonder about enthusiasm and about the importance of the exhibition of such enthusiasm.

I meet Graham and Denise from the office at Heuston station. Denise is quite pretty but sometimes I feel that I can put far too much emphasis on the word quite. She's a bit of a talker and I'm not a great one for it early on in the day, particularly when I'm travelling. It can be such a waste of effort especially with people of whom you know as much about as you ever really want to know. On the journey Denise insists on telling me how she is certain that we are going to have such craic in Cork. I tell her that it's going to rain for the entire trip. We eat sandwiches that taste of nothing from the trolley that comes around after an hour. I say that I feel like I'm on an airplane with nothing left to break the journey now that I have eaten. Graham feels the same, he assures me. Denise smiles at me and says that it's been a while since she has had a break and that she's happy to be going anywhere. I've heard something being bantered around the office that she's had some recent health issues. She looks fine to me.

When we arrive into Cork city it's pelting down just like I expected and with it is a wind that feels like it's going to slice through my body. I put on my new wax jacket and Denise looks at it with what I assume is weatherproof envy. I think about offering it to her but I feel that she might be too embarrassed to accept it so I say nothing. It's not my fault that she didn't think ahead. Cork is all bustle and I get an immediate buzz from the accents I can hear on the streets. We walk to the hotel down by the water because our legs are feeling cramped from the journey and when we pass Dunnes Stores I feel relaxed and at home. Cork is different to Dublin in so many ways and yet it feels the same. Dirty, yet forgiving. I feel a slight thrill that this might be an exciting trip and yet at the same time I am apprehensive.

I know it's never a good idea to drink with the work crowd but it's the first night and I am free from all domestic responsibilities and there's something about that feeling that's difficult to overestimate. I think about Jenny and about the drawing I have damaged. If anything I have done her a favour, I reassure myself, her second attempt at capturing a true sense of the Brother praying in the solace of the beach is in my estimation much better than the original. She has as much as admitted it to me herself and that's not an easy thing to do for an artist.

In the hotel Graham is attempting to treat me as his friend rather than my boss. It's intensely annoying. He's completely lacking in interpersonal skills. This is the warm-up to the flip charts in the morning. As I envisage the day ahead I begin to get drunk and I'm not slow to notice that Denise seems to be matching my alcoholic intake. Some of the office team are bearable, young, committed family men for the most part. I recognize a lot of myself in them, the need to talk about nurturing their children's talents, harping on about the good old school days, as if trapped in an adolescent world trying to keep up with traditions, the confident and ever so slightly aggressive talk about putting their children into the same schools that they attended.

Three of the younger girls in the office look like they would rather be anywhere than here. They too, it seems, don't have a choice and they are stuck tight together trying to avoid Graham, who's becoming lecherous after one too many. I try to act cool, humouring the girls saying things like it isn't that long since I was in their shoes when I was first dragged down to these team-building things but that there are some things in life that you have to put up with in order to get ahead. If it's meant to be reassuring it's not working. Judy, Graham's assistant, looks at me as though I'm nothing. I'm boring her and I am old. The other two smile nervously. I can never be sure of their names. I wonder if they think it's sad that at my age I still have to endure these expeditions.

I move over to the gilt bar to talk to Denise. She's that little bit more mature, it's all in the clothes, thirty-five I think. I have a recollection of a dry confectioner's sponge cake with the kind of pink icing that gives me an immediate migraine served up to me on a paper plate in the meeting room a while back. I often see these kinds of cakes in supermarkets in the chilled food section. It's always the same at the office. Friday night, someone's birthday. Someone I barely know. Someone that I have no desire to get to know. Who wants to know the people that you work with? All of these relationships end badly and that's the truth. You end up getting pissed with them for a couple of months after work at the end of the week and you bitch about the other people in the office and you say things that you shouldn't say. Regret is your middle name. And you are officially middle-aged now, bitter and bitchy, twisted almost. You go too far and you wake up on the Saturday morning with a bad head and then you remember the things that you have said the night before as your children ask you why there are lumpy bits in the orange juice. You want to puke.

The whip around after lunch for the present. The receptionist says a fiver is grand but she expects a tenner and you feel resentful because it's not like a tenner is a whole lot of money these days, it's just that you don't really have it to spare but you're too embarrassed to admit it, so you give it with sour reluctance.

It is no secret in the office that I kissed Denise at a party in the boardroom to celebrate the year end. I hate tax. Jenny is the only one who doesn't know and this breaks my heart but I console myself that it's something that happened a long time ago and it is meaningless. Vague recollections that Denise made the first move and the warmth of the prosecco that we'd been knocking back out of plastic tumblers purely because it was free kicking in. I cannot drink prosecco. Denise tasted like cigarettes and batter as we'd been eating a whole load of deep-fried finger food from the place across the road.

I remember how my main feeling was one of relief. That she was kissing me, that she was taking the lead. I like that. So not Jenny. The thing about the deep-fried platter is that it allowed me to become greedy and undisciplined and I bit off dried-up prawns from their tails and I gorged myself on cocktail sausages and I shoved potato wedges into my mouth in between and in the end my puke was a measure of my greed and nothing more.

I'm showing signs of enjoying Denise's company that little bit too much and I've got to watch myself. It would be so easy to have another go at it. Pity fuck if it's true that she's been ill. If that is the case then it's highly probable that she hasn't had much action going on. And I want sex, I want it very much. It is Jenny that I want but in my eyes that doesn't seem to be the real issue at this particular moment in time. I am getting such a rise out of Denise with my jokes. I have always believed in my dry wit and with a bit of lubrication it feels effortless. Denise is enjoying my stories, whatever it is that I am narrating to her with conviction. Everything feels right.

Time moves much more quickly than it does normally for me when I am drunk. I wish that the night could last forever. The bar is practically empty apart from the two of us. Graham and the younger girls have gone. The rest of the clientele have hiked off to bed because it's a Tuesday night and the kind of people who are staying here in this establishment are the kind of people who have early meetings in the morning and they are the kind of people who will take a flight back to Dublin rather than take the train. Because of these observations I rationalize the need to get another drink in quickly in case the staff decide to close the bar. After I order more drinks from the lounge boy I call him back over to me to ask him what time the residents' bar closes and he says 4 a.m. It is half three in the morning. We have enough time.

Later on we each clutch at our room keys in the lift. Her room is number 401 and that is where we go. Denise opens a bottle of prosecco from the mini bar. We sip it from plastic cups. I tell her all about Jenny and Jerome and what I did to Jenny's work and the group show. There is nothing that I don't tell her. As she listens to me I start to kiss her. It is sloppy and I try to undress her, to remove her bra but I can't undo the catch and it's as if this very problem is enough to bring me to my senses, the realization that I'm going down a road that I shouldn't be going down. I want to go there, I want to go there very much. I cannot drink prosecco.

I remove myself from Denise and I touch her face and I tell her that she is very pretty and kind because she is both of these things. But she is not beautiful. I keep that to myself.

Each time I put my plastic key into the door of my room and take it out again immediately as instructed by the receptionist when I arrived at the hotel but the door won't unlock. Even though I can hear a clicking sound after I remove the key I cannot open the door. It takes me three attempts to let myself into my own room. I fall to my bed and the blanket is soft on my face and I am much too warm. I set the alarm and I get up at eight in the morning. I have had two hours' sleep.

I want to tell Jenny about love. I want to tell her about denial and my restraint, about what she is doing to me. Driving me away. Crazy. Not touching me.

29. Good Times

Jenny was a dreadful cook and she announced this to me with a pleasure that I found endearing and I honestly believed at the time that there was something exciting about a woman who wasn't bothered with the trivialities of creating interesting meals. Her passion for art seemed noble to me, somehow. She entertained me with her stories of culinary failure. We laughed about burnt risottos and soup with no real flavour.

She kept in touch with the group from art college and they met up every now and again. When she returned she was always in a good mood and I could feel her excitement as she told me all the news. I listened, not for the sake of it but with genuine interest. The group evoked a kind of vibrancy in her. Her eyes filled with concentration as she told me about various projects and collaborations that they were involved in. She was part of it and her inclusion in this set of people was something that I knew she was proud of and it was important to her and that made it important to me. She told me about friends who were sleeping together and friends who wanted to sleep with friends. And I listened, safe in the knowledge that she was happy with me, that I was enough.

And I believed it, I believed her. Her with her fine smile and the almost shy way she would reach out to touch me, to indicate that she wanted to make love. She did that back then and I loved the feel of her fingers, her touch was pleasurable in the extreme and it made me feel incredibly special.

It was the simple things, the way she cooked when it was her turn, with a belief that this time it might be different, that it might turn out to be a success, and I graciously accepted anything that she produced and even if it was awful, I would act like it didn't matter. And it didn't truly.

I was living on the edge of extraordinary happiness. We always ended a night full of joy, walking back to the flat with a sense of exhilaration. Ambition fuelled this lightness. They were satisfying days. Days when I would leave the house for work early and Jenny would leave for the studio. Notes were left for each other about what time we would be home or where we should meet later on for dinner. Occasionally she drew a love heart on the note. She would often add that she couldn't wait to see me before she signed off, love Jenny. Sometimes I wrote, darling Jenny, and although it was slightly formal it felt right. Once she wrote, love your wife, Jenny. I knew that she was just testing it out but I was very pleased and I told her so later on. It was a dangerously romantic moment and we both recognized it as such and this made us laugh. I remembered how her laughter sounded, strong and full of gusto.

30. Running the Gauntlet

August 2017

A Saturday should be filled with fun. This is what we are brought up to believe and I believe it. Sitting on the couch working on my laptop I feel like my head is going to fall on to the keyboard. Maeve is lying on her stomach, on the floor, her head propped up with her hands watching TV. Mikey and Joey are arguing. We need very much to get out of the house and soon enough the lethargy that has a hold on me will only get more of an almighty hold and I will be no good to anyone, least of all my family.

Maeve is changing. She hardly speaks to us and she's showing signs of being excessively concerned about her appearance. I ask her what's going on and she says that there's nothing going on but I do not believe her or take her dismissal as a proper answer. Something's not right, call it a father's intuition. A walk, I suggest. Something as a family. A stroll to the top of the hill to the Obelisk. Her eyes are filled with boredom verging on tears, such is the glossiness. I look away because I am embarrassed by my suggestion, my predictability. So I laugh and I try to add a touch of excitement, an ice cream – a triple chocolate Magnum as we walk along the coast road, to the bay, to the cove at White Rock.

This is the stuff of childhood dreams.

We agree on White Rock and I rather fancy a swim now that the very notion is in my head. Mikey and Joey want to join us and I make a pathetic way-hay sound that causes me to flinch and I high-five them because I am a cool dad. The only one left is Jenny. I find myself promising her that I'll entertain the kids at White Rock and that she will be able to sketch in peace. I just want her to be with us, I tell her. It must be great to be told that you don't really have to do anything beyond a bit of light sketching, it must be bloody great. If only my life could be like that, if I had the time, I too could be a creative type.

We reach the beach and we walk down towards the Tea Rooms. I walk over to the outcrop of rocks which shows both the granite of Killiney Hill and the adjacent Ordovician schists of mica. The granite is so beautiful and I point out to the children the quartz schist which is a glossy grey and the white feldspar and the little pieces of mica which cause the granite to glint in the sunshine.

Look how it glints, I say to them.

I notice how the sun changes the hue of the water, it is that wonderful turquoise that fills you with an energy that feels urgent somehow, as if it is irrepressible and the sun is magical and enveloping. The workmen at the Tea Rooms heave with the effort of hoisting up a long plank of wood on to the roof beams that they have carried all the way from the jeep, which the new owner has parked illegally on the beach, but I am in no mind to mention legalities to anyone. I nod to the workmen and I holler to my family that the tide is coming in and that in order to reach White Rock we need to think fast and to act accordingly.

We go on my count, I roar and even though the air is calm and collected I still feel the need to raise my voice. That's what comes with trying to compete with the swish of the sea and I feel very lucky to be alive.

We go when the seventh significant wave is receding, I say, every seventh one is the big one.

They know all this because I tell them about my wave theory all the time and Mikey and Joey and Maeve give me the thumbs-up. It is a lovely thing to have the respect of your innocent children. I only hope that I still have a bit more time with Maeve. The years go so quickly. Fridays keep coming around and although this isn't a bad thing in the sense that my working week is over it is, however, disconcerting the way time keeps moving on and it's moving on too fast and I think about Johnny Cash and I think about freight trains and the fact that I know that Jenny has brought cigarettes to the beach – I can discern the compact shape of her twenty Camel Lights in the back pocket of her jeans. My heart falls. She turns to me and I touch her lips with my lips and then I look into the hazel of her eyes, eyes that could swallow you and I ask her not to smoke on the beach, not in front of the nude people and not in front of the children.

She looks at me as if I have lost my mind and I hold out my hand to her, Jenny, I say will you go on my count?

And as the seventh wave recedes my breath quickens and we dash over from our beach to the other side, to White Rock, and I want to sit down on the first flat piece of rock that you meet and I want to look up to the sky and I want to feel calmly the heat of the late morning sun. Instead I am faced with the prospect of Frisbee as Mikey and Joey race past me and strip down to their swimming shorts that are decorated with surfers and palm trees. I undress hurriedly and already they are throwing the Frisbee at me. It hits my ankles sharply and despite this I launch myself into the game and I am running around the compacted sand and the heat emanating from the sand feels absolutely glorious and we are so alive.

There's still lots of heat left in the summer and there's still lots of time left for swimming and that is what we must do, as a family. I play Frisbee with the boys for probably the guts of an hour but it feels less like that because I am having such a good time.

I know that Jenny isn't mad keen on getting into the water, it's been this way ever since I slapped her, things have never been right with Jenny and the sea and for this I blame myself. I figure that this might be the right time to make amends, it is not too late. Even though I have told her that all she has to do is come to the beach to sketch, I now feel like it wouldn't be a bad idea at all to convince her to swim with us. And so I set about it.

Nudity is common on White Rock and it doesn't bother me as such. Normally the nudists keep away behind the rocks beside the old mining shaft known as Decco's cave. Today, however, there's a naked man sitting on a wooden chair that has been left behind in the shelter and he's drinking champagne and it's some life when you can just do that, take off your clothes and drink champagne, out in the elements.

I don't push the swimming with Jenny in front of the kids. I don't want to push her after all these years have gone by. The little slap I gave her on her face. The coolness of her cheek, how I remember that stark fact. Instead I talk to her calmly from the water. I say the water's at its best ever and that there's no sudden sea shelf – like there is on the Killiney side of the bay – and that she can stand, and even though there is some movement in the water, it will not drag her out. All she has are my words. But Jenny is in the other part of the shelter, the one beside the naked man drinking champagne, and she ignores my encouragement from the water and takes out her sketchpad.

I have brought swimming reward goodies for the kids and I use this fact to encourage them into the sea. I shout but it is happy shouting. I tell them I have King crisps and suddenly they are in the water with me and the boys call out that they are cold but yet they laugh and I stay close to them. We throw the Frisbee about and time after time they miss a catch and they have to dive into the water and their happiness is music to my ears. Maeve does handstands and I give her marks out of ten for each one like I used to do on holiday in Spain. The naked man is like an actor in a play and I take stock of the latest graffiti offering on the shelter wall – *Fuck Israel*, in huge black letters. Mikey asks me what it means and I tell him that I don't know and that he shouldn't worry about it and then I go and suggest a game of Tip the Can.

Beside Decco's cave someone has placed pieces of drift-wood, upright in a circular pattern away from the rock, the uneven rock is the can. I spot little crevices where I will hide chocolate coins covered in thick golden foil for the kids later, after the game. I touch the rock, I can feel the warmth eman-ating from it and I close my eyes and I count to fifty.

There is no rush home.

31. Festering

For days we live with the delight of White Rock in our veins.

It's a bit of a blow when Jenny informs me that Jerome has asked her out for a drink on Friday night. That's three sleep nights away. I am once again a child counting down the arrival of Santa. And she tells me that she has agreed to it. Why? I ask her. I am deeply confused. She asks me why I don't trust her and I tell her that nothing could be further from the truth.

What I really want to know is how and when this drink was arranged. But Jenny to her credit is straight up. She tells me that Jerome mentioned it at the senior league match way back and that she agreed to it then. She says that she tried to tell me about it when we went to Glendalough on the picnic but I wouldn't listen. I think back to the picnic, how we fought on the way there and how I called her a fucking whore encouraging her ex-boyfriend to hang about her sniffing her out like a dog. I think back to the senior league match. How I looked over to see Maeve giving me the thumbs-up through the window of the clubhouse when our side scored. And I remember the ecstatic joy of the victory. Mikey and Joey were more interested in their sweets rather than the game at that stage and I remember how I didn't care about that, I was just happy in myself that we were having a good night out as a family. And I remember too that I couldn't see Jenny. Now I know why I couldn't see her. She was probably hunched over the table, more interested in arranging the drink with Jerome than anything else.

I become fixated on the possibility that they have been engaged in a phone relationship. I ask her outright if this is the case and she assures me that I am mistaken and that I am rushing to conclusions. She asks me again if I trust her and while she asks the question she flicks her hair that has fallen over her eye and I feel like I have a pain in my heart.

I tell Jenny that I am here in this world to love her. I have loved her since the day that I spotted her in the gallery on Lennox Street. Nothing has changed, I assure her. She is loved and my love for her is as deep as a vast ocean. It is longer than the distance to where the sea meets the horizon. I notice that there are tiny splashes of freckles gathering at the top of her nose from the recent bouts of sunshine.

I keep away from trust.

But only for a moment. This drink idea seems wrong somehow and I come straight out and ask her what the fuck she's at agreeing to meet his highness for a drink. I feel like we've been through this before, some kind of a warped emotional déjà vu. I want him away from her. He's hanging around, I tell her. Why else would he have put his kid in the same club as Mikey and Joey? Of all the fucking clubs in Dublin he chooses the one our kids are in. I ask Jenny if she is capable of seeing how this might appear, of what it means. She tells me that Jerome is on his own and that he is lonely and that it's the least she can do.

Where are you going? I ask her.

She doesn't respond as she goes to her desk. I follow her and I tell her how I am trying to empathize with Jerome fucking Fagan but I end up by saying that he has a fucking nerve. She sits down and takes up a bottle of rapeseed oil. She takes a pencil from an old Golden Syrup tin, filled with pencils of varying weights and textures, and makes some initial swoops. I am no longer a living being in the room with

169

her, it's like she's lost to herself after making sweeping statements like they mean nothing – a casual mention of having a drink with an ex-lover and I'm supposed to just take that and get on with it, move on to something else. Making these fucking arrangements behind my back. It's not right and I examine the cuticles on my fingers and I pull at loose skin and I feel a sharp sting as I tear a thin strip of skin away, too deep.

My mother had a thing about keeping her cuticles neat and her nails manicured. Sometimes she would let me paint her nails. It made me feel important and it is a wonderful thing to have a sense of one's importance, especially so at an early age. It occurs to me that the word importance isn't too far off impotence and I consider this fact carefully.

Jenny has such a fierce look of concentration on her as if her very face carries a do-not-disturb sign but I have every intention of getting her attention.

I think to bring out the bins because it occurs to me that it's bin day tomorrow but I have time enough to do that later and right now I want to keep this conversation going and there is nothing I enjoy more than a debate. I stand behind Jenny as she works and I massage her shoulders and I ask her what's for dinner. And I ask her if she's really looking forward to this drink business with Jerome.

There's a silence as I pick up a canvas that's covered with an image of scattered rocks and the sea. It reminds me of Strindberg's painting *Night of Jealousy* that I'd spotted in one of Jenny's art books with its energy and its violence. I use my forefinger. When Jenny isn't paying attention I spit a fairly significant amount of saliva on to the canvas and I rub my finger into the depths of the charcoal and the pencil marks.

It looks like a dog's dinner.

I resolve to go upstairs and take a shit. My bowels have

been acting up for the last number of days and I might be able to use the process of defecation to distract my mind from focusing too much on Jerome Fagan. I study the tiles above the bath. They weren't my choice and it certainly wasn't my choice to adhere them as I have done. I remember now how I forgot to wash the excess grout off and how it stuck in places where it shouldn't have. I look at my work noting my skill level. It's not that terrible. I am sure that many other men have failed miserably to grout successfully. As I am drying my hands I have a longing to get one of Jenny's art tools and scrape off the vile flocked wallpaper that Jenny insisted on sticking on with thick gooey paste.

Her feature wall.

32. Her Father

February 1997

It felt so wrong being there, meeting him – having already effectively stolen his daughter. I figured that if he had a problem with it, I would tell him that I was protecting Jenny from Jerome.

Over dinner – which we had brought with us – we talked about his life with Jenny's mother. I hadn't expected that and I felt quite uncomfortable, as though he was unburdening himself. It was too much. He asked me about Paris, what I had hoped to achieve by bringing Jenny there. I said that it was just a notion I'd had. I couldn't understand why he was particularly bothered. I didn't believe that he overly worried about Jenny and yet I found myself steering clear of offering any information relating to where we had stayed. I didn't want to discuss our sleeping arrangements with him.

He told me quite clearly that he hadn't liked Jerome. With such an admission made, my nervousness dispelled. If he hadn't liked Jerome, the simple fact that I wasn't Jerome might be enough for him to like me. I kept the conversation going, talking about the quality of Jenny's art. After a while, I got the sense that he didn't believe me.

He spoke in a way of his disappointment with his daughter. How he would have preferred if she had pursued something with an ounce of practicality. How she wasted her time with strange people and paints and her constant battles, believing in herself, when no one else believed. It was demeaning. I knew it was only talk coming from somebody with gener-ational obstinacy but I felt compelled to defend Jenny. I told him all about her wonderful paintings of the sea that I first saw exhibited in Lennox Street. I didn't tell him about the impact her work had on me, how I had been desperate to meet her. To be near her. To talk to her. To love her. I didn't say all that. Instead I said that she was brilliant and I hoped that it would be enough to put an end to our conversation, which was going nowhere good.

I got up and brought over the chocolate ginger cake that I'd bought in Tesco and I opened the cardboard box it came in. I cut three slices of the cake and put each one on a separate saucer. The icing was too sweet, and unnecessary, but we ate it regardless. I didn't appreciate the way Jenny's father was quizzing me about what I did, about my prospects. I was looking after his daughter and I was bringing her to exciting places and that should be enough.

I got up from the table and began to clear away the dishes and I brought everything into the kitchen. I made sure that I cleaned the sink the way you are inclined to in old people's houses. He wasn't that old but it felt that way, his loneliness seemed to leach into him. He didn't understand Jenny like I did. He couldn't comprehend what drove her. He knew nothing about her desires, how could he? He was her father but a father can only have access to a certain part of their daughter's essence and then they have to let them go to find out about life for themselves.

33. My Lovely Rebel

August 2017

Conflict can only lead to one thing – a state of unhappiness. As if you're floating over a lake, its surface calm, unruffled, and the conflict breathes anger into the water from above and the rage ripples across the silvery blackness. I want very much to keep calm yet there's something not right about the way Jenny is behaving. Covering up her excitement about the drink with Jerome, pretending to be interested in feeding her family.

It's been on my mind, this self-sacrificial thing that I got myself involved in with Denise in Cork. How I pulled away, how I knew when to call it a night.

I should have fucked Denise. I might as well have considering she's been going around telling everyone in the office that I did. But that's not true – what is true however is that I missed out. It's tormenting me, this wasted opportunity for a bit of sex. After all, it's what I needed, still do. Seeing as Jenny's in housewife mood I ask her what's for dinner, if she's decided yet. It doesn't take me long to realize she doesn't have any coherent plan as she lists at random the various staple foodstuffs that we have in our food cupboard, things like noodles and pasta in all shapes and tins of pulses. There's more than fusilli, she assures me. There's tagliatelle and rigatoni and penne.

Don't you have a plan? I ask. I always have a plan.

Denise's smile, her fuck-me warm Jack Daniel's lips.

Impressionable Denise. Up for a laugh. I stopped it to save me from myself. I know now that I shouldn't have bothered my arse being so self-righteous. Nobody at work believes we didn't fuck. I cannot think about that now.

So you're going to go and meet Jerome then? I hold up a packet of penne. I know it's what she's going to resort to. I may as well start to prepare the tomato sauce. I think about adding a squirt or two of lemon juice as well as the obligatory tablespoonful of sugar because I've seen somebody at this, possibly on last year's *Bake Off* when they were making pizza for the technical, but I'm not sure. It doesn't matter somehow, the only thing that matters is that the knowledge has been absorbed.

Jenny wants to know what I'm doing and I tell her calmly that I'm making an arrabbiata sauce and that I'm going to add some lemon juice to lift the flavour, to provide a touch of acidity to counterbalance the sweetness of the sugar just in case I add too much. She informs me that I always add too much sugar. This is true and yet I don't feel ready to admit as much. I ask her to put on the penne. She sighs as if I have asked her to perform a difficult task.

A drink with Jerome for old times' sake, well what do you know? I shake crumbs from an empty bread wrapper into the bin. I wipe the counter with a damp tea towel. Jenny fills the kettle with water and sets it to boil. I listen to the radio and the music isn't particularly good and I switch to *Arena* and there's a poet reading from her latest collection and her voice is grating and northern Irish and I have no surrender stupidly in my mind.

Stop, did you say that we have fish fingers? I say.

She tells me that she doesn't know if we have fish fingers but that the last time she looked for them in the freezer she couldn't see any. I open the freezer and shove my hand into the top drawer where we keep the ice. I pull out a box that calls itself fish fingers but there's no mention of cod and I feel my familiar fear of pollock and dogfish.

Why did you buy this cheap shit? I ask. My eyes are on her and she looks like she's afraid of me.

I don't know, they were good value I guess, she says.

There comes a time when you begin to equate your situation in life in terms of nature. This development comes from growing older and it seems to have little to do with anything else. If things aren't going well you think about things like natural disasters or earthquakes or tsunamis, basically general shit that shouldn't happen but just does. Not things like mass murders – lone gunmen shooting indiscriminately. A cosmic plate shifting in on itself on its own people, and for that I blame God. God and his way and his own problems turning into my problems.

This fish finger problem isn't like this.

I bought them because they were on special offer, she says.

If God could see me now getting all heavy and bolshie with my wife. I'm not in the habit of eating cheap shit. We're not poor, I yell.

Jenny says that she has to get back to work and she tells me to calm down and really and truly they're all the same. All fish fingers are made of pollock and she wants me to get over myself. But I find that I can't and that I can't let it go and that I'm repeating myself. Jenny tries to move away from me and the thing is that I don't want to turn into my father but I don't want to let this thing go either. So I ask Jenny if this thing with Jerome is a fucking joke and I push against her.

I open the box and I take out the frozen orange fingers. With the last of the evening sunlight coming through the window they look almost beautiful, they seem a brighter orange than normal. I look at Jenny, she is on her hunkers cowering by the bin and she has her hands on her head as if protecting herself from an onslaught of hailstones. I continue to admire the tone of the fish fingers – how they are almost reminiscent of the bright oranges that you see in the orchards in Spain heading down towards the Mar Menor. And all of this sense-triggering is wonderful as I fuck the rock-solid breadcrumbed fingers on to the kitchen floor and then use them as miniature fish stepping stones. I walk over a couple of them and I mash a couple more into the soles of my shoes.

Jenny moves her hands from her head and snatches at some fish fingers on the floor beside her, and sticks them, fuzz and dirt and all, under the grill. She has her back to me and I whisper into her ear that I'm not sure about all this business with Jerome.

I push her to the floor not violently but with enough force. I'm a bit worried that I've hurt her and I call her name. I notice that the white wooden floorboards, worn down by the rushing of the children's feet, could well do with another lick of paint. I call her name again, but she is staring through me. She sits up and there are flecks of self-raising flour that Maeve has sifted on to the floor, instead of into the baking bowl, in her hair. There are orange breadcrumbs in Jenny's hair.

She walks to her desk and I hear her banging about. I crush dried chilli for the tomato sauce and she comes over to me and places her arms around my back and it feels welcome. She places her head into my back and I can feel the hardness of her forehead and her breath. Through my light blue linen shirt I can just about make out her breath as she speaks and despite the warmth of her breath she tells me that if I ever lay my fucking hands on her again that she will take the children and that she will run from me. I am cold. I push down on her hand and she is clenching a chisel. There is a certain clarity when you are surprised.

She tells me that she will indeed be meeting Jerome for a drink and I don't say anything. The regret I feel for pushing her to the ground is beginning to ferment inside me and the passion that I feel for my wife is somehow mixed up with trepidation. She turns around to face me and she holds the chisel very close to my face and I feel particularly vulnerable now that I have lost my beard. I am a child once more, being threatened with a beating with a wooden spoon. She leans in so close to my face that I can see the pores in her nose, the small hole which now looks like an enlarged pore where she used to wear a stud. The delicate hairs above her upper lip, her coffee-stained teeth, her breath – the words I want to hear from her mouth – I love you. And not those other words – words that if strung together in the correct order will make the sentence that she'll leave me and that she'll take the kids.

All the time the chisel in her hand.

I will have to watch myself.

I have a vision of Jenny sucking his penis, hunkered down in the darkness of the street outside the pub. I have a vision of the trouble I went to, trying to open Denise's bra, down in Cork, and how this difficulty was my trigger to stop doing what I was doing.

34. Jenny's Walk

I rush the whole way home from work. I even miss out on a free bottle of Lucozade being given out at the train station by two cute but slightly overweight Lucozade girls. As I'm running past them, in my haste to get on to the DART I cannot but wonder what in the name of God, the good, if any, they might do for the sales of Lucozade, if anything sales might plummet. Being home early is the first sign that I am making amends. Jenny will want to get out for her walk.

As soon as I come in the front door I have a heavy heart. Not the everyday type of heaviness – this is worse, far worse. I am dead inside. Once you make a threat there is no going back, I am now faced with a real possibility that she might leave me. I'll have to let her go out for this drink with Jerome.

My breath is straining a bit because the place is in such a fucking mess but I know that I cannot say anything after the incident the night before. The pale blue tiles behind the stove are splattered with grease and I think about scouring them with a wire brush. Jenny is preparing dinner, she has flung a whole load of ingredients on to the counter. There's a bag of red onions, a blue plastic box of mushrooms, wrapped neatly in cellophane, there's an assortment of peppers. It's as if she has come in and emptied out the entire contents of the bottom drawer in the fridge. I think about warning her about how to cook steak. She has a habit of completely destroying good meat.

I ask her why she is wearing her coat. She tells me that she took her walk and hasn't had the time to take it off. I'm not one bit happy that she left the children on the green playing, essentially unsupervised, while she was out walking but I figure that this is a battle that I am surely going to lose. Jenny sees absolutely nothing wrong with leaving them by themselves for short pockets of time. She thinks that it is vital to their personal development. I strongly disagree with her thesis as I see danger in every crevice of a footpath, every stranger that walks by the green – a potential kidnapper. Over-heightened fears are one thing but Jenny not being completely straight with me is another thing entirely. I ask her why she couldn't wait for me to come back from work this evening before taking her walk. She is fully aware that I don't enjoy my job, and that I am highly unlikely to spend extra time there unnecessarily and that she ought to know that I'd be on my way. I don't wait for her to answer my question before I ask her where she walked.

I know her route, every evening the same. Every evening she tackles it with the exact same level of enthusiasm. She sets off quickly as if to give to passers-by a sense of her earnestness. She walks down the end of our road, takes an immediate left, then another left at the traffic lights and she walks briskly all the way along the main road until she reaches the Graduate pub, with its outdoor decking area, enclosed by large plastic sheets to insulate the smokers from the grip of the early evening chill that hits once any amount of leftover sunshine dissolves into the air. She wears white earphones that fit snugly into her ears and she listens to bad music as she moves, oblivious to cars and bicycles, the pub is directly in her vision as a guiding sign. Once there she goes around the back of the pub to where the bicycle racks are nestled in a corner. She rests awhile and then she cuts across the road and makes her way towards Maxwell's Park. She enters the park by the playground and the rugby club, then she heads out beyond the athletics track, which is nothing more than a couple of paint marks on a crumbling grit stretch. She finally goes by the smaller football club which is also housed in the park like our boys' club. The difference being that this club is also in the part of the park that the council don't bother keeping up.

I put some linguine on to boil and I take the striploin steaks out of the fridge. I know she's bloody well lying because if she has been back for ages like she has said she would clearly have taken the meat out of the fridge to settle because she knows that I like the meat to have that time out before I griddle it at a scalding temperature. Plus she wouldn't be still wearing her coat in the house. I can feel the cold emanating from the meat through the white plastic bag. I cut the little red piece of thick Sellotape from the twisted neck of the bag and I turn the steaks out on to a floral plate that my mother gave to me. I treasure it. I keep my irritation with Jenny to myself because I don't wish to turn into my father. I'd witnessed this carry-on from him when I was growing up, criticizing my mother, checking up on her, always asking questions, too many questions. If she came up short with the answers he might well have given her a dig. I don't have it in me to go down this road.

I often think about my mother. She was a beautiful woman, elegant, always so. I remember that her nails were often painted beautiful colours, crimson or coral or mauve. And even then, much like Maeve does now, I recall her shaking glitter over her freshly painted nails, as decoration. I remember as a young boy that she sat alongside me as I was reading or doing a jigsaw and rubbed my head. I laugh now thinking about how I made her list all the colours of nail varnish that she possessed and other colours that she could only imagine. The memory of laughing so much that I felt like I was going to puke, the same way I feel when I drink two cups of black tea straight in the morning, one after the other.

I remember how she claimed that she had always longed for a son because she herself had grown up in a house full of sisters and all they did was fight bitterly all day long, over hairclips, tights, makeup, records, and which boy loved which sister in school. I know that because I was the youngest she doted on me and that's what made it so hard for me when Brian was killed. I know well that my mother was devastated but was thankful that it wasn't me who had perished. When you're seventeen and you lose your brother you feel like you can never overcome something like it. You lose some emotional ability and you gain something else. You can sense other things more acutely. Things like pain and relief. Like the feeling of being blind, I imagine, and your other senses rising to the challenge, to block out your darkness. And your fear.

I know that my father wasn't an easy man to live with, that sometimes he gave our mother a slight slap if things weren't up to scratch after checking the condition of the house in the evenings, looking to see if the two toilets had been cleaned while he was working in the shop. I wonder how my mother put up with him, watching, as he removed his shoes and his wool socks from his jaded feet as soon as he closed the front door with a firm slam, the procurement of a beer, the nature programmes on television, the sighing and rubbing of his bare feet, massaging them, trying to absorb the tiredness into his fingers.

Whenever I hear David Attenborough's deep voice today, I remember my father and I think of how he quelled his disappointments in life by drowning them out with Attenborough's authority. To this day I find it hard to reconcile the two disparate parts of my father, the solid strong man who could hurt my mother and the gentler more passive man who could only marvel at the love exhibited between any two animals, no matter how insignificant they were.

I still do not understand how a man that could possess such empathy for all creatures, no matter how small, could simultaneously reveal himself as being a coward capable of hurting his wife, my mother. It is difficult to describe how much I loved my mother, hugging me, her long arms like a comfort blanket even though they were thin, I could feel the heat of her as she held me close. I know it was the right place to be. It is incomprehensible that my father could be unkind to a person as wonderful as she was. I don't recall him beating her, I remember discipline. Discipline can keep things afloat.

And yet I know with a certainty that I loved him as any son can attest to loving his father, watching out for his mood swings, being careful to remain the favourite.

I can still see my father's shop, his pride and joy; full of herringbone jackets, soft-wool socks in attractive earth colours, limestone green and charcoal and putty brown. Soft machine-knit sweaters in vibrant green like a Connemara ridge, the mauve of Connemara seaweed. Fishermen's jumpers composed of elegant tweed wool that mirrored the mussel shells that you find on the shores of the West, woven ties the colour of fuchsia and silk scarves of burnt orange like the Atlantic sunsets.

Women's underwear, fully cotton Sloggi knickers with thick elastic tops. I recall how I once placed a pair of these knickers over my head and charged about the shop when my father wasn't looking and my mother laughed her heart out. I remember that as soon as my father saw me he ran after me, shouting at me to stop, and I couldn't stop because if I did I would wet myself because I laughed so hard and my sickening laughter was turning to a kind of uneasiness. I will never forget how in that moment I recognized in my father that transformation from having fun to the realization that the fun was over. I still have the memory of having gone too far.

When we finish our dinner it is close to eight. I ask her where she's meeting Jerome and when she says, the Grange, I tell her that the place is full of wankers and I remind her that she has said this on numerous occasions. I want to put her off. The idea of herself and Jerome cosy as fuck in the Grange and me at home with the three kids like an idiot worrying about whether or not they will get a good night's sleep and cleaning the little bits of Astro that fall all over the boys' bedroom floors as they discard their football boots without a care in the world. Scraping unidentifiable black muck from underneath Joey's and Mikey's nails with a cocktail stick. By the time I get rid of them to bed I'll be too flaked out to even watch television.

35. Migraine

April 1997

I sat in the darkness, and looked out the front window and watched how the light from the street lamp spilled into the room, filling me with control. I told Jenny I loved her and I waited for her to respond and hoped she would say she loved me. She stroked my face and said, you too.

There were flashes where Jenny thought she was about to genuinely make it and that shows would be forthcoming. Maybe her patience had been worthwhile and finally she was moving beyond a place where she experienced an absence of recognition to a place where she might experience its presence. It seemed close. It was within touching distance and I could feel her hope, like a dying man experiences air hunger.

She worked so hard. Collages — surges of rubbish from the city, the flâneuse in her collecting detritus and not poetry or words. Hers were walk pictures. She still had most of her sea paintings from the group show on Lennox Street where we'd met and I urged her to try and push them out again to the galleries. She told me that she'd moved beyond that work and that they felt amateurish to her and partially untrue to herself and to her ability. I loved her so much, more then, with her vulnerability so evident, and I massaged her neck. I talked about the glory of moonlight, how it is something vivid and how it is obvious that it can offer you spiritual enlightenment. I had belief and I told her to hold her nerve with the work. I felt her fingers pressing into mine in response. It felt so good to help her.

Jenny was suffering from migraines. She went quiet in those moments and she couldn't work properly, sometimes for a day or two at a time. I was the fixer in the relationship and there was a time and a place for everything and when Jenny had migraine, it was healing time.

At first she didn't let on that there was anything wrong with her. But that particular morning I knew instinctively she was suffering because her movements were lighter than normal, as if the very sound of her feet as she moved around the flat could hurt her. She picked at her lunch and as it was a Sunday I had gone to a bit of trouble over it. Fresh hake with baby potatoes and a salad filled with colour, a salad like my mother would make. I was suffering a little from the night before, I had drunk a couple of beers after Jenny went to bed and I could really have done without the fish but it had been in the fridge for two days and I didn't feel right letting it go to waste like that. I fried it in a dollop of butter even though I would have preferred a heavy fry with black pudding and eggs.

Migraine was a bit like depression in my book. My natural reaction was to tell Jenny to get some fresh air in much the same way you'd tell a depressive to get out of bed and take control over themselves. But life wasn't like that and Jenny wasn't a depressive, she needed sympathy and understanding, and I did my best to be patient, I told her the pain would go away. And I did it all not with a heavy heart but with a lightness, a lightness that I'd discovered in myself since we'd been together.

Jenny picked at the fish and said she wasn't hungry.

She needed darkness and I led her to bed. I stroked the centre of her back. I removed her T-shirt. I rubbed the back of her neck willing the pain to slide down from her head and move through her body and to her hips and down to her feet and then out through her toes, out of her body completely, utterly and then she would be free of it.

Free of its anger, its force. I pulled at her hair lightly and I gently stroked her head. I heard her utter a sound and then she fell asleep and I put my arm across her back lazily almost and I drifted asleep.

When we woke up almost two hours had passed. My mouth tasted like stale beer. Jenny told me that the pain had receded somewhat, like a lazy tide with a forgiving shore, the water pulling away from the pebbles and the masses of grey flat stones. Jenny was cradled in my arms and it was lovely having just woken up like that, together, and still it wasn't that late. It was four in the afternoon and we still had much of the day left and we lay there not really talking but resting in each other's company and it felt comfortable and I thought there was nowhere else that I would rather be.

I had lifted her pain and she was left only with the after-pain, a pain that wasn't physically debilitating any more but was a kind of lighter dull ache. She wasn't proud of the fact that she was struck down by those migraine clusters from time to time, almost as if there might be something wrong with her, as if she was the cause.

And I thought that there must be other people in the world lying down together the way myself and Jenny were, in a different country, in a different time zone, with a different language for love.

I suggested air and that we head out to Killiney beach. Then I tickled her and she begged me to stop. I told her I would stop tickling her if she said she loved me. But when the threat from my fingers had gone away and she lay once again in my arms she said that she did indeed love me and it was in a very quiet and beautiful voice and I held that information so close.

Love was the thing that you couldn't discuss. You ought to keep well away from it, it was a train crash coming. It would get you in the end and leave you crushed and severed and fucked. I held Jenny again and this time the grip wasn't as lazy, it was tighter and I could feel her body sinking in against mine. I was her natural protector.

We got ready and we headed out to the beach. It was cool enough on the train so I closed the two windows above Jenny's head. We talked about music and books and she said she wished there were more hours in the day. The time she needed to study her old art history books and to hold on to her inspirations was endless. She felt she wasted time flitting from one artist to another but I assured her that this was her brain's way of exercising and it had to be good for her. Nothing was a waste, I told her.

Once on the beach I rolled out a bamboo mat and we lay huddled together and I covered Jenny's torso with my jacket. The beach was sparse of people and this suited me because I figured if we were going to kiss and if I was going to allow my hands to wander over Jenny's body, to touch maybe her fine stomach or maybe between her legs, I wanted it to be a private gesture and I wanted her to feel comfortable. We lay still and Jenny began to come out of the after-pain and she was in high spirits, and kissing me back in between her laughter. I had gone from doctor to lover. I was close to her face and I couldn't see any flaw in her, no pore too large, no wrinkles hollowed into her cranium, only a couple of laughter lines, only the mirth.

And Jenny's hand in my boxers. She moved her palm slowly at first. Her movements became almost lethargic as if her hand had a mind of its own, as if it was no longer in the mood and then the movements became faster but the increment in pace was gradual, it was barely noticeable because I was focused on the water and the sound coming in off the sea. I wasn't thinking about what Jenny was doing because I was enjoying it so much and I was thinking vaguely about the sudden depth of the water in Killiney and about the dangers of that and it was a surprise when I felt the wetness and the warmth of the sperm on my stomach.

I used the sleeve of my jacket to wipe myself and Jenny said that the semen would stain it and she suggested that it would be a good idea if I rinsed it in the sea.

I walked to the water which was only a couple of feet away because that is where I had chosen to park ourselves so that we could have this time together and be able to hear the sound of the light waves close to us as they lapped against the shore. I was careful not to get my shoes wet and I rinsed the sleeve of my jacket, imagining my sperm floating away amidst all the flotsam and swimming faster than anything I could imagine and I didn't know how I felt about what I was adding to the water. I couldn't work out if I was enriching it or polluting it, but there was one thing I knew for certain, Jenny was good with her hands and doing things with our bodies felt amazing. The clamouring and the rushing of tongues and the heat and the tips of our tongues, twisting and probing. Anywhere felt wonderful and once that kind of physical contact between us was moved outside into the fresh air our actions were pure exhilaration.

I had her. I had to keep her. I had to continue to make her feel special. I wanted to do it like a mother's natural inclination to protect her newborn, the delicate skin, the tiny fingernails. My mother always protected me but she couldn't protect everyone, she couldn't keep Brian safe. I had to make it right.

I thought about meeting Jenny's father and how I defended Jenny and her art. How would he feel about Jenny making me come all over myself on the beach, with the sound of the waves gently breaking on the shore and the warmth from her face? Her secret breath.

Through Jenny my interest in art was revived, a world that I thought I'd left behind after art college. One day I picked up my end of year book from college. I was drawn to some work from a guy who I remember. He had taken a photograph of a girl wrapped in plastic. She was naked and the expression on her face was of horror and I found that I was uncomfortable with the image and that discomfort was what made it interesting. I didn't like it particularly, yet the guy was doing quite well, I had heard people talking about him.

I wasn't sure how I felt about Jenny's work, whether it was good enough to provoke such a strong feeling. I talked to her about it. I asked her to sell me her vision. I made all the right noises, fed her with compliments.

She had to be grateful. She often said that she was. She told me that she felt an enormous sense of relief that I understood her work. It was hugely important to her, that I could appreciate the power of it. I told her that it was filled with substance and hope and promise. You had to nourish it like you had to water the remaining buds on an apple tree after the first drop of October.

36. Hanging Out in the City

May 1997

We needed a date night. When I called to her studio she wasn't ready. She had a couple of paint spatters on her face and she was still wearing her wrecked jeans. I asked her what she was playing at and she started laughing, of course, she was about to change. I joined in myself and I felt a bit strained laughing away like that, she had almost taken me for a fool, something made me want to twist her arm and I grabbed it and I said to her, I could twist your fucking arm.

I started to tighten my grip and then I stopped and apologized. I wasn't able for ingratitude after all I did for her. There was silence in the studio. I had brought a bottle of wine and I rinsed two small glasses that were slightly dirty and chipped. I poured the wine, a slight tremor in my hands, and I tried not to touch the chip on the rim of the glass with my lips while I sipped. I was prone to cold sores and I was afraid of them, of the scabs they turned into, the weeping, the stinging. The scab that appears well formed until you pull at it prematurely, and you remove some of the skin from your lip unintentionally and you wish you had the discipline not to do that but you are without it.

Hanging from the screen was Jenny's turquoise dress which she often wore with a belt, cinching it in, accentuating her narrow waist. Her suede jacket was on a chair. She took off her jeans. There was a bit of bad feeling in the place because of the way I had grabbed her and it made me feel uncomfortable looking at her stripped down to her knickers.

She said she was sorry that she wasn't ready.

It wasn't about that, the not being ready, I told her it was the way it made me feel, as if I wasn't worth getting ready for. She was becoming complacent. There was a tension between us that wasn't there before and I felt remorse for what I had done. I put my arms around her and pulled her close to me and I could feel that her flesh was cold due to the chill of the studio. After an initial resistance I felt her relax into me and then she extricated herself from my arms and sat down on the chair and she faced me.

She asked me if I liked what I saw. I looked at her, draped on the velvet chair – its tattered tassels, the embroidered edging marking her thighs. Her vulnerability in her naked-ness except for her knickers. But she wasn't asking me about herself, she wanted to know what I thought of a painting she had been working on for most of the day. She pointed to a canvas on the floor, which showed an image of a young woman slumped on the side of the road, her arms raised above her head, a small pool of liquid beside her that was brown and looked like stale blood. Jenny said that it was heroin. I told her the painting was incredibly moving, magical. The sense of magic like you have when you are a child and you just believe things.

I leaned over to her and started to kiss her and I was ten-der, as tender as I dared, and I felt her reaction to my touch to be natural and she really wanted this, God I could feel it. I removed her knickers and I moved on top of her, on the chair. It was a bit awkward and after a while Jenny told me to get off her because she was becoming claustrophobic. I lay on my back on the floor of the studio and she lay beside me and I felt in between her legs and it was the right thing to do because I could hear her groan. I had never before felt so close to what I believed to be primal and when I came, I wanted to shout but somehow manged to suppress the urge.

The floor consisted of sheets of plywood covered with a slate grey floor paint. I was on a section where one sheet of wood joined another and the seam was digging into my back. I didn't care because Jenny's naked skin was against mine and her smell and her loveliness was all over me. I whispered into her ear that I loved her and when she said it back the importance of it felt magnified. I said again that I was sorry for hurting her earlier on – I merely wanted her to be ready, that was all.

It was getting on and I suggested that we change our plans for the evening. We had missed our early bird booking at the Mermaid, the launch on Strand Street would be winding down – it was past seven. But when I saw that this wasn't what she wanted to hear from me I told her to get dressed. We would go to the gallery, but we had to hurry.

Jenny got ready. She looked so beautiful and I told her so but she laughed it off. I thought how impressive it is to be so unaware of your own beauty. If Brian could see me with Jenny. I knew that he would have considered her beautiful. Brian, who had practised his sexual exploits with the Spanish girls that came to Ireland to learn English in July and August. Brian, who imagined that he would marry a Spanish girl because he thought that Irish girls weren't pretty enough. How I would have loved Brian to have been alive so I could introduce him to Jenny, so he could see how beautiful Irish girls could be.

37. The Grange

August 2017

The Grange is one of those suburban pubs that makes you want to take a DART into town as quick as you can but you recognize that you are essentially trapped due to the cost of taxis. I'm not happy that Jenny is going to be overly-glammed up for a local bar tonight with Jerome. It's killing me but I figure that the sooner it's done with then the sooner it will be over. I cannot, in all honesty, believe that he doesn't want anything more than friendship from my wife but I try to be upbeat. I squeeze my eyes really tight and I see red and red is the colour of depression. I am not depressed.

Jenny arrives downstairs wearing a dress that seems to me to be highly inappropriate for such an occasion. A catch-up drink, old friends – look at my arse, notice me, is what it says. The demon is in the detail. It's bet on to her and that's that. I send her up again and she is back within a couple of minutes in a pair of white trousers and a top that I bought her in H&M. I tell her that she has chosen well and that she looks fine. I don't wish her to reach any level higher than fine tonight. She is wearing Quorum and it is so sweet on her that for a moment I forget that I am deeply unhappy about this evening. The kids are skulking around and they seem uneasy as to where Jenny is going.

Your mother is meeting an old friend tonight. There is nothing to worry about, absolutely nothing, I say.

Jenny eyes are unwavering and I go into the downstairs

bathroom. I am weak at the knees and I can feel the linguine and the steak that I have eaten earlier on sitting at the bottom of my stomach. It's there but it's not comfortable. I have no option but to shove my index and my middle finger down my throat. I gag and it takes a couple of attempts and at first I don't think that it's going to work because I am only puking up small droplets of bile. But I give it one more go, I make a push for it and the red gush is so acidic coming up that it hurts my windpipe and I am without hope.

Jenny is standing in front of the mirror in the hall, putting some last-minute touches to her makeup when I come out of the bathroom. I think that it would be a great thing if we were going to the Grange together despite my misgivings about the place. I feel it in my bones that she wouldn't be going to as much trouble with her clothes and with her eye-shadow, if that were the case. I don't know what to say so I ask her if she has her house keys and she nods. Then I tell her that she doesn't need to bring them, as I'll probably be up anyhow when she gets home.

This is as good a time as any to ask her what time she expects to be back. She is, I notice, unflinching in her eva-siveness and I choose not to dwell on this, instead I ask if she liked dinner and I mention that I am now vehemently com-mitted to the use of linguine as opposed to chips to accompany a steak. Jenny answers by covering her cheekbones in a face powder that I notice in this light has a certain luminosity. She dabs her thin lips with a dark red stain that makes her look as though she has been eating blackcurrants, such is the way she absorbs colour. She tells me that I am allowed to continue the book that she is reading with the children. I thank her for granting me permission to read aloud to my own offspring, that I feel privileged to have such an honour bestowed on me.

And with that she is gone.

38. Destruction

The boys look out the window as if with hope that Jenny might come back and tell them that it's all a terrible mistake and that she is in fact not going out tonight. Maeve is reading and I don't think it even registers with her that Jenny has left. I make a show of telling the children that as their mother has decided to go out gallivanting for the evening perhaps we might have a game of Monopoly. Mikey and Joey rush over to the shelf and pull down the Monopoly set. They are in good spirits now and I do my best to muster up some enthusiasm, after all it is my suggestion.

For half an hour or so things are grand, I even find that I am enjoying myself, much to my surprise. But after the initial high of who is buying what, things start to go a little sour. Mikey is using up too much energy trying to purchase all the utility stations on the board. He makes the childish mistake of telling us his strategy and it isn't long before Maeve buys up the water works and his whole plan now it seems is in jeopardy. I try coaxing Maeve into being a bit softer and to give her brother a break but Maeve I've noticed can be quite stubborn, much like her mother, and she refuses to bend. Tears are the inevitable outcome and once one starts it isn't long before they are all at it and I think that I'm going around the twist.

That's it, I say, off to bed.

I fold the board in anger and their little green houses and their slightly larger red hotels are mixed up and some of them are scattered now on the coffee table and I feel slightly repulsed by what I have done but I figure that they haven't left me with any choice. Such is the way with children, there comes a time, and it always comes when you have to make a decision on your feet that you are not putting up with any more nonsense and that enough is enough. As if to put salt into their Monopoly war wounds I instruct them to clean up the mess and I stomp upstairs with the intention of running a bath for them. I'm tempted not to bother as I'm slightly concerned that there will be insufficient hot water for all three of them but they haven't had a bath in four days now and I worry about hygiene.

As I sit on the toilet watching the water flow into the bath, I think that Jenny will have made it to the Grange by now. I wonder if she will head straight to the Ladies to check her appearance before she looks out for Jerome. I imagine that he will be waiting at the bar with a pint of Guinness for himself and a red wine for Jenny in situ in anticipation. It irks me that I remember that Guinness is the drink he ordered from me all those years ago in the Crown. I can hear the kids downstairs fighting amongst themselves about whose fault it was that the game had to come to such an abrupt end. They are all blaming each other. I stick my head out of the bathroom door and I shout down to them that they are all equally to blame and that one of them better come up here and get into the bath first before I lose it. I turn around and I choose not to look in the mirror above the hand basin because I know that I'm likely to see anger and contortion. I push the lid up on the toilet seat and I take a piss. It feels right to dispel whatever fluid is left in my body after getting sick.

Bathtime is the greatest test of one's sanity as a parent. Everyone is always tired and tempers are frayed at the edges like old cloth. Each kid has many needs. Maeve is adamant that she will not use the same towel as Joey because he seems to permanently have worms. I tell Maeve to get into the bath first as she is a girl and is less likely to be as grievously dirty as the other pair. This will serve two purposes, she will get clean water and she can have first dibs for the towel. We joke around about boys being disgusting in general but the humour doesn't last on my part. The problem is that Maeve is taking far too long for my liking, five minutes at my last count and the whole ritual seems interminably long if things are going to continue to move along at this wretched pace. And I need a drink.

Half an hour later and they are all decked out in their pyjamas. I have only the story to go. I start off in earnest but I am only two sentences in when Joey says that I'm deliberately using a boring voice. I respond by saying that I find it torturous to use any other kind of intonation when reading about wizards. I don't wish to be a spoilsport but I do believe that there is significant truth to be gleaned from such a statement. Joey asks me what torturous means. I say, this. I tell them that if there are any more interruptions I'm going to stop reading. Mikey interrupts to tell me that he hasn't interrupted. I close my eyes and I try to mentally commit to what I'm trying to do. I'm attempting to make my children happy, to settle them down so that they will have dreams, warm dreams, dreams that they can hold on to. Memories that they can keep for years to come.

I am a good father.

That's it then, so goodnight, I say.

We haven't finished the chapter. I tell them that they will appreciate it all the more if they are left hanging. Maeve argues that this is the whole point of chapters whereby the author has decided the perfect place to pause. She says it's up to the author to decide at what point the reader should be left to hang. I know she's absolutely correct but I don't have the presence of mind nor the patience to have an argument. I tell them enough is enough and that it's one thing that I have to put up with their mother going out for a drink with her ex-boyfriend without having to argue the toss about chapter length with children. I make it very clear that he's an ex-boyfriend and I'm careful to explain that it's a good thing that he's an ex because if he wasn't then they wouldn't have me as their father. They want to know if they would even exist if Mommy's ex-boyfriend was her husband and not her ex-boyfriend.

I tell them that they will always exist.

I say that they will exist until they die.

I tell them that I love them and that I'll see them in the morning as I'm walking down the stairs.

I grab a beer from the fridge and I turn on the TV. I put on a CD and I play with my phone. I put my phone down and pick up a book about wine-making. I read a passage with a semblance of hope and newfound possibility. My mood dampens somewhat when I see the words demijohn and siphoning. Perhaps the better option is to stock up at O'Brien's. Plus, I tell myself that any efforts on my behalf will probably be undrinkable. I am aware of very industrious people who are quite capable of making wine out of such things as parsnips and blackberries. I'm just not sure if it is for me.

I find myself at Jenny's desk and I look fondly at some of the pieces that she has ready for the show in Gallery One. There's the series of pencil drawings of the sea at rest and the sea at turbulence. There's the wood carving of the lobster pot. There's the drawing of the Brother that she has redone since I cut the original. There's the collage that she has called *Shards*. It's a rather interesting piece that takes up a significant portion of her desk. The base is essentially plastic cut from old fish boxes that she has found on the beach over the last year. To me it looks like a storyboard. At a first glance there is certain innocence to it, as though on some level a child has been involved in the process of choosing some of the items that are adhered to the rough blue plastic, sea glass and feathers. Sailors' lace – the spaghetti of the sea – has been dried out and it acts as a frame. As a contrast to all the beach innocence Jenny has stuck a syringe into the centre of the piece.

I check the time. I have been sitting here at Jenny's desk for an hour. My beer is finished and the empty bottle is testament to that. I am lost. Do I think this is any good? I ask myself, could Maeve do this?

What could they be talking about? Must be hard being a widower, Jerome. I think about this for a moment and I realize that I'm experiencing schadenfreude and that I'm glad that he's in pain, that he has lost something. I'm losing many things now as I sit here and dwell. I am losing her laughter, her eyes flitting, the way her clavicle is so fine, slender, the way she leans her head to one side when she is listening to something that she finds deeply interesting. I can't remember the last time she has looked at me with that same inclination of her head. Jerome the fuck. I recount my stories of the sea and of the surf these days mainly to Maeve.

I go to the fridge and I get myself another beer and I drink it but I'm not tasting it. It's just cold and wet and I realize that there is no sweetness to it. I like things to be sweet. I open up a bottle of specialized craft glue and I know how expensive this is yet I pour some on the desk, not on the collage but very close to it. I take a palette knife and I use it to slather the glue on to the collage. I start with the syringe and the pickaxe isn't the correct instrument at all to use so instead I take hold of one of Jenny's large brushes from an old watering-can wedged under the desk. I sing under my breath as I sweep the glue over the entire work.

I get up now from the chair with an urgency and I walk into the kitchen and I fill my arms with the tea caddy and a large jar of turmeric. I go back to the piece and I have a very acute picture of Jerome touching Jenny's face with his fingers and then touching lightly her clavicle. The top that she chose to wear, I remember now, has a low neck and it's an item of clothing that shows her vulnerability. Lace does that to Jenny. I hear Jerome's voice, gravelly, telling Jenny how he's trying to move forward after his great loss. His beautiful and talented wife, he's trying to get his life back together, he places his whole life now in the hands of his little boy and as he admits this to Jenny his voice catches and he has to swallow to fight back his tears. The lying cunt.

I rip open Barry's tea bags and I scatter the fine tea leaves all over the syringe and I sprinkle the turmeric on to the sailors' lace and then I tip the jar upside down and everything is turmeric yellow. My fingertips are stained good as if I am a hardened smoker and there is something right about this night after all.

I sit here and I destroy the sketches of the sea. One by one. All of them. I add drama and depth to the delicate seas. I rub out great tracts of waves from the rough waters. Everything is upside down, you can tell a story any way you want. I am upside down. There are two sides to every story and this is my side. I add colour to the drawing of the Brother as he is kneeling down in a religious trance gazing out to the horizon. I draw fish – stupid fish that you learn to draw in school with three-quarters of their bodies covered in tiny waves that look like the imaginary mermaid's tail of childhood. Its glimmering sheen. And the one big fish eye that seems ever so important. This is realism as any kid under the age of ten will tell you. I line up the empty beer bottles in straight lines much like I used to do in the Crown with Andy when things were quiet.

I check on the kids.

I check that the immersion is off.

I check that I can puke.

I am sitting on the couch at one o'clock in the morning when I hear a scuffle at the front door. Jenny. I can go out and open the door for her but I don't. I hear her throwing her bag on the floor and as she puts one foot on the stairs I call her to me.

She looks like she's had a grand old time and here am I sitting on the couch listening to the Smiths. I am old.

Well, how was it? I ask.

My voice is sneering and I don't mean it to be but that's the way it comes out. She sits down and I can see the effect of his attention on her. Her gait, her aura, all different, a bit like the way she was when she came back from the meeting with Simon Thompson from Gallery One. All hope and ambition and for a split second I sit here and I wonder how can my wife be so full of herself. I ask her if she wants a beer and she says that she's had enough to drink and I tell her that I would like very much for her to have a beer with me, her husband. I get two beers and I hand one to her. She cradles it. I open my beer with my teeth and I throw the bottle opener to her. With a clink we are both sitting now comfortably. I ask her about Jerome. She says that he's fine and that he wanted to catch up and hopes that his son might get to know our kids now that he is living in the area.

It is a strange thing when you lose control of your body. Your voice. I want very much to say that Jerome has another thing coming if he expects it to be all roses in the garden from now on but I don't laugh, instead I say, why not? I sit beside Jenny and I prise the bottle of beer from her fingers. They are so graceful and self-assured and I try to lift up her top but the delicate lace clings and it only rises to her navel.

I open the top button of her trousers and she tenses. I read this rapid movement as desire and I push my hand into her crotch. She clings to me. Her hair falls over her face and she uses her hands to brush it from her eyes and she looks over to her desk and then she looks at me and her eyes are not like my Jenny's.

39. Everything Moved So Fast

July 1997

It felt like a compulsion, a shotgun and I was holding the trigger. It was in my hands, the relationship, and I didn't know exactly what to do with this control.

And it came suddenly, surprising almost like the arrival of the first dew on the grass in the morning.

I was in the part of the flat that I liked to call my office. It was nothing more than a large shelving unit where I kept my favourite books, ones that I couldn't part with. I had thrown away a good many before, books that I had no particular love for, but I kept all my favourites for no particular reason other than sentimentality, which I was taught was somehow wrong. It was erroneous to allow yourself to become too emotionally attached to objects, this was something my father had told me.

I cleaned the bookshelves. I relished the fact that we were living together. Having her there when I came home from the magazine. Having her there after I had finished a late shift at the Crown, even in the long summer when the tourists coming through the doors reached saturation point and the only languages that myself and Andy seemed to hear were full of Mediterranean-soaked fluidity and whatever Irish voices were in the pub were overwhelmed. The Spanish were so polite but they didn't drink enough and in order to attract more locals we decided to hold a weekly draw. It worked in rural parts, why not Dublin?

I didn't like the idea of Jenny being alone in the flat when

I worked late, despite the fact that she said that she didn't mind. For her, there was something about all that quiet time, the calmness, the all-encompassing sense of being content with your own company. I didn't agree with her, I was never completely happy on my own. I was propelled by fear and I was afraid of my memories of Brian. How I knew early on about his potential. He had that type of personality, warm, modest, ambivalent about his good looks. People often commented on his empathy, his kindness, how he let me win our penalty shoot-out games because even as a child he understood my love for football, completely got how important it was for me that I was good at it. It was as if he wanted to show me that I could excel.

And the black biker jacket that I bought him for his sixteenth birthday present, I used up all my savings on it. It wasn't new, I'd bought it in a vintage shop in Temple Bar — thirty quid, probably owned by somebody who was dead and their wardrobe had been cleared out following their demise, perhaps weeks after or maybe months. Those sorts of details probably weren't important but they mattered to me. How was I to envisage that Brian would be wearing that same jacket on the night he was run over by the car and left for dead? I felt as though I had bought him his shroud early on in life. I had bought him his death costume.

Those thoughts of Brian would come back and then the loneliness would creep up on me, the way the power of alcohol in a gin could seep greedily into my bloodstream and those were the times when I was self-congratulatory about being sure to have a bottle to hand to fuel those very times when I wanted very much to introduce that feeling into my body. I had seen heroin addicts at play on the Quays hanging around dealing and scoring, morning or afternoon or evening. The disconnected facial expression on the addict, the soul-searching, the dismay, the forgotten babies in buggies, the hooded hysteria of the crazed 'athletes' in their leisurewear pacing, pacing.

It was a relief not having to rely any more on quashing my anxiety with gin, I had Jenny. One night after I arrived back from a late shift at the Crown she wanted to talk to me about a piece she was having trouble with and I kept looking around the flat happily as she spoke, not really concentrating on what she was saying, just looking. I noticed the way it appeared, now that she had moved in. I ran my eye over the vase of purple tulips, nice and straight and not bulging or falling over on themselves. They were a welcome addition, added some joy, more joy as if we didn't have enough of the stuff. There were other things about her living with me that brought joy. I wasn't alone any more, my aloneness was dispelled. The place was untidier than it would have been with just me but I didn't care about that, a happy place was meant to look lived in.

40. All Her Fault

August 2017

The day after I attack Jenny's work is a dark day and it is my day of reckoning.

I am not going to be that man. That man who cannot take a good hard look in the face of things, a man who refuses to admit that he has done something wrong. Something ignoble. I don't act unless there is good reason to do so. But Jenny, even Jenny has to understand that there comes a point in a man's life where he has got to call things as they are.

I could have destroyed everything, I say.

I hold Mikey's football that he has left on the sitting-room floor. And I look at it intently, counting the parts where its lining has been ripped from all its use on the road. I tell him constantly to only play with it on the green, that it's not designed for tarmac, but he says it's not his fault, that it's easier for him to practise his keepy-uppies on the road. He insists that all the great footballers practised on their childhood roads. I have reminded him that he's lucky to have such an expensive football to practise with, that Pelé had to make do with a potato or a grapefruit wrapped in a sock. It is a wonderful thing, a child's gullibility.

I keep my eyes away from Jenny, I'm afraid to look at her. She is crying and I am deeply aware that this is not an act that she succumbs to easily. In fact I rarely witness her tears.

How could you do it, Des? she asks.

And now she wants me to look at her because she needs to

see my eyes. Needs to work out what is going on in my head. I tell her that the eyes are devious or perhaps I mean to say that they are deceiving and I lift up my head. I'm still resolutely holding the football, as if it can offer me some protection. I want to feel cocooned. For some reason I want to speak to my mother but she is dead and I talk softly to her in my head. I hear her voice and I remember how she used to tell me that kindness is everything and that I should always be kind.

I am not a perpetrator of evil, I say.

This is not about the perpetration of anything, this is about me – my work. You destroyed everything. What about the show?

I admit that I am at a loss and I pull at the tiny slivers of thread that have come undone at the seams of the football. I am sad in myself that we are having this conversation. I tell her that what I have done is fixable, retractable.

It will make your work stronger, I say, to start at the beginning, afresh. It's what all artists do, great artists.

I tell her that the pieces weren't right, that they didn't do her justice.

She gets herself together and says that she will have to ring Simon to explain what has happened.

I go into the kitchen and I don't know how to react to this news about her phoning Simon so I start to make guacamole. I peel a red onion and the purple skin lies on the chopping board and now that it's been taken away from the onion, what it has exposed is a paler mauve denuded bulb and it is slippery and I have to use control not to cut my finger while I am dicing it finely. Red onions do not make my eyes fill with tears the way regular onions do. I thank God for this one small act of mercy.

I can hear Jenny's voice, she is no doubt sitting at the bottom of the stairs where she makes calls when she wants privacy. I can hear her voice but I can't make out exactly what she is saying, however I can tell from its tone that she is apologizing. I slice an avocado down its length and I breathe a soft sigh of relief that there is a certain give in its flesh. Too many times I am faced with unripe avocados. I begin to worry about the world's current lack of the fruit. How much can I expect to pay for an avocado in the future? I take a tub of natural yoghurt from the fridge and I spoon a generous amount into the clear bowl, I crush garlic, I squeeze lime. I am on automatic pilot.

I grab my wallet and as I pass Jenny at the end of the stairs I go to touch her but she flinches. Her head is down and her long fingers are twirling her hair. I head over to the Centra to buy tortilla chips.

They don't have plain tortilla chips so I settle for cheese-flavoured. I buy a lottery ticket and I avoid small talk with Geraldine, at the till, I just don't have it in me today.

On the way back I meet my neighbour and he tries to engage me in a conversation about the hedge that divides our gardens. I tell him that the hedge as it is holds little interest for me. I walk on back to the house. The kids are out on the green playing tag and I shout that I am making lunch. There is no response, I wave the bag of tortillas, I sense young feet behind me.

Jenny is gone from the stairs. I can see her through the kitchen window out in the back garden. Crouched down, she has her back to me and she is weeding the flowerbed by the tree. She is also smoking. The kids want to know where lunch is, I tell them that it is in mid-production. I open the tortillas. I put a pot of water on to boil and then I take out a bag of pasta. The children watch television as the kitchen window steams up.

Destruction, she calls it. I have a good mind to start

another conversation with Jenny. To tell her that the use of the word destruction in my mind seems awfully dramatic when one is talking about a few drawings, a wooden sculpture of a bird. Destruction seems more appropriate if one were to consider, perhaps, the collapse of a city. I sometimes forget that Jenny has a tendency towards exaggeration.

But we don't have that conversation. The day moves on. I notice the changing pattern in the weather. The initial humidity of the morning is gone and now the cool breeze of the sea is making its way up into the village and hitting the front garden. I'm outside cutting the grass and our garden seems entirely insignificant opposite the green. How I long in my heart for a large garden, it's what I always dreamt of, why don't I have one? My neighbour, spotting an opportunity, tries once again to talk to me about the hedge. I ignore him and he walks back into his house. I wonder why it's so difficult to regurgitate penne, perhaps it has something to do with its shape.

Evening draws in and the children have to be looked after. Now is not a good time, I sense, to ask Jenny to give me a hand, so I go about boiling potatoes and grilling pork chops. I peel some smoked salmon from a packet for Maeve. I wash my hands quickly while avoiding breathing in its oily fumes.

We sit down together at the table and we each have our own way of eating and that's fine, but Joey is bolting his food as if he's not expecting to be fed for a very long time. It's too hard not to mention it so I do. If I don't give these instructions what kind of a father am I? Jenny is quiet and I feel that I need to break down this barrier she has erected so I ask her if the pork chops are overcooked, if she likes the sauce? She nods and I'm not sure if she means that I've ruined the meat or if she is enjoying the medley of flavours I have created. Maeve can sense something amiss, she can be very perceptive. She asks Jenny about the upcoming show and if Jenny is excited about it. I feel like laughing. My children do not know what I have done.

What did you say to Simon? I ask Jenny.

She ignores me. Maeve waits for her answer and I wait for mine. I feel like I could cut through this tension with a knife. When Jenny speaks it's as if she has been storing up her speech all day and it feels rehearsed. She explains to Maeve that she has made the difficult decision that she isn't happy with the work she has done so far for the group show and she is going to start all over again.

I keep my head down.

When I am tucking Maeve into bed we have a brief discussion about disappointment and how that very notion means different things to different people.

I mention to Jenny that there's quite a few out-of-season cooking apples going rotten in the wicker bowl on the kitchen table and perhaps she might do something with them. Anything at all. I'm quite partial to a bit of apple tart but she knows this so I feel disinclined to actually suggest rustling up something so obvious. I pick up a large apple at random and I check it for patches of wrinkled skin and for any other kind of blemishing – bruising or a sneaky infiltration of insects. I take a tea towel that is hanging from the handle on the oven and I polish the skin and I try not to press down too deeply on the fruit in case I hurt it because the way I'm at odds with myself today I imagine that apples have feelings.

There are more apples rotting prematurely in the house. I come across a plastic bag under the stairs with the Tesco logo and the shit about how every little helps and in this bag are a whole load of unripe, bitter apples given to us by some generous spirit in Jenny's art group. And despite the fact that they have been picked too early, the smell is so delightfully pungent that I put my entire head into the bag even though I have always warned the children to never ever put their heads anywhere near a plastic bag. I leave my head in the bag for a couple of seconds but it feels more like a few minutes, allowing the cider aroma to build into my nostrils. My cheeks begin to feel hot – like they are covered in a blush of sweat, and even though it's a bit early in the season for apples, there's something about wasting food that is unforgivable.

A certain part of me is sad that Jenny won't be able to showcase her work. She obviously has talent and that's the pity of it all but when you're slicing through drawings that your wife has spent hours over you don't see the consequences. All you are capable of seeing is Jerome Fagan laughing at you because you're at home playing dad while your wife of many years, your beautiful wife, is out with him, filling him in on her artistic endeavour.

You don't see or indeed fully comprehend what you are doing to your wife's meticulous work as you admire the grooves she has carved in the wing of the turnstone, carefully constructed by tiny soft taps to the wood. You don't taste the salty saliva that is slowly accumulating at the base of your mouth, mimicking the sensation you get when you are about to purge your system of excessive nourishment. You are alone. You don't see what this one chance, perhaps this only chance will do for your wife. You are blind to her potential, all you can see is Jerome's face, his widower's face looking at your wife pretending to be simply hooking up with an old acquaintance, settling himself in nicely into your neighbourhood. No, all you see is your fear of losing your wife's love. This is not envy, this is jealousy.

41. The Football Trials

It's an important day for the lads. The football trials. Our lot have to perform well if any of them want to move up to the As next year. Otherwise they'll be staying put with myself and Maurice on the Bs. It's a serious business.

At the pitch I place the enormous emerald green kit bag on the hard grass, unzip it and begin to dish out the balls to the lads. They go at them in a frenzy like they've been imprisoned for months and are desperate for release.

It's a scorcher of a day and Mikey and Joey push out into the thick of it. They're red in the face. I shout at them to stay focused, that they're doing great. I say it but in my heart I know they're not good enough to be moved up, and as the first phase of tests begins my thoughts are confirmed. I split the lads either side of the goal for one-on-ones, an exercise that can very quickly draw out a player's deficiency. They have to run to the far cone, around it and then into the penalty area where I play a through ball. All the time I'm worrying about Mikey and Joey that they won't let me down.

The lads run through another few skills and I can hear them shout excitedly as I outline the instructions for the Barcelona drill. This is a favourite even though it's overly complicated for their little bodies to get to grips with. It's all about the glamour. I blow the whistle and shout, normal. The lads start playing as if they are playing an ordinary game. I shout out, possession, and they have to keep the ball in their side and they cannot take shots on goal. After a while I shout, Barça, and this time they have to keep the ball in the other side's half. I'm beginning to get a stitch from all this running around and the lads look half-dead. I call time out and I make my way over to Maurice while the boys spray each other with their water bottles.

Maurice asks me if I heard about the family whose house was burnt to the ground in Shankill back in July. He's at it again getting the tragedy juices going. I tell Maurice that I have indeed heard about it and that it's a bloody awful thing to happen to anyone. And this admission of mine leads to a discussion about dodgy domestic boilers. This moves us on to the dangers of electrical appliances that are reaching the end of their lives in general terms; Maurice is particularly interested in washing machines. It seems that Alison is on at him to buy a new machine and he describes how he's refusing to budge. As I holler at the lads to stop mucking about, Maurice is listing the benefits of Calgon to me and revealing what he terms the truth – that washing machines really do live longer with it. And now the jingle is stuck in my brain.

We talk about the wonderful spirit and about the strength of our team considering the age of the lads. I think about the horror wreaked on the family from Shankill. Three kids now without a mother. I look over to see Joey lying on the ground, clutching his ankle. I can tell he's faking, call it a father's intuition. I go over to him and I tell him to stop messing or he'll lose his chance. I tell him to be ferocious. Joey asks me what ferocious means and I grunt at him. Martin Coyle, the selector, is watching, he's the guy to impress and I look Joey in the eye and I tell him to cop himself on.

Martin Coyle splits the boys into groups for a game. As I'm watching Mikey and Joey being handed bright yellow vests, Maurice tells me about the snake that was found up a tree the week before in the village and he assures me that it wasn't dangerous. He also tells me that a group of local women have got together to reclaim the streets, to send a message to the guy hanging about the DART station scaring women that they will not be threatened. Maurice is convinced that the women are drawing unnecessary attention to themselves and that this may not be a good thing.

I look over to Maeve and I imagine her being attacked and I picture her running away from someone with the stature of Maurice and then I shudder because I shouldn't allow myself to think of Maurice in this light. And Maeve, despite her fitness for her age, cannot get away from him. And I start to believe once more in the notion of the wrong time and the wrong place.

The trials go on for another hour and on the way home in the car I try to tell the kids the story about the snake. No one is listening.

42. Proposal

June 2003

I had a job interview with a company that sold life assurance. The manager, Graham O'Neill, sat across a veneer table from me. He asked me a series of questions, including where I saw myself in five years. It was preposterous but I went along with it anyway. How would I feel about working in an open-plan environment? I was used to that set-up, coming from the magazine, I assured him. If I had worked out a way to play Tetris when I should have been closing in on sponsorship, I could manage anything. I got the job – a middle management position telling people they are going to die.

I would have agreed to anything because I had an exquisite plan for Jenny that night. I knew well where I saw myself in five years, with my darling Jenny and with children tugging on the cuffs of my shirt. All the way through the interview I only had thoughts for my plan.

I landed the job. I could finally give up the Crown. Jenny wouldn't have to worry about anything. We could travel to splendid cities. She would create great art. We would have blessed children. She would be all mine. I had secured a vintage engagement ring for her weeks before. The look of it was so Jenny.

I went home, full of joy. Later, when I heard her opening the door of the flat, I seriously thought that my heart might stop.

I felt sick but it was a heady sort of sickness and I told myself to stay strong. I focused all my strength to the top of my legs and I concentrated on my breathing. While Jenny put her bag on the kitchen table, I inhaled and I popped the cork from a bottle of champagne. I poured two glasses and placed them on the table beside her bag and I got down on one knee, as I had dreamt of doing, and I asked her to be my wife.

Her eyes seemed to glisten and she gave a gentle cough and then she said, yes, she would marry me, and I felt my strength waver momentarily and then the euphoria that rose in my chest was like something that I'd never felt before.

We drank champagne and I babbled nervously. I started to cook – the fillet steak rare, the spinach wilted perfectly so you could easily absorb the iron in it, the thin chips cut with precision. The scent of the meat cooking in the flat seemed to bring calm.

I couldn't believe she would be my wife.

We finished the champagne and I opened a bottle of red wine and we drank some and then we took our glasses to bed. Jenny turned to me and touched my face. She was so tender and it felt like we were once again in Paris, I felt so in love, we were so in love. To think that a feeling like that could allow itself to be duplicated, to think that it could travel across France to Ireland and instil in us the certainty of togetherness.

It wasn't the fact that the Pompidou Centre was constructed from the outside in, it wasn't that the place seemed to reflect me, the way I wore my heart. It wasn't that our efforts to escape bumping into other tourists were successful, that is the way of Paris. It was the way Jenny linked my arm, lightly, as we strode about the city, how she waited while I bought the carnets and she passed her ticket into the turnstile, always after me. And the way she stroked my fingers, gently, as I studied the Métro map in the stations, working out which exit we should take. I could have been leading her anywhere. I had led her to stay with me, forever.

There was moonlight shining into the window of the flat. I told Jenny not to sleep, to stay awake; to hold the night's happiness. She said that the light meant something and she felt safe with it. I held her close. Perhaps there was something to be said about all the fuss about the darkness into light walks that would spring up about the country, years later. Light, it seemed, was so amazing it could even prevent suicide.

I was careful with the weight of my body as I lay on her and the penetration I performed was weighted in its own gentle way.

We were getting married.

43. It Couldn't Get Any Better

July 2004

We were full of the early flush that you get as newlyweds which people warn will quickly disappear, but you hope won't happen. When we decided we needed a house of our own to feel like a proper married couple, it wasn't like the lights went out at the end of a party and we were told politely that we had to leave. It was dangerously exciting.

It was at that stage where you could lie about your salary and it was decent of Graham to exaggerate mine on paper for the bank. We managed to buy a place. It wasn't Killiney but it was close enough to the beach and that was all I cared about. There was a shop, a pharmacy and a pub. It served our needs.

Jenny started to consider having children, she wanted life to grow in her body. I was delighted. We finally seemed to want the same thing and this unleashed an optimism from inside my heart and my bones.

She must have told Jerome about the wedding, even if she didn't invite him, because we got a present delivered to the house. A throw from Avoca – a mixture of turquoise and cream and grey and its texture was mohair-warm and I imagined it would scratch your skin but Jenny didn't seem to worry about such a thing. To her it was fluffy-perfect. In the evenings, in the early days, before we had Maeve and Mikey and Joey, Jenny would lie on the couch, snuggled into it. She often covered her legs with it when she was working at her desk. It was spattered with paint and she didn't care about the stains. Jenny saw them as testament to the fact that she was working.

I continued to sell life assurance and although I'd only been in the job a year, I felt as though I'd known Graham O'Neill for a significant part of my life, but with the mortgage repayments, I had no option but to put up with it.

Graham paid for me to do a part-time business course. The people. Dullness seemed to be etched on to their faces. I thought that perhaps Graham or God might be playing a joke on me, that this was all that I had to look forward to, courses with the aim of allowing me to climb the corporate ladder, rung by rung to dizzying heights and then maybe later, if I was successful, a retirement plan.

Graham was trying to bond with me at work, and I didn't like it, putting a bit of pressure on me to go to the Friday night drink. I was scared of going out with the work crowd, scared where it might lead. The job I had was a means to an end, and nothing more. The course was a means to an end. Our children would be beautiful and gracious, and our house would be painted with heritage colours throughout, and Jenny's face would be full of pleasure in the evenings. Our future happiness was secured.

Despite the monotony of the job, there was a kind of holiday atmosphere to the way we lived. Jenny finally taught herself how to cook. I came home in the evenings and we would talk and she often had pleasing meals prepared, salads and cold ham and shepherd's pie, in the winter, and French onion soup that I felt was every bit as flavoursome as the one you could get at La Maison des Gourmets.

Our place, in general, spoke of kindness and of two people who didn't have it all yet, in terms of the perfect house, but at least had a fairly decent home, a place they could call 'theirs', and the jam jar filled with Michaelmas daisies on the kitchen table in the late summer reflected that. And for a long time Jenny seemed content and she made me believe she didn't miss town, and the dirt and the grime and the sort of beauty that's in that, and she didn't say that she didn't enjoy fixing those meals to share together in the evenings and one evening after one of those lovely meals of hers – a beef and olive casserole – Jenny told me she was pregnant.

And that's when I truly believed.

The knowledge that we were absolutely meant for each other, forever, felt warm to me in my blood. We were having a child together, we were unstoppable, us. The beautiful calm knowledge, the perfect evening, the perfect news.

I wanted to run to my books. I wanted to read poetry. I wanted to scream verses by John Donne and other verses like Bukowski's 'the trash men' because that is what the euphoria felt like, if you could describe it as a mood. I didn't care, though. I felt ambidextrous to life, like I could take it in my two hands and juggle the happiness around, it was unbounded and I no longer had anything to fear. She was mine. Jenny was mine. We were having a child.

When Maeve was born and, later, Mikey and Joey, my Jenny was there for them. Their demands were so encompassing that it meant Jenny's work suffered. As soon as I came home in the evenings they were mine to deal with. And slowly I realized that the flash of life that she'd shared with me in the earlier days was a flash, and nothing more. And I was jealous and I wanted that flash of our old life back. The time when she wouldn't bother staying up late to work but would come to bed and, if the children were quiet, or later asleep, she would hold me and I could feel the glisten of perspiration on her chest when we made love and I wanted to be able to smell that sweat.

The belief in our happy life that I gifted her. The way she listened to me and took from it what she wished and the freckles on her nose, accentuated in summer, and our garden freshly planted and the children growing with it and the slips of plants from Jenny's father's garden, whom we would occasionally visit on Sundays. He was a coffee man and I was a tea man. He never really bothered talking to the children. He didn't seem to talk much to Jenny either, and hardly ever to me.

And yet we took his slips.

44. The Portuguese Man of War

August 2017

I lie in a foetal position on the urine-streaked ground beside the shelter at the end of the ramp on our beach where I used to come often with Jenny, just the two of us. The shelter has some great graffiti from time to time but mostly, inane messages like 'Bono doesn't pay any tax' or 'Kill all singer song writers'.

I can feel the uneven-lumpy ground digging into my bare back and then I can't feel anything of the ground. Only a peculiar mortifying pain. A pain that is so magnificent that I do not have the words or the breath to describe it. For I am without breath and even through this pain I am not without hate. Hate for Jerome. As I drift in and out of my orbit, my reality, my day off, I can hear the frantic voices of Mikey and Joey and Maeve asking me if I'm all right and do I think that they'll still be getting an ice cream? I can hear them discussing how unfair it will be if I don't follow through on my earlier promise as they'll be going back to school and that the Mr Whippy van will be gone for good if I don't get up off the ground and do something.

This agony leaves me breathless and I'm not even sure of my own name now and I will myself to come out of this but at the same time I'm not strictly sure if that is actually what I desire. Because now I realize that in another way I feel quite contented with my lot. I have three beautiful children and a wife, who is at once attractive but also artistically talented. My whole body is burning and I feel like I am crawling with itch and my skin is so uncomfortable that I feel like I could scratch it off but my nails are insufficiently long.

I shout out. I tell the kids to open my wallet and take out the money for the ice cream. Contractions of pain shoot up my spine and I have a flashback to Jenny screaming to the doctors in the hospital to get Maeve out of her because she thought that she was going to die. I cross my arms and I rub my palms up and down the top part of my arms and I start to shiver violently even though I am burning up. I am rubbing bits of tentacles further into my body. Mikey asks me if he should get strawberry or lime sauce on his ice cream. I scream, strawberry, because even in my desperation I know that strawberry is his favourite flavour and it's what he wants to hear. I can hear Jenny asking me if I am all right, if I can breathe. And I wonder how it is that she's even here with us on the beach. She should be at home working on her paintings, her sculptures. And now I recall that she has joined us because there has been an overnight storm and there is no end to the possibilities of what she may find after the sea has ravaged the headland. I can see her standing over me and she is wearing a flowing white dress with a floral pattern that seems very much at odds with how I'm feeling now.

As I lie on the ground I make the decision to get dressed because I am shivering now in my swimming shorts and then I immediately reject such a decision because I am aware that I'm entirely incapable of doing such a thing. The cloud formation overhead is at once foreboding and poetic and I wonder in my heart why is it that there is a scarcity of what you could consider deeply attractive men native to the Irish hinterland compared to, say, the French. And yet Jerome Fagan must be doing something right and in my twisted agony I curse him for it.

It isn't strictly a jellyfish, the Portuguese man of war, and

of course I learn all this in time. A group of gelatinous cells –
a siphonophore – which occasionally hangs out in Irish
waters that I have been unfortunate to encounter. I get some
sympathy from Jenny the next day but it is insufficient compared to the magnitude of what I have been through.

45. Jerome Is in My House

I cannot control an emotion surfacing; I can, however, control what I do with it.

Days pass into weeks and I don't know how that happens but it does and still Jenny will not speak to me properly about anything. The summer holidays are coming to an end and you can see the shift in the way the flowers in the garden are starting to lose their lustre. The only things really hanging on are the stubborn geraniums. An anxiety begins to take a hold of me, a list of things in my head to be done. The kids need new school shoes, Maeve could do with another school jumper. I contact Maurice because we have things to discuss as the football season proper will be back upon us before we know it. Maurice is on about organizing tracksuits for the winter, something to protect the lads for when the weather gets really fierce. I agree strongheartedly but I don't have the inclination to discuss sponsored walks to raise funds with him, I have other things to worry about. There's the fact that my wife will not speak to me for starters.

We move in and out of each other's company, Jenny and I, and I feel as though I'm living alone even though I am surrounded by people. It's an incredibly frustrating way to conduct our lives but that is what we do now. The children are our fodder in this war. They soak up our grievances and yet they never show it. As if sensing our unhappiness they behave impeccably. I miss their antics. I miss the fights, the blame games, the moaning about not having mobile phones and being the only children in their entire school without them. I miss how they stomp upstairs, their tempers flared, the weight of the world against them. I miss them complaining that they have to come in off the green at night, that it's only ten o'clock and the kids that live across the road are thinking about heading down to the beach for a swim. And I miss telling them that they're different as they're French and that French children, much like Spanish children, never seem to know when it's time to call it a day.

I want to tell Jenny how I very nearly slept with Denise when I went to Cork on the work trip. I want to tell her how I was tempted, sorely tempted, because my wife will not physically touch me. Can she not see what she is doing to me? I cannot be a functioning man and not function. Surely there is something to be said about a wife's duty, it's not an expression coined for the fun of it. It has to mean something. Can she not recognize just how easy it would have been for me to do it? One quick fuck. And then back to our life together.

I want to tell Jenny that I didn't actually penetrate Denise because of my love for her. Because the love I have for her isn't just an easy love, it is deep and significant. I feel it when she is awake and I feel it when she is asleep and when she is asleep she looks perfect to me. As perfect as she was when I first clapped eyes on her.

But what I do not want to tell Jenny is that there is trouble in my veins and that my mild transgression is not only debilitating in its frustration, there is also the fact to contend with that Denise is now making official nasty allegations about me, that I tried to fuck her and it is most unfortunate, her pathetic version of events, she is not even that pretty but often, I find it is the women who have the least that make the most noise. Denise, seemingly, has nothing to lose for making up these lies, lies that are an attack on my very being and my standing as a good husband, father and provider, how fucking dare she.

But I'm ready to deny everything so help me God and if the worst comes to the worst I can find a way out.

I want to tell Jenny that I am not a jealous man, that I don't care about Jerome, that all I care about is the possibility that he might take her away from me, that I am afraid of losing love.

I don't say anything about love.

Instead I back her into a corner and I make her listen to me as I tell her that it's her fault that the show didn't work out for her. I make it clear that if she hadn't gone to meet Jerome I wouldn't have touched her art. I'm starting to come across as being aggressive so I go to put on a CD. I choose soft music, gentle undulations of an Italian church choir that I'm particularly fond of because it makes me melancholic. Sometimes it is incredibly uplifting to allow yourself to slip into this kind of a mood. To feel the splendid loss of control.

I sit down on the sofa and listen to the choir. My arms feel as though they are being caressed and I close my eyes, and I imagine that Jenny is running her fingertips along the inside of my arms. Don't stop, I say silently. I allow the music to do its work. Jenny is close by me, I can sense it. I open my eyes and her hand is almost touching my hand and I reach out to her. Her hand feels cold in comparison to mine and I smile because her heart is warm and I hope that she will forgive me.

This perfect moment.

The sound of the doorbell seems like a rude interruption. I walk to the door and I feel that maybe things will be right between us once again. We have our share of good times and bad times, we are no different than any other couple. My mood is light.

I open the door to see what I don't want to see – Jerome Fagan standing on my doorstep.

I turn and walk into the kitchen and Jerome follows me.

It's been a while since I found him here in my kitchen drinking coffee with Jenny while I struggled to lead the lads to victory out on the football pitch. Jenny doesn't seem to know what to do with herself so Jerome says that he is here to see me. How is it that I feel uncomfortable in my own house as if I am in the way, an outsider in some club, not part of some pact? Jenny mutters something about going to buy milk. I give her a look. I want to stop her in her tracks and demand to know why she is contacting Jerome behind my back but I don't. I've a good mind to scream.

Des, he says.

I don't like the way he feels he can use my name like he's a friend or something but I don't say it. I set the kettle to boil, and I stare at the neon blue light at its base. The kids run in to get water and their clambering at the tap dispels the tension in the room. Jerome asks them what age they are and if they like school – the usual stupid adult talk. Mikey and Joey don't respond and Maeve smiles her quiet smile. I smile back at Maeve because it's hard not to.

The boys go back outside as quickly as they came in but Maeve hangs back. I tell her to go back outside and to let us have a cup of tea in peace. She starts for the hall and I can tell she is reluctant because of the way she drags her feet. Jerome informs me that he wishes to be straight with me. Jenny has told him about what I did to her work, about her disappointment and how he feels he is to blame.

I don't need another man to tell me that I have let my wife down. A man who is the cause of all this trouble in the first place.

The Italian choir is a crescendo of voices and its beauty is somehow being distorted by the presence of this man in my kitchen, noble and all as he thinks he is with his surprise visit. Here to set things straight, I cannot believe such audacity.

Jenny comes back and makes a pot of tea. Without waiting for it to draw sufficiently, she pours three mugs and we each hold one in our hands. My mug is from Tesco and it doesn't retain heat well. Jerome tells me that he's sorry, that he wanted to meet up with Jenny as a friend because he doesn't know many people in the area, how he never for one moment intended to cause a rift between myself and Jenny. It's a flawed argument but I don't say anything. I am not a man to let myself down and so I play along with Jerome. I tell him that I don't know what came over me. I tell him that I curse myself every day about it.

Once the tea is drunk, there doesn't seem to be any reason for Jerome to extend his stay and I say that we have to think about getting dinner ready for the children. I ask him about his own son and as he is going out the door I tell him that I'm sorry that he has lost his wife.

46. The Innocence of Childhood

I spend my days now thinking back on happier times, like the time last year when we couldn't wait to sing 'Happy Birthday' to Jenny; the children and I. We, as a family, smiled at her face. Her eyes had a redness in them, as though she had been crying. I presented her with a sketchpad, made of pages of coarse undyed paper. The pencils I had bought to go alongside it were as dark as ebony and they came in a wooden box which I imagined Jenny could reuse to store tiny shells or fragments of sea glass.

The children gave her gifts: chocolate and bubble bath, and she thanked them even though bubble bath gave her a rash. I put on some music and Jenny danced with the children in the kitchen and their laughter was contagious and so I joined them and it didn't matter really that the kitchen was too small for that kind of behaviour and our bodies touched each other, in our tangle of arms and legs, and it was heavenly to be dancing like that, with my wife, and with my children.

After the dancing there was the cake and Jenny said that she didn't feel forty-one and I told her that she didn't look it. The process of ageing was, after all, something that you couldn't control. Life could not stand still for us to enable us to remain in that one moment of bliss when everything was great between us. Despite the pressure of caring for our children, who seemed to follow us everywhere we went, for the most part we were content with what we had achieved together. Special occasions made me philosophical.

Maeve had put forty-one candles into the icing on the

chocolate cake. Mikey and Joey had carefully counted them out for her. We would have preferred not to mark the passing of time with those small oblong twists of wax in white and sickly pink. We would have preferred not to have marshmallows stuck into the icing as a border, but I had crumbled under the pressure from the children.

Jenny sat on a kitchen chair and kissed Maeve and told her the cake looked delicious. The children produced the homemade part of the present. Their lovely drawings, a true representation of their innocence. The childish depiction of our family through splodges of paint. Two large splodges – Jenny and I. Three other smaller splodges – the children. Palm trees in the background of each picture, the simplicity of the strokes of the leaves, and the sun, a yellow ball in the corner of each picture, made me smile. Jenny told them the pictures were wonderful, they were so realistic. I told her to judge them. She looked carefully at them and said that each one had a particular quality that the other two didn't have. It was impossible to choose an overall winner.

This was happiness – her gentleness, her consideration. Laughter was the part of it that got to me, reached into my core, as I witnessed the children's delight in the simplest of celebrations. I cut the cake and we all had a slice, sweet and cloying. This was some party. The fairness, the way she made each of them feel so special, made me proud.

It was time for bed. Their arms were draped over our necks and it was all hustle as we climbed the stairs, Jenny holding Mikey and me guiding Maeve, Joey on my back too, a piggyback and I told him not to choke me. He moved his hands away from my neck briefly and placed them instead on my shoulders and I lurched forward, and his sticky palms were once again around my neck and I told him that I was going to kill him if he did that again, and he laughed. When the children had brushed their teeth Jenny read to them in the boys' room. I watched from the landing and it was just us, this unit, and the darkness outside.

Later, the way she touched my stomach, pressing on it gently. Stroking the hair near my groin caused me to moan softly and she was astride me then and when our bodies were truly locked together I felt like I could cry with happiness. We made love that night like it was the first time that we were together when the power of her and her wanting me felt so tangible. When I orgasmed I screamed out.

I eased Jenny's body off mine and I felt that sense of security fall over my body that I had before my mother died. It had been four years and yet it felt so raw. But even that security was tarnished slightly, it was fake. Losing Brian had messed with it and had exposed me to loss too early in my life. At least my mother had been alive to see my family, to get to know them for a while.

The calm I experienced lying beside Jenny was deeply satisfying. I felt the way the sea looks on a really close, silent winter morning a day or two after a storm hits – the surface lake-like and I would walk by the beach to take the train to work, to put in an entire day with Graham and think how I would rather submerge myself in the water. How I would rather dive under and stay down in the clear sea, looking at the stones and the pebbles and the small channel dug into the seabed, rather than face another day in a dull office.

I knew my sea.

47. My Fear

I recall now, how there was often laughter to behold in the ordinary little things, and in the evenings the children told us all about their day at school. I loved listening to their innocence and their earnestness, and I didn't mind at all that the house was so untidy or that there were scuff marks on the kitchen wall, that the boys could never wear matching socks. None of that stuff mattered. And Jenny's relaxed attitude to all the chaos didn't bother me as such, my mother had always been tidy but somehow with Jenny I felt safe in all this mess.

Things began to change. At first Jenny was attentive to our needs. She would often break away from what she was working on to dance with the children in the kitchen. They laughed at the way she waved her arms about. I told them that their mother was a good dancer and I would join in, my hands moving steadily, and I would wave my arms in the air until I couldn't stretch them any further, all the time showing them how to dance, how music could have power over your body. They would howl with laughter, tears on their beautiful faces when I told them that I was a cool dad, and that they were lucky to have me. Oh the laughter. I told them their mother was a fine dancer and that was one of the reasons I fell in love with her.

She was light on her feet, I said.

Jenny talked to me about her work all the time, and I listened. Nobody wanted to hear stories about hopes and dreams and ambitions. You had to know the right people in Dublin, it was as simple as that, and you were doomed if you missed the boat, but I didn't say that to Jenny. I listened to her banging on about the tangibility of dreams, how a dream can be so clear in your head but when you attempt to voice it, to extract it, like a painful decaying, festering tooth, it becomes fuzzy and not at all the way it is in your mind. The tooth hiding there in the recess of your mouth is causing you pain but the brain itself cannot feel pain and that is why it is possible to do brain surgery with a local anaesthetic. I wondered about the pain Jenny was supposedly suffering and I wondered if it was imaginary.

I was her sounding board, her first port of call. She would talk through her ideas about her work with me and I would offer whatever advice I had. She would take this counsel and play with it and oftentimes she would act on it. These were happy times. If she ignored it I would feel emptier inside than I had before she came to me for help.

I urged her to generate constant positivity around her. We were there for her comfort, the children and I, we would wrap her up. It was faith that pushed people to do great things with their lives. Nobody got where they were by just looking and not pushing. I was all talk about self-belief and motivation and Jenny, it seemed to me, refocused.

Her new project involved newspapers. She gathered reams and reams of print and it seemed as though the letters weren't just letters that made up words, and the words weren't mere words that made up sentences. She was looking at the print in terms of form and shape.

She talked about her fear of the sea. And I reiterated my love for the water and of my deepest respect for it. She said that it was her latent fear of the sea that had given her the inspiration to depict it, and that was what she had achieved with her work on Lennox Street. She was searching for some inspiration that could equal that fear. I didn't know what to believe, how she could fear something and be willing to explore it, it was admirable really. Her relentless depiction was her way of confronting her fear. I couldn't confront mine.

She had an idea of shredding the newspapers, tearing through all those letters, all those words. Mixing the pieces of torn newspaper with water and glue and then moulding them into bricks. She talked about wrapping the bricks in plastic and what that might achieve and then she considered wrapping old phone books in plastic.

It was as though if they were packaged they could speak to her in another language and the pain of the lack of belief in herself and in her work would disperse. She found a new energy. She started working late into the evenings, into the nights. She bought flowers for herself from Tesco sometimes when she was tired after working late. Tulips – often the purple ones that were that perfect mixed shade of bruises and hope.

I could have told her about real problems and fear of failure, of how I found it difficult as a child. How nobody picked me to join any team. Back then I wanted to be a football manager so I could get my own back. Nobody chose me, even though the coach said that I had great strength in my legs. Nobody cared about strength or its greatness. I was strong and nobody cared.

I hid my fear from Jenny. I told her that she wasn't to give up. I knew that she needed to meet other artists, to share ideas, but I didn't encourage that. I focused on her personal ambition. My dread of other people getting in the way, of us. I appeared sociable but I was burning up inside whenever we were invited anywhere. I was glad the children were young because they kept Jenny at home.

My fear became gargantuan but I couldn't let on to Jenny. I continued to talk at her, half-heartedly, and encouraged her to go along to gallery events. I would watch the children, I assured her. I was a puppeteer with an unruly puppet who was getting mixed messages from its keeper, go out and mingle, no, stay here, stay with us. I wanted Jenny to be successful, I wanted her name out there, truly I did, but I held the strings. And I felt tired and I didn't like all the work that Jenny had to do in order to achieve her ambition. I was using up my energy encouraging her and at the same time making her feel guilty for leaving us to our own devices. I was cooking all the time – Chicken Kiev for the boys and vegetarian dishes for Maeve.

And all the time I was suffering. I was trying to cover up my own disappointment, not getting anywhere with my artistic ambition. I was selling life assurance. I was tired, more often than somebody should be for their age. I would fall asleep on Saturday afternoons and when I woke up I would have a taste in my mouth that was at once sweet and bitter. People often say that you feel better after a power nap – twenty minutes or so. I didn't feel any better, I felt terrible, despite the fact that there was nothing physically wrong with me.

I started running more and maybe I was having a mid-life crisis but I felt I could exercise my way out of it. I was officially a Mamil. I knew the meaning of words like wainscoting and I could describe any astronomical phenomena to the children with enthusiasm. I was unstoppable, but I was boring, I was painfully boring. I was boring myself.

I was going through that phase where you wonder what you would do without the other person, your mirrored self, your other you. It wasn't a comfortable phase. I wondered about longevity and mused about Jenny's head and how she came about decisions, even small ones like what way to wear her hair, loose and relaxed or tied back. She was always messing with her hair.

And I wondered about the sky and its menacing dark

clouds and how its uncertainty could cause a small vibration in my stomach, a tiny flipping sensation of trepidation.

It wasn't an easy thing, being faced with the certain relief that you could love somebody that much and have children with them and that this would be enough. It was a wonderful feeling to know that this was sufficient to sustain you, I didn't need anything else.

But I still had the fear.

I kept everything in check, close to my heart – the knowledge that I was capable of hurting somebody else. It was difficult to imagine how events could have gone any other way.

The trouble I got myself into, as a young boy. It was a simple case of hitting a girl across the face, in the swimming pool. She wouldn't play with me. She was much more interested in the other children. I wanted her attention so much, for her to swim-chase me, to choose me, and she refused to do any of it, and the whole feeling was excruciating. During playtime, I shoved her head under the water; just for a split second. When I let her go she started screaming, so I slapped her, it was a reflex action.

I lay in bed that night and I imagined what it must feel like to drown and I wondered if it was true what people said – that it is a pleasurable way to die. I felt sick about what I had done but I'd get over it.

48. You Can't Make Tea

That tea was awful, I say to Jenny after Jerome leaves us.

I can't make tea, she says.

Something in the way that she agrees with her inability is sad. I sense that she is defeated and it appals me that I have contributed to her sadness. It's even more difficult when you know that you haven't been faced with a choice.

He's not a bad person, Des.

She might as well be telling me that he is in fact a good person. The CD has finished and I press play again as if the monks will lead me down a path of peace. Everything feels wrong now. I take a beer from the fridge. I open it quickly and there is a slight hiss. My hand is shaking as I bring the bottle to my lips. I try to think about what I shall make for dinner. I pick out some wilted spinach from the fridge and I figure that perhaps if I soak it in water with some added sugar it may regain its rigidity. I remember my mother used to do this with lettuce but I reckon with spinach it's probably a long shot. As I'm thinking about the spinach I look into the press under the counter for noodles or rice. All I can see is a giant packet of fusilli that seems to be staring at me. Jenny is curled up at her desk mixing oil paints on her artist palette. Silvers and blues and gold and I wonder if she is going to paint the sea. The sea has so many different forms that it's quite possible that she will never grow tired of depicting its movement.

The children come in and out of the kitchen on the hunt for snacks. I feel so irritated that I shout about the amount of obese

239

children living in the area and their general lack of self-control. I mimic the women whom I often spot in Tesco, pushing their trolleys full of processed food, their thighs rubbing together. I tell them that that's not what I want for my children. The first one's free, I say to them in a tone that's meant to be menacing but comes across as being highly amusing in their eyes and they start to laugh at me, at their father. I'm talking about Jaffa Cakes, I scream at them, and suddenly I don't see the humour of it all and in actual fact I'm becoming furious.

The kids head back out on to the green because they know what's coming. A lecture on the subject of cleaning. I haven't given them one in a while and anger does this to me. It makes me awfully pernickety about things left lying around the house and my children can recognize these little shifts in my demeanour because the sad fact is that I am too predictable, and that is something that a child will catch on to in no time whatsoever.

What they don't envisage, however, is my next move. I've had fucking enough of this I say to Jenny as I head outside to the green. The kids are with their friends and I can hear the laughter of children at play and rather than stand there and relish the sound, I start shouting my head off. I tell not just Mikey and Joey and Maeve that they don't do enough around the house to help me, but I tell their friends. I can see how their friends are beginning to look at me as if I've lost my mind or I'm a bit crazy and right at that moment I simply don't care. I tell the kids to get inside and to tidy up their rooms.

I am seething and I come back inside and the clatter of nervous feet, young nervous feet, follows me. And I feel their confusion because they know that their rooms are messy but they don't really know where to begin. I bark at them to get started and for a moment I feel that some order will prevail and I feel a semblance of hope.

But it doesn't last. I am tired. Why do I have to cook? I feel like something has snapped, some realization has just washed over me that I do pretty much everything around the house. I cook and I do the laundry and I work in an office that I detest. There is not a single person in the office that I would naturally gravitate towards in any other situation. Not one of them.

The least she can do is touch me. The least she can do is want me. She is concentrating so hard and her features are so becoming in this light that I find it difficult to be angry with her. She is all I have. The way she tucks her legs up underneath her knees, the way she chews the end of her paintbrush as she is deciding where to place her brush strokes. The way she smiles when I bring her a cup of tea while she consults her Hockney book. It's hard when you start to feel uncertain about someone's love for you. You doubt things that you once held to be true.

I visualize Jenny in another place at a desk, just a different desk, perhaps made of hard wood. And the children, Mikey and Joey and Maeve, happily reading or playing Monopoly in a corner. I can see how happy she seems, in colourful clothes and still painting the sea but painting other things as well, drawing from other inspirations. I see her David Hockney book facing out on a shelf above the desk, I can discern the ring marks on the cover from the many hundreds of cups of tea I have brought to her while she works. I see purple tulips in a vase on the desk. I see all these things and Jenny in the centre of it all, my Jenny. And I see a man touching her shoulders and I see her raising her face to be kissed and to kiss back and I realize that this man is not me. This man is Jerome.

As I'm rinsing the spinach I realize that I cannot let him take her and my children.

49. The Last Dinner

I often think back to Paris, and the cold. The type of cold where the street cannot warm up and you can see your breath in the air, as you exhale. But despite the cold, a sense of rapture makes everything seem possible; Jenny and I, there, together – wrapped up in our winter coats and our arms slung about each other as we manoeuvred our way through the streets of the city and along the river. Glorious – the aroma from the bakeries and the aroma from people smoking on the streets and although I hate smoking, and in a way smokers, there is something about Paris that makes it acceptable. I am a reasonable man.

I can still see the Pont Neuf. I can visualize the thousands of locks attached to the bridge, over the Seine. The swathes of people, the fluidity of the place, the sense of life. I often think about the graffiti in Paris, how it looked, so modern, so sharp, full of authenticity and sincerity and confident in its message. The bravery of the hip artists as they go to blank walls exuding a self-belief in the thick of the night. I don't see the designs in Dublin in the same way. They are too safe.

I often think about my level of happiness when we went on a family holiday to Spain. It was astronomical. The pinnacle of my happiness, the magnificence making me smile, on the plane with Jenny and the children. The collective hope that we would have a fabulous time and the very notion of Granizado de Limón and fried chorizo and salted almonds and beer and cheap wine would be enough.

Those two precious weeks, hanging out on the beach and

shopping in the market where we purchased the juiciest, choicest tomatoes that we'd ever seen and how we joked that any reasonable Irish person would attest that it is virtually impossible to get a decent tomato back home. I can still remember the pungent scent from my hands as I cupped them to my face, having secured a kilo of the best tomatoes at the market in Alicante.

I recall how I met Jenny's father for the first time when he reiterated the story Jenny had told me about Jerome and the wine and I didn't have the heart to tell him that I knew all about it.

And there's a crack on the ceiling of the sitting room. It looks like my mother's royal icing on the Christmas cake that she used to make. The crack starts off as a straight line and then it breaks up like a branch on a tree and it is shaky, as if a child has drawn it with an HB pencil, and when things are shaky like this everything is wrong. I am on the cusp of something terrible and the things that I know and the people that I love – they are cracking and crumbling away from me. I could leave the ground, couldn't I? I can imagine it. Take my eyes there, take my eyes; gouge them. If I take some drugs or lots of drugs then maybe I could rip them out of my head. But I am not a man for drugs.

I run a steak knife down my arm and I try to stick the point of it into a vein near my wrist. It is futile. The knife is too blunt at the tip somehow. It's like a bad oar on a paddleboard. I need balance. I need leverage at the top of the knife and from its middle, I hold the paddle in my mind's eye. I have never been on a paddleboard but I live with the memory of the documentary of a lifetime. A documentary about Australian paddleboarders that I watched with Jenny and Mikey and Joey and Maeve here on this couch two nights before, Jenny's eyes fixed on the television screen but not connecting with it. I know a thing or two about connectivity. Connectivity is everything and that is all that I know. And I get up and I stumble, but I do not fall completely.

I go to the kitchen and I look in the first aid press for Jenny's Valium. The sound of the television now and the children talking about how they could easily beat the Cube. Jesus Christ. A cube and that is it. Small feats and all of them to be performed behind transparent glass so everybody can see how stupid and clumsy you really are.

I have sufficient tablets. I find the mortar and pestle. The mortar bowl that we bought in Paris on account of its beautiful crimson polished finish and it feels strange not to be grinding spices or peppercorns and I hope the Valium tablets will be easy enough to smash. I grind 20mg for Jenny and I place it in a red ramekin and I crush 20mg for the children and I place it in a yellow ramekin.

My potatoes are cooked and I mash them using the hardwood pestle. I add lots of butter and a good splash of milk – three tablespoons but I'm not counting. I am merely gauging. It is a welcome trait, the ability to gauge, I remember I once told Mikey, when he asked me how much fusilli to add to a pot of boiling water, but that was ages ago and despite that I remember telling him to be careful in case he burnt himself.

And I do think that I'm happy often. At times this euphoria comes to me like a day off. A day off the lead, if I was a dog, humping and barking wildly and going for a stranger when I have been told not to run. I remember my mother telling me not to run and my father saying, stay and be kind and instructing me not to run, dogs can sense your fear. They cannot just sense it, they can smell it. I can sense my fear. There is blood sport for a reason.

I have fear – in our kitchen, but I cannot do anything to myself with the knife, proper. I try again. I see again if I have the capacity, the capability to stick the point of the steak knife into the vein on my arm. The vein is slightly pronounced now that there is some heat left in this evening, for it is the last day of the holidays and there is still warmth and very soon it will be autumn and the heat will have worn away like plastic spikes – worn down on used football boots. I know all about it. It seems as though there are football boots strewn everywhere here. It is a wonder that I haven't had a terrible accident, perhaps suffered a spinal injury.

I make a small puncture to the vein and it is astonishing really the surprise. I hardly feel any pain, a slight twinge, nothing more. I need to feel what it might be like, just a little deeper. And I am all about conviction and I am deeply scared and the Spanish for depth is profundidad and it seems so much more real. I am a tangible being and it is laughable. I am acutely aware now of my fear. It is eating me up. How I long for a cordless hoover but instead ours has a long flex and the suction is bad. It's terrible. I clean the filter often but it doesn't make any difference.

I suck in my breath, slowly through my teeth. I add a touch more butter to the mashed potato. I add more salt and pepper. I get a small cereal bowl and in it I mix the Valium from the red ramekin with roughly three tablespoons of mashed potato. I transfer it to a plate and add a pork chop and some broccoli. This is for Jenny. I place roughly the same amount of potato into another small cereal bowl and this time I add the Valium from the yellow ramekin. I divide this on to three separate plates for the children. I add some broccoli to each plate but I only add pork to the boys'. I try some potato with my finger and I cannot taste more than the potato and the buttery saltiness and it is great to be Irish with that smug false belief that we invented the potato and to know that we definitely invented Kerrygold.

I'll have to stay here. I will not be able to do myself the fullest of damage imaginable. I will have to stay here to explain to them, when they come for me. I could be running. It could be my last run but I am tired of running, running away from the fact that she wants Jerome. It cannot be. It cannot happen like that.

I adore Friday evenings because I can look forward to the big run on Saturday morning. The greatest sensation – free from Graham for two whole days but I am not free with my thoughts. I have my family. I have my family for the weekend and it starts off so positively but it doesn't always end up like that. Sometimes by the end, I almost don't mind the idea of seeing Graham again and the thought of this is disarming in itself and slightly sad. And I wonder how this absence from work which I assume should be so good for my soul can dissolve. Somehow it is not enough.

I think about the one time we went to Spain, as a family, and none of us could take the heat, not really. Not properly, or naturally the way the Spanish can, and all the irritation which we felt towards each other got slightly out of hand and I wanted to hurt Jenny but I knew in my gut the way you can recognize true pain that it wasn't right. Pain that is entirely unprovoked and irrefutable but exists, nonetheless. Throbbing away, inching towards you and I wanted to hurt her, to injure her somehow. I never said it but it's what I felt and I don't know if feeling something is the very same as doing something and where is my judge, hand me my judgement. Deliver me.

I think about the mosquitoes and how they seemed to go for me more than Jenny and I remember saying that it wasn't fair, that it wasn't right somehow. But it was the way it was and it wasn't right. Why me? Me with my limited pain threshold.

And that one day during our holiday when Jenny sat in the

living room at five o'clock in the afternoon, the sun had reached a fever pitch in our minds. She had laid her beautiful body on the floor. She had the air-conditioning on and I noticed she had the window open at the same time and the irritation I felt was way out of proportion. It seemed to take a fair bit of my resolve not to shout at her but my mother had told me not to shout at anyone, particularly not to a girl, so I didn't say anything. I calmly shut the window and our holiday moved along. Strange how it comes back to me now, my annoyance with her for the smallest thing, all the time besotted by her beauty.

Yes, mine was a keen love but I didn't truly understand the depth of my emotions at the time and I felt that the rapport I had with Jenny was verging on claustrophobia but it was a happy place to be.

I can still visualize those sweltering marks of reddened flesh left by the mosquitoes, how I picked at the blisters until a slightly yellowish liquid wept out and I could almost weep myself with the relief of bursting them.

I remember how Jenny arranged the bowls of olives – some stuffed with anchovy paste, some with stones – and how that made me smile, how I watched her as she sucked the olives, leaving the stones in a small bowl on the coffee table. I like watching her. My memory of how we read and drank beer in small glasses and added ice cubes to the beer because it was so hot and it is the only way to drink beer in Spain. Everything was right and Jenny spoke to me in her gentle voice, full of happiness and it wasn't nuanced with anything else. Her voice was earnest and it wasn't caged one bit. I remember how she touched my hand when she put her glass down after taking a sip of cool beer and the pleasure of that touch.

I know that despite the mosquito bites and the way they drove me crazy everything was perfect. I know now, that it wasn't difficult to measure perfection then. I remember we walked the paseo one evening when the sun was low in the sky and about to drop suddenly as it does in Spain and I wanted it to be special, and it was. I know all about the appreciation of simple things, the Spaniards ambling along the promenade stopping intermittently if they had something to say that they felt ought to be accentuated, such was the importance and how I loved the drama of it.

I remember we moved into a restaurant that had a kind of genuine simplicity at its core and this seemed to elevate Jenny's spirits. She found it charming and I was absolutely delighted with myself. We ate pork chops with garlic and the meat was so tender and the strength of the garlic was evident but it wasn't overpowering, not in any way, and I was struck again by the ability of the Spanish to turn basic ingredients into something really special. I recall asking Jenny if this was a symphony, was music food or as good as, and she said that with the right treatment it could be. I can taste the bottle of Rioja that we drank between us and I can feel the tranquillity of the restaurant.

I remember how we sat sipping a liqueur that the waiter had brought to us on the house. It tasted of oranges. It was a little sweet for me, too intense, but Jenny didn't seem to mind. The children were becoming tired and it was time to go. I left a tip that was probably too generous by Spanish standards because the waiter seemed a little flustered when I signalled to him to keep the change that was on the plate. I had succeeded in embarrassing myself. I didn't care, though. My heart was soaring and we laughed at how early it was that we were leaving the restaurant and the Spanish only beginning to arrive, whole families with their young children and grandparents. The jostling and the noise.

And I recall that Jenny held my hand as we walked back to

the apartment. I felt full of pork and garlic and if it is true that garlic is good for the blood then I figured my blood to be like gold. Jenny was wearing a dress that was covered in a pattern of tropical plants and she looked particularly beautiful in it and I told her that. It seemed like the best moment.

I remember putting the children to bed and feeling a pleasure deep inside me that I would have Jenny all to myself. I had bought a bottle of cava before we'd gone out for dinner. I opened it and we sat out on the balcony to enjoy the rest of the evening, listening to the crickets and to each other. There on the balcony, I reached for her and slid my finger inside her and I felt so lucky. And her response was so tender. And she whispered that she loved me, whispered it.

And I think how we saw so many cyclists making their way up hills and the stinking heat. The stinking heat and the murder of it and the mosquitoes. We agreed, myself and Jenny, that Mediterranean cyclists must have an inner strength.

And I recall the birds, in flocks singing together. I could see them from the balcony in the apartment in the morning while Jenny slept. The overriding sense of joy I had in telling her when she woke up. Keeping the children away from the railing in case they leaned over too far. I told Jenny about the birds later on in the afternoon. How it appeared to me, that they moved together as though they were dancing and the noise they made was like song and how I wanted to call out to her to witness it but I knew by the time I manged to go to her and rouse her that it would be too late. So I stayed and watched the birds on my own and sometimes being on your own is just the thing. When I finished describing it to her I could hear the chorus of crickets in the background. Jenny put her arms around my back and I felt so strong and I loved the way her arms were perfectly bronzed from the sun.

It is a simple fact that I plain adored evenings in Spain.

The way all the heat from the day seemed to come to a head. The balcony in the apartment was overlooking some mountains. They were much more pointed than Ireland's glacial offerings. We sat looking at the view and deciphered different shapes in them and each formation we found was unique to us and yet we shared the magic.

It is a terrible thing to cut down beauty, to shut it off just when it is at its peak, and that is something that is impossible. But she is not beyond her prime now. That is not what I am saying. It is not what I believe.

I remember Jenny giving birth to Maeve. I can recall clearly the way she screamed in her special language of pain, a language that I couldn't understand but somehow I could grasp and I was able to hold her down on the bed as she screamed and twisted. Screamed as though she was being attacked. A wailer, one of those people who scream their heads off in remote places. All for relief, as if the very act of shouting out will absolve the pain. I remember feeling so sorry for her but I was insistent that screaming wasn't going to do her any good and so I held her down. Nobody can hear those people in those places and I thought more's the pity for them. And she called me by my full name, Desmond. Nobody ever calls me Desmond, except for my mother when she was angry with me. I remember the time I hurt Brian. It was his birthday and I was disgruntled because it wasn't my birthday and everyone was making such a big deal of him and I was used to my mother making a big deal of me and I wasn't comfortable with this switch in equilibrium and I bashed his head against the kitchen wall and then I punched him in the face, until I drew blood.

I remember my mother finding me in the kitchen, with my head in my hands after I hurt Brian. It was unprovoked and it wasn't right. Brian lied to her and said that he had stolen money from my room and that is why I attacked him. I think Brian could recognize how I was feeling, he understood my jealousy. He was so wise. I miss him but it's not desperate; it's more of a dull ache that I get on with. I hold my head in my hands in mock horror.

It comes back to me now, the present I bought Brian – a water pistol. How he threw it on to the kitchen floor after I hit his head against the wall. I remember that he destroyed it. I recognize that now, as a sign of retribution. What I wouldn't give to have him here with me now so I could crush him with a hug and tell him how sorry I am that I ruined his tenth birthday. You can never know love or rivalry until you have a sibling and now I have none. But I still recall love and I still recall rivalry.

I think now about the days after our wedding and the fuss and the whole bother of it and the incredible sensation I had in my heart that day, like I could sell love and emotion, or both. I had so much to spare. But I'd keep it all for her, for Jenny. How stunning she looked – the dress that she spent ages choosing and how she did it all on her own. It was a pity her mother wasn't there to see her.

Jerome and his fucking notion of taking her now when she has been through so much, her angst, artistic in nature and having those children. Jerome only has the one so he has no fucking idea how hard it is to have three. I still dream of Jenny begging the doctors to cut Maeve out of her. Like a sacrifice, how she would have agreed to anything to stop the pain, how she had screamed at them to claw her out, to use their knives. How awful it was, how Jenny thought she herself was going to die and I remember that I thought Jenny was going to die although at the same time I had no real idea of what was going on. But die she didn't and that was a pure gift. As soon as I knew Jenny was going to be fine I

251

became petrified, it was like a delayed reaction. When she had Mikey and Joey things were much better. Maybe she became used to having children after Maeve. Perhaps her beautiful vagina, or her birthing canal as the doctors called it, had stretched.

It still feels tight to me and secure, when I can feel it.

I set the table with knives and forks. I make sure there are spoons for the children for their mashed potato. I call my family and tell them dinner is ready. The children are watching a documentary about the Japanese tsunami and I figure that it isn't a bad thing for them to know about the fragility of nature. I can hear them talking about it. I yell out that the people didn't have time to get out of their cars, they were trying to get away as the wave levelled out and the bits of floating wood and general debris acted as rafts. They didn't know what they were doing. How were they supposed to know what to do? I shout, even though I am only a couple of feet away from them. I am still here. I am still here thinking about the Valium I have added to the potato and wondering if I have added enough salt. The children try to leave the television on while we are having dinner and I tell them if they don't turn it off I will switch it off myself.

I am nervous. I have sliced the pork chops thinly as they have a tendency to do in Spain. They have developed an attractive colour from the olive oil and the razor-thin slices of garlic that have caramelized on the frying pan. This aroma is one of my favourites. I have made a salad for Maeve. I have also cooked petits pois. I spoon the peas on to the plates and they move about. They are out of control. I am out of control and I hope I have added sufficient Valium to Jenny's mashed potato because I have a thing about her tolerance levels and the noise of the Spanish children on the paseo comes back to me and the sensation that seemed to engulf my body that I wanted Jenny and I will always want Jenny. I have young voices of our very own to guard, and to protect.

They are hungry tonight because we have had a day out on the beach. We took a kite on account of the breeze and what started off as a pleasant experience became a little fraught with arguments over whose turn it was to fly the kite and whose turn it was to gather the string. The string became knotted and I was forced to keep my patience in check. The kite is in the boot of the car now. I didn't want to drive to the beach today but Jenny said that she was tired and there might be some driftwood lying about on account of the overnight storm that seemed to take everyone by surprise. I don't particularly want any more wood lying about the place, nonetheless I agreed to drive.

We start to eat and I have been careful to make sure that Jenny eats all of her mashed potato so I haven't given her a large portion, three tablespoons, enough so I know she will eat it all and that the Valium will sink into her body. I look at my family, really look at them now as we are halfway through this meal and I realize that I cannot go back. I get more water and I go to the photograph on the wall, above the mantelpiece, that I have had there for years.

Jenny calls me back to the table and I tell her I'll be there shortly. The image is something that I can file away. The people in the photograph – my family – are my possessions and they are not something that I will be giving away any time soon to anyone and especially not to Jerome Fagan. These people are my cargo.

I know I promised. I swore in front of God's eyes to honour Jenny and to love her and not just then and not only in sickness and in health but for all the days of our lives and that is what I am doing. They don't say until death do us part any more. And I meant it too, clearly about welcoming any children that we might have. We were meant to have an open heart while we were doing the welcoming. We ought to cherish them too.

I fetch ice cream from the freezer. HB Vanilla and there is a whoop of delight from the children when I dish it out. And then Joey says, I scream, you scream, we all scream for ice cream.

And then our meal is over.

After dinner I look at the photo again. We are all full of a heightened happiness in it and I didn't realize it at the time – that emotions could be so elevated like that but they can be and this elevation can be captured. Maeve is young in the photograph, five years of age maybe, I cannot really remember. Her hair is seaweed-strewn and the freckles from the Connemara sun are visible on her nose. They add a kindness to her face as though you can paint on characteristics in pointillism. An innocence on her too and you can tell she's been pulling faces just moments before I took the snap because her eyes have a devilment in them which I love about her. She is wearing a pink dress that my mother bought for her and I remember how Jenny thought it was somehow odd that I would want to hang on to this dress when we were clearing out the children's old clothes. And the way Jenny, I remember now with a clarity, how she wanted me to move on quickly after my mother died. I was expected to get on with it, we were so busy with the children, too busy to waste time on grief. Jenny's mother was gone and now mine was and I was to get over it.

I remember how I couldn't and she began to haunt me. Images of the vibrant nail polishes she wore. I woke often in the middle of the night with an ache in my stomach and a feeling that I was hungry but then that feeling would pass and I would lie on the bed beside Jenny and I would clench my hands into fists and I would imagine my mother holding on to my hand as we crossed the road together. Her grip was tight and strong. I started to push her hand away from me when I was ten years old. I wasn't a little boy any more and she wasn't to kiss me at the school gates. I suppose it was normal, natural even, but still I felt as though I disappointed her. And I would lie beside Jenny listening to her breathing beside me and what I wouldn't give now to have another chance to touch my mother's hand.

The photograph captures wonderfully the stretch of Dog's Bay and the brightness of the day and Jenny's face, in between the children. Jenny's hair – windswept by the Atlantic wind and I can feel the wind. I can almost feel it touching my face but that is not true, it is not the wind but it is my hand and I touch my face and I feel the beginnings of stubble. Perhaps I will allow myself to fully regrow my beard, perhaps I will not.

The children continue to watch the rest of the documentary about the tsunami. Jenny goes to her desk. After a while I go to her to see what she is doing and she is sketching an outline of the sea and I place my hands on the desk. There is a certain roughness to her sketch as she adds an outline of a kite and I hope she isn't going to add small blobs that are meant to signify young little people on the beach. I hope she's not contemplating that, not now.

But she does. She uses her brush to signify the little people. Each little person is comprised of two blobs of paint, one vertical blob and a smaller blob placed on top, horizontally like a clumsy cross. I remember her teaching Maeve how to paint people. And I remember that she mentioned potato figures or butterflies, I'm not entirely sure, the crosses were enough to represent people and she told Maeve not to bother with features per se. It was all in the eye and, Jesus what am I doing?

Three such crosses. One cross, that has to be Jenny. Another figure behind the dune in the distance – another cross. It is slightly bigger, that must be me. And beside it another smaller one and that cannot make any sense. Three crosses, we are a family of five. It is then that I realize it's not me at all. I am sure that the bigger one is Jerome and the other one, the smaller one behind him, is his son.

A watery sensation in my stomach and then a cramp. The feeling I get when I go to a place where there is proper sun and I drink coffee because the tea there is shit and no other reason. And I forget that I cannot stomach coffee and the shit that emerges from me with all the coffee and the olive oil is liquid and the aroma in the toilet, the aroma afterwards of me and my bodily functions.

The counting to ten. The counting of my strides as I visualize myself running up the Cat's Ladder, two hundred and thirty-eight steps.

Wait for us, Daddy. I recall the one time I brought Maeve and Mikey and Joey with me and how they tried to keep up with me but because of my adult addiction to rhythm I found that I was afraid to decelerate in case I wouldn't be able to finish going up and down with the children, like I'd planned. I have read that extreme exercising is a form of mid-life crisis. I find this interesting. I went on ahead of the children that day and when we finally got home Jenny berated me for pushing them too far. The words she said are still in my mind.

Remember, Des, they're only children.

They are not only children. They are my fucking children and Jenny is my fucking wife and if I get my hands on that cunt for messing my family around I don't know what I might do.

The tsunami documentary is opening up a series of questions from the children and I answer their natural disaster queries with a reluctance from the kitchen now with a notch of irritation because I am out here cleaning. Clearing away dishes, scraping the pork fat from the plates and putting it into the bin. There is a stale smell coming from it and I know that Jenny has been up to her tricks. She runs her cigarette butts under water and she wraps them in fragments of kitchen towel. She does this because she doesn't want me to know how many cigarettes she is smoking when she is working downstairs and I am in bed. It is pathetic. Her smoking and me trying to instigate sex and calling her upstairs and me wanting her to want me.

I scour the hob and I clean the back splash with a squidgy sponge that is meant for scrubbing pots and pans and there are specks of green fuzz stuck to the grouting in the tiles and I think about grouting and what a pain in the arse it gives me. I think how futile it is, but perhaps not quite as futile as ironing. I sweep the floor and then mop it out and I use far too much bleach while I'm doing so and the fumes start to engulf my nostrils and Jenny shouts at me from her desk not to bother, that she'll do it tomorrow, now is not the time.

Their sleepy faces. I am filled with a short jolt of tenderness and I can feel my cheeks blush with a compassion that I didn't know that I possessed until this moment and I shake it away. I am not without resolve.

They agree to come to bed because it is Sunday and they are due back to school in the morning, after the holidays. It is officially a school night and half past nine is beyond reasonable in my estimation and this is what I tell them. They say goodnight to Jenny and she tells them that she is feeling very tired and that she will be up to them shortly because she'll be going to bed soon herself. It is good that she is tired. I follow the children upstairs.

I stand in the doorframe of the bathroom and I look at

them play-acting with the toothpaste and I look at the grouting over the bath and I can see only my mistakes.

And later I plump Mikey's pillow for him just the way he likes me to and I kiss him goodnight, and his hair – the fly-away bit that sticks up and makes him look as though he has a Mohican. I push it back down into its place. I kiss his soft cheek and I feel the softness and my heart lurches. I do the same to Joey who is in his bed beside Mikey's. Joey asks me how high the wave would have been in Japan. I tell him that it would have been taller than he could imagine.

Joey – how tender his skin and the smell. The smell of the unknown and that sense of belief in what a great life they have. They don't have myself or Jenny arguing when they are about to sleep. They are merely caught in the glorious sensation of another good day as only children can.

Goodnight, Dad, he says.

I tell him it's Daddy, always Daddy, and I turn off the bedroom light but I am careful to leave the light on in the landing.

Maeve is very sleepy. Her head is on her pillow with the picture of the unicorn and the words, Unicorn Dreams. And I think how lovely it is, this whole unicorn business. I almost want to believe in unicorns if only for Maeve's benefit. And I think now of Maeve and what a beautiful name it is, a bit old-fashioned maybe but I recall that Jenny had envisaged this as a strong name in adulthood.

Maeve will always believe in unicorns.

I can sense Jenny's presence behind me in the door of Maeve's bedroom. I lean over to kiss Maeve, one last goodnight kiss. One last time to feel her silken skin. I count the freckles on her nose, at least twenty, accentuated from the summer and I think now that she only had about five in the photograph from Connemara. More freckles over time.

Jenny touches my arm and says, Des, thanks for today.

I want her to thank me not just for today but for other days. For instance our wedding day when I did everything in my power to make her believe that we were going to have this wonderful life together, that we were about to embark on this amazing journey together, this journey that would take us to a land where we would be deliriously happy and Jenny's art work would flourish. A place where we would have beautiful children and that would all be enough. It isn't enough.

I want to thank her for bringing Jerome back into our lives. For her audacity and above all, her bravery for holding out on me in bed at night repeatedly, and having it off with Jerome. It's possible. Nothing is impossible. To thank her for allowing that prick to take her away from me, to destroy our perfect nest.

And the fire in my belly and my beautiful daughter, her hair strewn on her unicorn pillow and her dreams are not far off now. Jenny tells me that she is exhausted and is off to bed and wants to know if I'll come too.

I lean to her and I place my lips against hers and I tell her that it is the beach that has made her tired. I tell her I'll be up in a while, that I have a bit of work to do on a project for the office.

I go downstairs and I watch television. It is about time now for *The Week in Politics*. When it starts I'm watching it and I'm not watching it. There is no real distinction between the two acts. I am in a political trance. I grab a beer, a can of Pražský which I notice has now become my mainstay beer, when did this happen? I look at the photograph again. The beer goes down my throat quickly but beer can do that sometimes. I take a second can from the fridge and go back to the sofa. I get up and take the photograph from the wall and I sit back down. The cottage we rented was close to the beach. We couldn't actually see it from the cottage but that didn't matter to us then for we could smell the Atlantic and we could hear it and we could feel the mist on our skin. It was like satin.

The mussels that we collected and I ate, and the chowder that we gorged in bars alongside the single pint of Guinness. You only need the one in Connemara. I don't recall the black stuff ever having tasted so sweet, so sweet the froth on your lips. I remember the children's delight at being allowed to dip their fingers in to taste it. I remember laughing at the facial contortions they made as the sweetness became bitterness to their childish palates. Their delight with their little bags of Bacon Fries and Scampi Fries and their Cokes, in the pub. I remember that I asked the barman for bitter lemon but he didn't stock it and instead I bought a couple of cans of Fanta Lemon and I showed the children how to mix the minerals, like I used to do as a child when I was on holiday in Ireland: two parts Coke to one part lemon. Bitter lemon is in my opinion far superior to Fanta and somehow I am happy that I kept that thought to myself and didn't even allude to it, in fact.

It is still with me, the sand on the bay, soft like Spanish sand or Brittas Bay sand but far removed from the grainy compacted strip offered on Killiney beach that I run on in the evenings during the winter and early in the mornings on work days. I am careful not to move beyond the strip where the stones are scattered all along the rest of the beach right up until the wooden fence.

And I think about rhyme and the importance the children place on it.

50. What Am I Doing?

I will never forget how we couldn't decide for ages on the song for our first dance and in the end Jenny suggested 'The Garden' by Van the Man. She always seemed so at peace when she played it and as we moved slowly on the dance floor together she made some joke about it being entirely irrelevant to love and I told her that it was perfect. She beamed with her own perfection and I felt so proud that she had chosen me to have this dance with.

I know now that it was the right thing to allow Jenny to sort out the venue for our wedding – that perfect place in Wicklow, where there was a great big open space at the back of the hotel, and the added bonus of a walled garden with its formality of box hedging and bursts of colour from the montbretia and the terracotta pots distributed amongst the beds filled with rich pelargoniums. I have always loved these plants, they remind me of the West and the trips we took there, just the two of us and then later with the children.

I laugh to myself about how Jenny had insisted on playing her music on the way to Connemara and how the children looked horrified as she sang along to the Cure and despite the shrieks of objection coming from them, Jenny continued and the children became car sick from laughing. Jenny too, there was something about her on that trip – her flushed face, a kind of radiance as though she'd left behind a trouble or a worry. And the excitement of choosing who would sleep where and the enthusiasm of her picking wild flowers and grasses in the meadow outside the cottage.

I know that the thing that struck Jenny most about Conne-mara was the peace. It took two days to fully realize it but it came to her in the end. Two whole days to register that level of relaxation overtaking the body and I agreed with her wholeheartedly — it wasn't a sudden sense of quiet that you got when you reached smaller roads and began to notice the appearance of dry stone walls. It was more gradual and it was like recognizing Geist, creeping into your corporeal being and triggering all the sense pleasures you could find there in the recess of your mind.

I feel glad that I had showed her a place where she could be herself and feel wild and free and we made love when the children were playing outside the cottage and afterwards we went out, wrapped in dressing-gowns to check on them. I believe that in that special moment I felt so proud to have this family. The pleasure that I derived from these people in my life was immense and I felt so fortunate, so much so that I had difficulty measuring it.

And now I have difficulty measuring my breath. A breath that normally comes easy for me is laboured and I must stay sitting here for that is what a sitting room is for. I must sit and I must be still and I must be quiet and I mustn't allow myself to stumble for I am here after all, and this is my plan and it is imperative to go along with a plan once it's been made. I never backtrack. It's one thing that I don't like to do and I think now that it might be why I didn't fuck Denise in Cork when I had the chance, despite her insistence to the contrary. It wasn't only about restraint, it was about making the same mistake twice and sometimes there are things that you can only do once.

I go into the kitchen and take another can of beer from the fridge. I pop the ring and I do it softly, slowly so the sound will be weak but measured and I don't know why I'm worried about the noise yet I must be quiet.

I check on the children.

I check on Jenny.

The children are in a deep sleep and Jenny is motionless apart from her steady breathing. It is soft but hoarser than normal and the Valium is working. I never doubted that it would and yet I did.

I creep silently down the stairs and I am careful on the last two steps even though it's not like we live in an old house where I have to be mindful of this idiosyncracy. Ours is modern but I go through the motions nonetheless. *The Week in Politics* is winding down and I feel like I've learnt nothing but that is not something I feel bad about.

The children's school bags are in the corner of the sitting room, not where they should be. They should, rightfully, be underneath the stairs, alongside the coats. Jenny organized their new school books earlier on and she mentioned something about them not being covered and that she was quite certain she had requested that when she was ordering them from the bookshop. She had ordered them in June just before the old school term finished up and that uncertainty about the weather had set in when everyone wondered if the sunshine that we had enjoyed during the June bank holiday weekend had marked the beginning of the Irish summer and the end. The summer hadn't in fact panned out too badly and I was glad for the children. I am glad now.

I wait with a greediness for it to be later and yet I don't wish time to move forward. I wait the same way I waited impatiently for darkness to come as a child at Hallowe'en. It never seemed to come fast enough so I could go out to the neighbours and beg for chocolate. The chocolate and the sweets were scant and I laugh aloud now in the sitting room about how many times I have told the children that they are destroyed by sugar, by junk when they go out on their rounds.

I have to sink my teeth into the soft skin of the token apples that are left at the end of each of their bags underneath all the junk that they upend on the floor to segregate. Good lollipops and less good ones, and cheap and dangerous ones where the stick comes out when you least expect it to, and you are left with a lump of something horrible that tastes like nothing in particular. Mikey and Joey and Maeve rolling around the floor surrounded by heaps of mini Mars Bars and fun-size Smarties and Haribo jellies and crisps, smoky bacon Wheelies and Hula Hoops.

The beer is cold, never getting any warmer. I go to the downstairs toilet and my piss is wholehearted. I go back to the sitting room to my sitting position and I am beginning something here.

I wait until it is half one in the morning and then I go to Jenny. I place my hands on her throat and I squeeze and it takes so much effort and I have got somewhere and I have to go further and I have to be careful that I do enough. And there is fight in her as she wriggles violently, I think, but I cannot be sure because I am so caught up with her neck that I cannot properly register her body, not fully, but I am aware of her beautiful arms flailing and it seems to go on forever but then she no longer moves and her arms are just there.

I go into the bathroom and I vomit beery sick and that feeling you get when you know that you've drunk too much as soon as you wake up and you take an Alka-Seltzer and you knock it back too quickly and you puke it up around ten minutes later after you have crawled back to bed to lie down and try to get yourself together. And my vomit is like that vomit. It is violent and then the retching starts and then it stops and I wipe my hands on my jeans and I move into the boys' room.

I am here because I cannot let them see what I have done to Jenny and I go to Mikey first and I have to move his head because he has his face flat against the pillow and my hands shake as I manoeuvre his head towards mine and every ounce of resolve I have is here as I place my hands on his throat and I squeeze the innocence out of him.

And I stop then with Mikey unmoving before me and Joey stirs in his bed and I go to him and his eyes open slightly and it is breaking my heart and I place my hands around his throat too and I don't do anything else but place pressure and I am under pressure and pressure is looking down on me.

I stand now on the landing and I place my head in my hands and I try to count and now I have to go there.

Maeve is the hardest. I go into her bedroom and I move towards her bed and she lies there and her eyes are closed now, her soft childish breath, I can hear it. I touch her hair and I am about to touch her neck but something holds me back. I am stumbling and it is a real nightmare and I am in it and there is sweat under my arms and I don't know what in God's name I am doing but it doesn't stop me placing my hands on her neck now and whatever strength I have left in me now I muster and this is my resolve. Maeve's beautiful face and her head and I dismantle her beauty and her grace and I am crying while I'm doing this and it is so hard to breathe and it is so hard to focus and it isn't supposed to be like this but it is and Jerome cannot come into this house any more and none of them can enter any of these rooms any more.

And now I have to check and this is what I have to do because I cannot guarantee that I have done enough, maybe they're not dead, the boys, maybe I haven't used enough power and maybe.

And a run now is out of the question. I recognize that almost immediately like a child who has done something terrible and is awaiting punishment. There will be no more Christmas presents to confiscate. How about that?

265

And, Jesus, the way I tried to make amends for bashing Brian's head against the wall on his birthday when I was jealous because it wasn't my birthday. And the way I slapped Jenny in the water and tried to make out like it was a bit of fun. And the way she wouldn't have sex with me afterwards and the way she sometimes used sex as a weapon punishing me with her abstinence and the way I hit her once more when she complained about the fact that I'd produced spaghetti bolognese two days running and I told her that she could go and fucking cook something more interesting herself, what was stopping her?

And the way she was so worried about her precious exhibition in Gallery One.

Well, picture this, Jenny and I will not do anything more now tonight and I will wait here, sitting much in the same position that I sat, what, an hour ago? and I'm singing 'Here Comes Your Man' in my head. It's going round and round like the way I used to go round and round on the Waltzers in Bray and the pizza I had devoured beforehand made me want to spew and that is the same way I feel now.

And now I'm up, out of my seat and I'm moving around and there isn't adequate space in this room to get any decent movement going. I go to my CDs and I put on music, unnecessarily loud, the way I like it. I don't even know what artist I have chosen, all I know is the heft of it and the drum beat is heavy and is reverberating into my loins, or so it seems.

And this isn't like how I imagined it to be, at all. They are gone, but I imagined my legs running quickly, covered in Lycra – a steady rhythm, mimicking my heartbeat, possibly, and a glass full of freshly squeezed orange juice drunk beforehand quickly, greedily. I imagined the sun on my back and possibly on my face and my shoulders. It was never my intention to execute this deed under the cover of darkness in the dead of the night, when everyone should be sleeping, and yet I am conscious that there will always be somebody awake in a different part of the world. I could always run later when the light comes up, I do not have long to wait because even though it is the end of the summer, the light may still come quickly and it will be a guilty bright light like what you get on your way to an early house, and you are loaded with regret that you have over-indulged in the hours leading up to this. But it seems definite now that my planned run is out of the question, heading up to the Obelisk on Killiney Hill and giving myself that special moment to admire the sweep of Killiney Bay, its magnitude, and to decipher the glint of light that marks the tunnel from Bray Head to Greystones. And I am contemplating many things here tonight, as I do my stretches, but I will not be contemplating the proximity of Dalkey Island and berating myself for never having set foot on it. Oh the waste.

And the music is thumping and I suppose this is my tribute to Jenny and to Mikey and to Joey and to Maeve and I go into the kitchen for water or possibly beer and I notice my Lycra leggings hanging on a kitchen chair by the radiator and they are inside out and the label is exposed, The Great Outdoors. I shake as I open my jeans and I push them down my legs. I can see my reflection in the kitchen window as I stand there. I grab my Lycra leggings from the chair and I put them on and it isn't easy because I am using too much haste and it is not helping in the speed department. Finally I get them on, fully, and I think that I could still make a run but it will be a different one. I fill a water bottle, it is a recent purchase, one of those bottles, its interior comprised of metal enabling me to keep my water at a satisfactory cool temperature. Only yesterday I used it and the way the water slid down my throat was something wonderful and it caused me a degree of pleasure and there is significant pleasure to be gained in the smallest of things.

I think about setting fire to the house. I have no fuel. I imagine going into the garden and siphoning petrol from the car. I have in fact siphoned petrol before, as a child, with my father when he ran out of it for the lawnmower. Oh the memory, the taste of money.

I go out into the front garden and I look at the car and I imagine myself down on my hunkers sucking fuel and I realize that it is an impossible task. And there is a loud awful wail and the sound is guttural and brutal and it takes me a moment to realize that the sound is coming from my own body. I take the sweeping brush that is beside the porch that Jenny never took in after I asked her to, even though it was me that had used it to wash the car at the weekend. And I begin to bang the bin with the sweeping brush, a beat like a crazed drummer keeping in time with the band, no, leading it, and I am shaking and I am violently cold and I look around the small garden and it is a frantic movement of the eyes and I look up and I can see my neighbour, the light is on in his bedroom window and he is watching me.

I am pacing up and down and I am jumping from one foot to the other foot in much the same way that tennis players do in the moments before the umpire flicks the coin to decide who will serve, only my movements are exaggerated. I am a natural server. I decide to run now, anywhere, even though it is dark and I am screaming. It seems like I should just go, but before I run down the road I pull the black bin to the front of the footpath, so it will be obvious to the bin men that it is indeed ready and waiting to be collected in the morning. When it comes to the smallest of things, of duty, I remain a good father.

Epilogue

When you die is it true that you see those whom you have loved on this earth in heaven? If so, if this is the truth, I will meet Mikey and Joey and Maeve on a rollercoaster. I will hold their hands as we rush down great ramps and I will whisper reassurances into their ears as we once again make our ascent. I will tell them that I love them and I will point down to Jenny beneath us and I will say that their mother is afraid to go on a rollercoaster. I will ask them, who is afraid to go on a rollercoaster? And they will answer, laughing, Mommy. Their little eyes will be filled with tears, tears of excitement and joy that I am here strapped in beside them telling them that everything is going to be okay and that we will reach the end of this ride, unscathed. Joey will ask me what unscathed means. I will shout that he's one of the cleverest boys that I have ever known because he never stops asking questions and that this is a sure sign of intelligence.

At the end of the rollercoaster ride we will wait for the man who runs the show to unstrap us and we will run to Jenny. Her arms will be outstretched and she will be smiling, enjoying her children's excitement and admiring her husband's forbearance. We will eat candy floss from a woman who will have set out a pretty stall with the sole intention of pleasing little girls and boys.

The art and how I have destroyed it won't matter any more. The memory of what Jenny has created will live on because it is enough that I alone have seen it exhibited solely for me in my own house. There will be no more talk of galleries and group shows. There will be no more talk of Jerome.

And when I get to heaven we will walk together hand in hand.

Acknowledgements

Thank you to my editor, Claire Pelly, for believing in this book from the outset, and for all her work and attention to detail. To Michael McLoughlin, MD, Penguin Random House Ireland, copy-editor Annie Lee, editorial manager Ellie Smith and all the Penguin Ireland team.

To readers of early drafts of this work, Aodhnait Donnelly, Nicholas Kearns, Jonathan Williams and Gisèle Scanlon.

To my professors and mentors at Trinity College Dublin, Ian Sansom, Deirdre Madden, Sean Borodale, Colette Bryce and Sophia Ní Sheoin. Special gratitude to Carlo Gébler for all his support and friendship.

To Chris Binchy, who was the first to read my writing and the initial draft of this book. His early encouragement has led to this, my first novel.

To publishers of earlier work, especially Banshee and No Alibis Press.

To all my friends, especially my fellow sea-swimmers at Killiney beach who make every day special, regardless of water temperature, wave patterns and wind mutability.

My love and thanks to my dearest parents, Anne and Peter. To my sisters, Anne and Colette, Henry Seward, the Carrolls – Eileen, Patrick, Eoghan, Marian and all the Aldatz-Carrolls. To my late parents-in-law, Penny and Justin.

And finally, thank you to my husband, Dara, for all his love and support, and to my wonderful children, Kate and Ted: I am so proud of you both.